PURSUITS

Joshua Danker-Dake

Three Giant Elephants

PURSUITS
Book 2 of the *Projections* series

Copyright 2022 by Joshua Danker-Dake

Three Giant Elephants

Cover design by David Lange

This is a work of fiction. All names, characters, places, and events
are the work of the author's imagination.
Any resemblance to real persons, places, or events is
coincidental.

William Bernhardt was the straw that broke the camel's back,

so this one is kind of his fault.

ONE

"Bubble, bubble, toil and trouble, and so on and so forth! All right, let's see what our baby can do." Garcinia Cambogia, the elderly head of Xiong Holonautics' R&D branch, activated her newest holographic projector prototype, then stepped down from the display platform, an expectant look on her face.

Green Greene, Xiong's chief of security, watched as iridescent bubbles began to foam out of the top of the projector's glossy black casing. Piling almost to the knee in thick clouds, the suds spilled across the Portsmith Convention Center floor in every direction like an out-of-control bubble bath.

Greene stepped back instinctively as the froth reached him, but it flowed, unrelenting, around and beyond him. The sea of bubbles surged on past display booths and kiosks and dozens of early arrivals to the tech expo, until he couldn't see any part of the concrete floor that wasn't covered. Always moving, shifting, they reflected the light like a million tiny mirrors. The effect was utterly hypnotic.

"It's just for show, dear." Garcinia moved over to the small folding table in the corner of Xiong's designated area and began sorting through the pile of gadgets there. "We didn't bring the solid projector, and it doesn't do wet anyway. *Yet.*"

"I know. It's just reflex." Greene lifted one leg. His slacks were perfectly dry, of course, and none of the bubbles had clung to him. "It looks completely real."

Garcinia waved a hand. "Yes, of course it does. But today, we're going for *distance.*"

"You know, I think it's '*double, double,* toil and trouble,'" said her assistant, a young man whose name Greene couldn't remember.

Garcinia clucked her tongue. "Does this look like the time for literary trivia? Community theater? Take this walkie-talkie, follow those bubbles, and get me some data!"

"Yes, ma'am." Her assistant accepted the radio and headed away from the Xiong exhibit, toward the more crowded area where the smaller companies were setting up.

Greene watched Garcinia fiddle happily with several presumably hologram-related devices. "The tech expo is your favorite weekend of the year, isn't it?"

"Well, it's certainly in my top three." Garcinia rejoined Greene by the projector, brandishing her tablet. "This really is an exciting piece, Chief. It can project over one hundred meters without loss of resolution. Not only is that more than twenty meters farther than our last model, but it's also more than anything Algary's got. This is the next level in outdoor and long-range applications, and today we're going to show it to the world."

"Very nice," Greene said. "And those vendors over there are all fine with you spilling into their space like that?"

She waved a dismissive hand. "If I was going to worry about such questions, I wouldn't work for Xiong Holonautics, would I? They should have known better than to set up so close." She raised the walkie-talkie. "How far now?"

"I'm at fifty-three meters and it's still looking strong," came the reply.

"Very good, keep going. By the way, Chief, have you seen Max? He went off to make sure that Algary didn't swoop in and outbid us for the headline timeslot on the main stage, but he should have been back by now."

Max Fill, Xiong's twitchy little public relations expert. He'd be dialed up to eleven for this event, which was an even better reason than usual for Greene to keep clear of him.

"I haven't, sorry."

The walkie-talkie crackled again, and Garcinia's assistant said, "We're at seventy-five meters, but ... I think we need to stop."

"Stop?" Garcinia peered at her tablet. "What are you talking about? The system says we have plenty of range. We should be able to get another twenty meters at least. Xiong Holonautics doesn't phone in these tech expos, never has, and we're not about to start now."

"Yes, but we're up against Crestridge's floor space. They're giving me dirty looks as it is."

Garcinia snorted. "Crestridge? Pooh. What is that half-rate hologram company going to do? Those poor peasants are still using aerohaptics, bless their hearts."

"Uh, I think they heard that. I'm going to come back now."

"Oh, very well. I'll switch it off. For *now*."

Garcinia tapped at her tablet, and soon the bubbles receded, dissolving in concentric waves until they were gone as if they had never been, leaving no moisture or residue. They were, after all, only light.

"Well, there you have it, Chief," Garcinia said. "What do you think?"

"Very impressive range," Greene said dutifully.

"I know! Just wait until the demonstration this afternoon—then we'll show those Crestridge hacks what we think about their personal space. The nerve." She turned and wandered away, engrossed with her tablet.

Greene scratched at his forearm. It had been a month since he'd had it reattached, and it still itched—or maybe it was all in his head. That was what Mainprize, the Xiong doctor, had told him—after all, there wasn't even a scar anymore. But he wasn't sure.

"Excuse me, Chief?"

Greene turned to the athletic young woman in the black and gold Xiong Security uniform. "What's up, Sunny?"

"I've been around the whole place, and we've finished our last round of checks." Sonnenschein tucked a loose strand of purple hair behind one ear. "Everything's clear, nothing out of the ordinary."

"Excellent."

"Looks like a good year for Xiong, too."

"How do you mean?"

"Have you been around the convention center? Checked out the exhibitions? It's a weak crop. All Crestridge has are some new vacation programs. Algary has a new zoo and exotic animal line with 'unprecedented interactivity,' but we put out a version that was almost as good last year. You know, I wonder if it's something Shepherd stole from us and sold to them."

"Could be," Greene said. "We're still chasing down a few of those loose ends."

There was a chirp in his ear as his comm activated. "Chief, are you busy?" said a woman's voice.

"No, what's up?"

"If you're not doing anything pressing, I'd appreciate it if you would join me for a few minutes. I'm in C Lobby."

"No problem. I'll head over there now."

"Everything all right, Chief?" Sonnenschein asked.

"As far as I know. The boss wants me, though."

Sonnenschein gave him a play salute. "Have fun."

Greene started to walk, then realized he didn't know which way C Lobby was. He surreptitiously used his phone to pull up the Portsmith Convention Center's floor plan on his Spec-Tron glasses, oriented himself, and set off.

The wall clock he passed displayed 10:09. The expo had just opened, and the convention center was quickly filling up with people. Not just people—*consumers*, Xiong's marketing department kept reminding him.

Greene arrived at C Lobby and had no trouble finding his boss despite the growing throng—indeed, she was hard to miss.

Even without the two massive Xiong Security men flanking her, Marlena Ranga Rao commanded attention. Her copper hair seemed to catch every bit of sunlight streaming through the lobby's vast windows, making her radiant. And she was immaculately dressed, in flared slacks and a button-up shirt that seemed barely up to the task of containing her ample bosom.

Marlena was conversing with a tall, slender white-haired man in an expensive suit whom Greene recognized but couldn't immediately place. He too had a bodyguard—a burly man in a royal blue Algary uniform.

Victor Carandini, President, Algary Applications, Greene's SpecTrons informed him.

Greene brushed a bit of dust from the lapel of his suit, straightened his tie, and approached.

Marlena spotted Greene and smiled, showing preternaturally white teeth. "Ah, Chief, there you are. I'd like you to meet Victor Carandini, President of Algary Applications."

"Of course," Greene said, extending his hand.

Carandini took it in a not-quite-crushing grip. "At last, the rising star, the golden boy, the man who saved Xiong Holonautics from itself and showed the world that The Bear still has some teeth." He spoke in a rich baritone, with a Eurozone accent. "Shorter than I was expecting, but it's good to meet you, young man."

"Good to meet you, sir," Greene said, holding eye contact until Carandini finally released his hand. By their words and body language, it was evident that he had been summoned to play some role in a cordial dick-measuring contest between Xiong and Algary, and he would do his duty to the fullest.

"Yes, it's too bad we didn't review your job application with greater diligence some time back." Carandini grinned, his teeth unusually yellow inside the frame of his snow-white beard. "What might have been, yes? In any case, the responsible parties have been dealt with, and such a mistake will not be repeated."

"Algary's never too far behind," Marlena said.

"Not *too* far," Carandini replied, his smile becoming strained.

Greene cleared his throat. "If I can be of some service?"

"You know," Carandini said, recovering smoothly, "I was hoping to see Xiong's new solid holograms at this expo—if such a thing indeed exists. I've heard such delightful rumors, you know. Surely The Bear has not fallen so low as to resort to hype without substance."

"And surely The Dragon has not become so desperate that it must resort to fishing blindly," Marlena said.

"Far from it," Carandini replied. "But I do hope that today will be stimulating, even so." He nodded to them both in turn. "I look forward to our future meetings." He turned and headed for the convention center floor with long strides, his bodyguard in tow.

Marlena patted Greene's arm. "Thank you for that, Chief. I'm sorry to have inconvenienced you."

"It's no trouble," Greene said. "Is everything all right?"

"Yes, everything's fine," she said, a faraway look on her face.

"If there's anything I can do?"

Marlena shook her head and seemed to come back to the here and now. "He's just probing for weaknesses. With the loss of Shepherd and Raj, plus everything that Shepherd did—and now with a grieving widow at the head of the table—some of the corporations have gotten the impression that Xiong is ... diminished. Vulnerable."

Greene was impressed that she managed to say all this without a crack in her voice, without pain on her face.

She had a determined look in her eye. "It's taken some time to right the ship, and we may have lost some ground, but I have no intention of letting Algary or any other company overtake us."

"I have every confidence," Greene said. He'd learned well not to underestimate this woman.

"Thank you, Chief." Marlena tilted her head, peering past him. "It looks like someone is trying to get your attention."

Greene looked behind him and saw his wife, Nisha, bursting pregnant, her belly almost comically huge on her tiny body.

"You're dismissed," Marlena said. "Say hello to your wife for me. I have a couple more VIPs to go impress."

Greene went to Nisha and kissed her forehead. "Hi, baby. What are you doing here?"

"I came to see you do your thing in a suit." She grinned at him. "Wow, look at Marlena! She looks amazing!"

Greene shrugged, trying to be noncommittal. "I guess."

"And her boobs are still looking as great as ever! Are they real, or did she get them done?"

Greene sighed, reminding himself that on some level, he enjoyed the teasing. "I really don't know. Why are you here? You should be at home."

Nisha thumped him on the chest. "You sound like your mother. I don't get a break at home, you know that? You *don't* know, because you practically live at work."

Greene held up his hands in surrender. "If you want to have this baby in the middle of a convention center, far be it from me to stand in your way."

"You know, I've decided I'm going to do what I like, and I'm counting on your Xiong privilege to get me to the hospital in a timely fashion should the need arise."

Greene smiled. "I'm mostly impressed you got away from Mom."

"Oh no, she's here. She's watching entirely too much news, you know? She's gotten kind of obsessed with this ongoing story about dead homeless people out at the city limits. So morbid. Long story short, I needed to get out of the house. Anyway, she also wanted to come see the new India line of interior holograms, so here we are."

Greene didn't really keep up on the marketing details of Xiong's new products, but this didn't sound at all familiar. "Is that ours?"

"No, it's Crestridge," Nisha replied. "She didn't want to tell you. You know, she's been a little funny about buying new programs from other companies since you've had this job."

Greene shrugged. "I get paid either way."

"What about you guys? Got anything new and exciting?"

"We've got three full rows of displays, but I don't think there's anything you haven't seen in early access. We seem to be focusing on the commercial side this year. So unless you'd be impressed by a floor full of pretend bubble bath ..."

"I might be. *If* there's a place between here and there where I can get some form of potatoes."

"There's a good chance," Greene said. The convention center was ringed with concession stands.

"Then lead the way."

He took her hand and led her through the growing crowd.

"So are you going to be home late tonight?" she asked. "I saw the expo goes until nine."

"I shouldn't be," Greene said. "We're taking it in shifts. Deputy Chief Burg is responsible for getting all the tech back to the tower. I should be on time. Maybe a little early."

She snorted. "I'll believe it when I see it."

Greene tried to contain a sigh. Nisha accepted his long hours, and she didn't complain much, but he knew she didn't like them. It hadn't been a problem—at least not a big one—but now the baby was coming, and Greene had started to think about what he might be missing.

"See, what did I tell you?" he said. "Bubbles."

The glistening mass of bubbles had been reactivated—even restricted to Xiong's assigned area and the adjoining thoroughfares, it was an extremely impressive display.

They waded into it. "There's a big market for bubbles?" Nisha asked.

"Unprecedented range on the projector. See, it's way over there, where that tech in the white coat is working. What it means is larger holograms with fewer units. Great for public spaces and big events." Greene realized that as a member of the Xiong organization, he felt a sense of pride in this innovation even though he'd had absolutely nothing to do with its development.

"Very fancy."

"Anyway, there's a Carbotarium booth past our big projector, by the elevators. That's probably your best bet for potatoes."

"Ooh, Carbotarium." Nisha patted her belly. "Your daughter and I can work with that. Would you care to join us?"

"Sure," Greene said. It was too early to eat, but he could go for something to drink.

The sea of iridescent bubbles flickered, became opaque white, and vanished.

"What in the world?" Garcinia exclaimed.

Greene looked up at the projector. He knew a malfunction when he saw one. No techs were around now, but the lights on the machine flickered.

The projector sparked twice, sending out long arcs of electricity. A searing flash blinded Greene for an instant, and just as his vision started to clear, the projector exploded.

TWO

As the projector blew apart, Greene had just enough time to throw himself in front of Nisha before the blast knocked them both down. Then the back of his head struck the floor, and everything went white.

He heard screaming—a lot of screaming. Through it all, he could hear his wife desperately calling his name.

Greene sat up, his ears ringing, his eyes stinging from smoke, his nostrils filled with the stench of burning plastic and the fishy odor of scorched wiring. A dozen sharp pains stung his back. His sight returned, but his senses were overloading.

The fire alarm activated, adding to the cacophony, and the convention center's sprinkler system kicked on.

The spray of water brought him to alertness. "Nisha!"

Beside him, she grunted and tried to sit up, and he helped her.

He looked her over, trying not to show his anxiety. "Are you hurt?"

She shook her head. "I'm all right. Just a little bruised. And wet. But the baby ..."

Greene froze. "What about the baby? Is she hurt?"

Nisha scowled, and Greene knew she was fighting panic. "What am I, a doctor? I don't know. I landed on my back. I think we're okay, but I don't know. But I'm worried, Green."

Greene jumped to his feet and received pounding pain in his head for his trouble. "We have to get you out of here. Can you stand?"

"I think so. Give me a hand."

Greene grasped her arms and pulled her to her feet.

"Chief! There you are! Are you all right?"

Greene turned and saw Sonnenschein, wet, as they all were, her Xiong uniform shredded down one leg.

"We're okay," he said. "Are you—"

His comm activated. "All staff, this is Marlena Ranga Rao. I need help. I—" Marlena broke off in a fit of coughing, and then the line went silent.

Greene glanced around frantically, feeling torn between duties. As best he could tell, the destruction was localized to their area, but the chaos was everywhere. Most of the crowd had gotten well away from them by now, but there was no guarantee that this area was safe now, that there wasn't more to come.

He took a deep breath and decided. "Sunny, are you good?

She nodded, her purple pigtails bouncing. "I'm good, Chief."

"Get my wife out of here. Get her to a doctor. I'll help Marlena."

"On it." Sonnenschein put a hand around Nisha's shoulders and began leading her toward the nearest exit.

"That's right," Nisha called over her shoulder. "Pawn me off!"

"Nisha—"

"Just go do your work!"

"Thank you," Greene murmured.

He realized his Spec-Trons weren't on his face anymore. He spotted them on the floor several meters away, and retrieved them.

One of the lenses was badly cracked, a nearly opaque spider web. He forced it loose with his thumb and tossed it aside. The other lens, thankfully, still worked.

Greene pulled out his phone—the screen was damaged, he noted with annoyance—to zero in on Marlena's signal and then headed toward her. The multitude of pains in his back intensified—metal and plastic shards from the exploded projector, he figured. Nothing he had time for now.

He saw no one else around—they'd all had the good sense to flee. And the convention center's fire suppression system was making progress in subduing the startling quantity of acrid black smoke that burned his eyes. Small mercies.

He found Marlena pinned under an enormous toppled souvenir cart, with little boxed robotics kits, children's STEM projects, and crumpled T-shirts scattered around her. Her eyes were closed, and blood streamed from a gash on her forehead.

Greene crouched beside her. "Marlena! I'm here."

Her eyes fluttered open. "Chief!"

The heaviest part of the cart rested high on her chest, restricting her breathing and giving her no leverage.

"Just hold on," he said. "Do you think you can move? If I lift it, can you get yourself out?"

"I think so."

He squatted at the end of the cart closest to her and tried to find a good grip with his wet hands. "Ready? One, two, *three*."

He heaved, and the cart lifted, although not as high as he'd envisioned. His pulse pounded in his head like a hammer.

"Can you move?" he managed to grunt.

"Yes, I think—" She broke off, hissing with pain.

But she wormed her way out. The instant Marlena was free, he dropped the cart and stood straight, trying to stop the pain in his back.

Marlena got to her feet, clutching her ribs on her left side.

Greene drew near to be heard over the fire alarm. "Are you all right?"

"Nothing a trip to a doctor won't fix. But I can walk." She said this casually enough, but he saw pain in her eyes. "Thank you, Chief."

"Glad to be of service." He offered her no support. "The exit is this way."

She nodded, and he allowed her to lead the way.

Greene activated his comm. "I've got Marlena. We're on the way out."

"What happened?" Marlena asked. "I heard a *boom*, and the next instant, that cart flattened me. Was it an attack?"

Greene's suit jacket had become heavy with water, and it clung to him. With his adrenaline spent, he suddenly felt tired. "I don't know. Our projector exploded. The new big one. I didn't see why or how."

Marlena's mouth fell open. "*Our* projector? *Exploded?* With all the fail-safes and redundancies, I don't know how that would be possible."

He shrugged. "Or was blown up."

"Damn it." She jabbed a finger at him. "Chief, I want this treated like an attack until proven otherwise. Job one is to figure out what happened, and then you're going to figure out who's responsible."

Greene nodded. "Yes, ma'am."

"Who else was hurt? Do we know?"

He shook his head. "There was so much going on, and my wife— But it was big. It could be bad."

She took a deep breath and let it out slowly. "All right, one thing at a time. Let's make sure our people are safe, and then we'll get the facts."

Greene's comm activated. "We've got most of the Xiong people outside on the east side of the building," Sonnenschein said. "Chief, we put your wife on the first helicopter out of here. We've got a couple of people still inside, though."

"I'm still in the building," Greene replied. "What can I do?"

"You want to go find Garcinia?" Sonnenschein said. "We aren't super worried about her because her chip data says she wasn't anywhere near the blast, but she should have made it out by now."

Marlena met Greene's gaze, then motioned to her own ear. "I heard. Go on. I'll be all right."

Greene nodded, pulled out his damaged phone, and set the single lens of his Spec-Trons to track Garcinia. She was at the far end of the convention center, near the freight entrance. She'd probably been headed to the Xiong truck for supplies. If so, odds were she was safe.

Greene left Marlena and walked briskly through the now-vacant convention center, passing stand after stand of upturned tables and soggy electronics. Everything smelled of smoke and wetness—or maybe it was just him. The sprinkler system had deactivated, but the alarm continued to clang away. Now that the ringing in his ears was subsiding, the sound was harder to ignore, and more annoying, much like the stinging wounds in his back.

He reached into a jacket pocket and pulled out a small bottle of Pain-Kill. He unscrewed the cap and swallowed two capsules dry, then thumped himself on the chest to get down the one that had stuck in his craw. He had a long day in front of him all of a sudden, and it was best to get on top of things now.

Ahead, he saw a line of food booths, the doors to an emergency stairwell, more booths, and then the doors to the loading docks.

Greene passed the Carbotarium and felt a sharp pain in his stomach as he thought of Nisha. Was she all right? Was the baby all right?

Stop it, he told himself. Pay attention. Focus on what you can control.

One of the metal doors to the stairwell banged open, and a tall, fit man sprinted out. Jeans, a leather jacket, a ponytail tied up on top of his head—

Greene was stunned into motionless. "Juha?" he said.

For the briefest instant, the two men made eye contact, and then the running man bulled into Greene with his shoulder, dropping him to the ground.

His back burning, Greene sat up. The man—Juha, there was no doubt in his mind he had seen his old partner Juha Karjalainen—had dashed on across the convention center floor without pausing.

Alternatively, maybe Greene had a concussion. He didn't really know how to make sense of what he was seeing otherwise.

The stairwell door slammed open again, and a second figure emerged, a woman close to fifty years old, wearing a hunter green and orange security uniform, her long hair wrapped around her head in intricate braids.

She stopped, raised a pistol, and drew aim at the fleeing figure.

Without conscious thought, Greene launched himself at her, targeting her arms, trying to knock the gun away, or at least to spoil her shot.

She fired as he knocked her down—Greene had no idea where the shot went—and her smartglasses went clattering across the floor.

The woman shoved wildly at him, then thumped him in the arm with the butt of her gun, and he scooted away from her.

"What the hell? Who do you think you— *Greene?*"

Her sophisticated African Alliance accent was familiar, he realized—and in the next instant, he recognized her, too. "Ojukwu!"

The athletic woman jumped to her feet and pointed a finger at him. "You stay out of this. This is the one time I'm going to warn you." She scooped up her smartglasses and sprinted after Juha.

Greene rose, rubbing his bruised arm, trying without success to get a grasp on what in the world might be going on.

He activated his comm. "Sunny, is there someone else you can send to collect Garcinia? I'm going to follow up on an ... incident. Not sure if related."

"Will do, Chief."

"Thanks."

He took a deep breath and ran after Ojukwu, who was halfway across the convention center by now.

Could he even catch her? His stamina was pretty good these days—better than it had been, certainly—but his tattered, wet suit hung on him like a weight. At least he would finally get a chance to see how these running Oxfords performed. And the Pain-Kill had started to kick in.

Greene went into a full sprint. He had to close the gap now, before she got outside and he lost her.

The floor was wet here, but his traction was surprisingly good. And the cushioned heels were superior by orders of magnitude compared to the other times he'd had to run in dress shoes.

What in the world are you thinking about, he said to himself. Shoes? Focus! How hard did you hit your head?

Greene hurdled over an obstacle in his path and realized mid-leap that it was a body. The sobering realization brought him directly back to the present.

He reached the end of the main floor and emerged onto the concourse, now devoid of people. The sunlight streaming through the immense windows was dazzling. The remaining lens on his Spec-Trons tinted accordingly, and the light disparity between his eyes quickly became disorienting. He yanked the glasses off and thrust them into a jacket pocket.

He paused for only a moment to determine which way Ojukwu had gone, spotted her, and resumed his pursuit. Juha was nowhere in sight.

If it *was* Juha.

There was no question he had recognized his friend, but that meant little these days. Now, illusion was king. After all, a month ago, Greene had been completely fooled by a man wearing a holographic collar.

But what would someone have to gain by impersonating Juha? Alternatively, why would Juha be here, mixed up in all of this, whatever *this* was?

Then again, with Juha, Greene reminded himself, nothing was completely off the table, no matter how ridiculous.

Greene wasn't sure he was closing on Ojukwu, but he was keeping the pace. She'd maintained her conditioning since the last time he'd seen her, what, three years ago?

Greene ran through B Lobby, where the dazzling morning sun blazed through twenty-meter-high plate windows. His breathing had gotten heavier. He fumbled in a jacket pocket for his Power-Through inhaler, took a puff, and ran on, energized.

He reached the main entrance, where the automatic doors had locked open, and sprinted through them.

The emergency vehicles were just arriving—at least five fire trucks, plus ambulances and police cars, blocking the street and filling the convention center's plaza.

Greene ran past them all.

The late morning sun burned high in the cloudless sky, its reflection off the clear water of Reclamation Bay blinding.

Greene had been on this very sidewalk before, numerous times, with Nisha. It was a wonderful place to take a walk, with the beauty of the bay on one side and the grandeur of downtown Portsmith on the other, and, usually, a cool sea breeze on top of it.

"God, please let her be all right," he muttered as he ran down the seaside path, past strolling pedestrians and the occasional food cart, hoping and striving not to collide with anyone or anything.

The bright orange trim of Ojukwu's uniform made her easy to spot, about thirty meters ahead. Perhaps twenty meters further, he could see Juha—or whoever it was.

Greene realized he wasn't actually sure which of the two he was chasing. *Keep her from shooting him*, that was the sum total of his plan.

Juha ran straight on, seemingly content to stay on this path rather than try to cut across the busy street toward the congestion of downtown Portsmith. But where was he going? Straight ahead loomed the Waterfront Amusement Park. On a gorgeous day like today, it would be packed out. A perfect place to shake pursuers.

Greene felt good thanks to the Power-Through, even though his heart thundered in his chest. But, he realized with profound annoyance, he wasn't gaining.

"For God's sake," he said. Here he was, thirty years old, in his purported prime, and he couldn't catch up a pair fifteen and twenty years his senior.

Sonnenschein could have run them down with ease, he thought. But they were all natural athletes, and although he'd never been a slouch and he'd worked on his fitness in the months since he'd joined Xiong Holonautics, he wasn't at their level.

Greene dodged a lady pushing a stroller, nearly barreling into another pedestrian. The Power-Through was doing its part to minimize the burn in his muscles and in his lungs, but he could feel the strain he was putting on his body.

He had no chance of catching either of them, he admitted to himself as his fatigue mounted. In fact, the longer this went on, the farther behind he would fall. The only way he'd get a chance to make up ground was if Ojukwu caught Juha—but if she was closing on him, it was only gradually.

If. So many ifs.

And meanwhile, what was happening at the convention center? The explosion, his wife, his coworkers—those were his priorities. He had profound obligations there.

Was the blast related to this chase? Greene didn't believe in coincidences, but he didn't have anywhere enough information to make a guess as to how the two might be connected. What was it all about? What was Ojukwu doing here? What would happen to Juha? His curiosity burned white-hot.

But he had to let these questions go—at least for now.

Filled with regret, Greene gave a last look at the sprinters ahead of him, then stopped, took a deep breath, and jogged back toward the convention center.

THREE

The elevator doors opened and Greene stepped out onto Xiong Tower's one hundred and seventy-fifth floor.

The décor here was as lavish as that in the Xiong lobby. The glossy onyx walls and floor were inlaid with golden geometric designs, and elaborate light fixtures hung from the high arched ceiling.

At the end of the hall stood the desk of Marlena's executive assistant, Sundstrom, a tiny man with a thick beard and shoulder-length hair who looked like he'd be more at home on a heavy metal concert stage.

"You can go on in, Chief," he said, nodding at the immense pair of leaded glass sunburst doors behind him.

"Thanks."

A good man, all business. No remarks about Greene's torn suit and haggard appearance. No requests for updates from the convention center. He knew he would get the information when it was his time to get it.

Greene pulled open one of the heavy doors and entered.

Marlena's office was somehow even more impressive than the rest of the floor. It was done up in a similar Art Deco style, but with rich reds dominating the palette. A golden Xiong logo taller than Greene, an X and an H overlaid to form two thin triangles, dominated the wall behind the desk, commanding attention.

Marlena Ranga Rao sat stiffly in her chair, wearing a rigid brace around her torso. Her face was still dirty, and she wore the same ruined outfit she'd had on earlier.

She looked up from her terminal as Greene approached the desk. "Ah, Chief, come in, sit down. I'll have some coffee sent in."

"Thank you." Greene sat in one of the four low overstuffed leather chairs flanking the desk, grateful to be off his feet. "Are you all right?"

"A few cracked ribs. Nothing I can't get fixed up downstairs when I have the time. And you? You've been through a lot."

"I'm fine." It was true enough, he supposed. The Pain-Kill was still working, his ears had stopped ringing, mostly, and his clothes had dried to a vague dampness.

"You haven't been to Medical." It wasn't a question.

"It's on my list of things to do."

She nodded. "As long as you're functional. How's your wife?"

Greene tried not to show his considerable concern. This was his problem, not Marlena's. "When I talked to the doctor, she thought Nisha would be all right, but that was a while ago, and I haven't gotten an update."

"I'm sure that's high on your list. It's better for all of us if we keep this meeting short. What have you got for me?"

Greene took a deep breath and let it out slowly. "All of our people are accounted for. Garcinia is fine. Two of our technicians are dead. Four more of our people are injured. Of those, Max Fill got the worst of it. He's in critical condition."

"Damn it." Marlena tugged at a stray lock of copper hair. "He's here?"

"Yes. Medical was giving him most of their attention the last time I checked in."

"God, I hate losing people." She sighed. "I don't know how to say it in a way that doesn't sound trite or corporate, but I mean it. Keep going."

Greene shifted in his seat to retrieve his phone from his pocket, noticing as he did so that he'd tracked dirt across Marlena's pristine cream carpet.

He pulled up the footage from his Spec-Trons and cast it to Marlena's wall screen. "As you can see, that looks like Juha Karjalainen. My Spec-Trons IDed him as Juha."

Marlena leaned back in her chair, winced, and sat up again. "Yes, that's Juha, all right. I don't blame you for going after him."

"Firstly," Greene said, "I'm open to the possibility that it is in fact Juha, although at the moment, I'm at a total loss as to why he'd be involved in something like this. However, you remember that Shepherd had a holographic collar, which wasn't our tech, and was impersonating—"

He closed his mouth, cursing himself inwardly. Of course Marlena remembered—Shepherd had used the collar to masquerade as her dead husband.

"Anyway, I have no idea why someone would impersonate Juha," he concluded lamely.

Marlena didn't appear to be offended. "You know, it's funny that you bring that up, actually—"

She broke off as her console beeped.

"Come in!" she said.

Deputy Security Chief Burg entered. She wore her usual black and gold security uniform, which stretched tight across the muscles in her shoulders and thighs in a way that always pricked the tiniest bit of jealousy in Greene.

Behind her came Garcinia, looking no worse for wear.

Greene nodded to them both. Garcinia patted him on the arm and sat next to him. Burg remained standing.

Marlena studied Burg's grim face. "I'm not expecting you to have anything good to say, so let's just have it."

"It wasn't a bomb," Burg said.

"Not as such," Garcinia added.

Marlena looked as surprised as Greene felt. "What do you mean?" she asked.

"The projector itself exploded," Garcinia said. "The power core overloaded."

"That's not supposed to be possible," Marlena said.

Garcinia shook her head. "No. It's not."

Her face hard, Marlena leaned forward, elbows on the desk, grimacing from the movement. "So what are you saying? We have two people dead and more in the infirmary because of our own staggering incompetence? How could that happen?"

Greene met Burg's gaze, and she shrugged slightly.

Garcinia turned her palms upward. "You know that it's not *impossible*, per se. But it *is* extremely unlikely. Yes, it's a new model of power core, but we've tested it extensively."

"Yes," Marlena said. "I've seen the reports. It's supposed to be very stable."

"Oh, it is, it is," Garcinia said.

"Then give me an alternative hypothesis."

"Someone could have attached an explosive device to it," Burg said.

"Perhaps," Garcinia said. "Although that would have certainly been sufficient to destroy the projector, it's unlikely to have caused the power core to overload."

Greene stretched in his chair, fighting the fatigue that pulled at him. "We should have CCTV footage from the convention center for the whole time we were there. If somebody tampered with the projector, it should be easy enough to determine."

Based on Burg's response, or lack of it, Greene guessed she didn't know about Juha—or his doppelganger.

Marlena returned her attention to Garcinia. "You have a different hypothesis?"

The old woman nodded. "I think the projector itself was sabotaged. Deliberately overloaded. I certainly don't mean to tell you all how to do your jobs, but I think that's the way we should be investigating this until we have a compelling reason to do otherwise."

"Could it have been sabotaged remotely?" Marlena asked.

"Hm. I want to run some tests, but it's possible. It would take access to our system, which is of course concerning on a much deeper level, but if you had that, I don't think it would be difficult if you knew how."

"Everything's easy if you know how," Greene muttered.

Marlena frowned at him. "What do you mean?"

Greene shook his head. "Nothing. Sorry. Just thinking out loud."

"Would remote access be something you can prove?" Marlena asked.

Garcinia shrugged. "Possibly."

Marlena's intercom chirped. "I apologize for the interruption," Sundstrom said. "I thought you would like to know that the police are downstairs. They'd like to have a word, and possibly a bit of a statement."

Marlena thought for a moment, then activated her panel. "All right, I'm coming. Have the lawyers meet me down there in fifteen minutes. No, thirty. Let me tidy up a bit first. This is too disheveled for Xiong. And send down Max Fill— Oh. Send down whatever media people are available."

"Very good, ma'am."

Marlena turned back to Burg. "Follow Garcinia's lead and stay on this. I want an explanation, but more than that, I want *evidence*."

Burg nodded. "Understood." She waited for Garcinia to rise from her chair, then opened the doors, and the two of them left.

Marlena swiveled in her chair. "Now, Chief, I have something else in mind for you."

This remark pricked at Greene's heart, and he tried not to show it. "This is priority one for the entire company, isn't it? Why am I not on it?"

Marlena gave a little sigh. He was trying her patience.

"Chief, would you say that Burg has as much experience with explosives as you do?"

"She's ex-military," Greene said. "I'm sure she has more."

And he was sure that Marlena knew this as well.

"Do you have some other concern about her ability to do this job?"

"No, not at all. I—" He broke off. There was no good way to say it. And possibly it shouldn't be said in any case.

Greene felt, not for the first time, excluded from the company's most important affairs. Xiong had hired him as chief of security over more qualified candidates, including Burg—had hired him to be the fall guy for an internal conspiracy, as it had turned out. But even though he had proven himself to the company, the same insecurities persisted. He possessed that much self-awareness, at least.

Whether Marlena knew about or suspected any of this, Greene had no idea. But it didn't matter.

"I have a task that's uniquely suited to you," Marlena said. "And it might be a chance to kill two birds with one stone. You know we're still cleaning up the mess that Shepherd left when he tried to steal this company out from under us. We've recently identified a property he leased that he may have used as a safehouse for his tech smuggling. I want you to take a team and check it out, recover what you can, and back bring anything you find."

Greene scowled. "That's important, of course, but I don't see how it's more urgent than today's disaster. Doesn't that take precedence? Of course, let's send a team over there. But you don't need me to lead it."

Marlena opened a drawer of her desk, pulled out a brush, and began to pull it vigorously through her hair. "I am willing to discuss your duties, to an extent, but I am not willing to spend time arguing about them. Am I clear?"

Greene realized that the battle had been lost from the start. "Yes, ma'am."

"First of all, it *is* urgent. This might finally be our chance to find out what exactly he stole from us. Second, I want you to see if you can track down Juha and take him along."

Greene looked up sharply. "Really?"

"Just see if he's available as a freelancer for a few hours. If Shepherd used holographic defenses to protect his assets, which I think is likely, it will go a lot more smoothly with Juha helping. Plus it would give you a chance to talk to him about today. I know you want that, and we need to in any case."

Greene didn't find this plan appealing, but it made sense. "You think I'll be able to get a hold of him that easily?"

"Why not?" Marlena said. "If you're right and he wasn't involved, if it was someone impersonating him, why wouldn't he want to talk to you? Odds are, once he hears about it, he'll want some information from you. And talking to him might give you insight one way or the other."

Greene shrugged. "Fair enough."

Marlena replaced the hairbrush in the drawer. "Have him help you find whatever's there in Shepherd's place. But make sure he doesn't take any of it. Don't even let him get too close of a look at it."

Greene found himself both surprised and relieved to hear that he was not the only one holding lingering suspicions of Juha.

"Agreed," he said. "Anything else?"

She shook her head. "I've taken the liberty of having a team prepped. They're going to meet you at the site, secure it, and wait for your arrival."

"I'll leave immediately." Greene rose from his chair. Stiffness had begun to settle in.

Marlena held up a hand. "No. Change first. You look like hell. Don't forget: you're representing the company, and the company is strong."

"Yes, ma'am."

Greene left, grateful for the opportunity to get into some dry clothes. He nodded to Sundstrom on his way out—the man rose from his chair immediately and headed for Marlena's office.

As Greene headed for the elevator, he pulled out his phone, took a deep breath, and called Juha.

To his surprise, Juha answered immediately. "Green Greene. What can I do for you?"

"Hey. Where are you right now?"

"I'm at FatAss. Just finished a class. What's up?"

"Are you free in thirty minutes?"

"Ooh, that's mysterious," Juha said. "I can be, if it's for something sufficiently exciting."

"I think you'll be interested," Greene said. "I'm on my way. I'll see you soon."

The rest of the questions could wait.

FOUR

Greene's autodriven company car diverted the crush of traffic at Morbid O'Beefity's Triple Bypass, which now featured a huge sign reading *Try Our New Sausage Gravy Fountain!*, and parked across the street in front of FatAss.

Greene got out of the car, brushing a speck from the lapel of his fresh suit. He entered the gym, wishing he'd had time to shower.

The FatAss lobby had a simple layout, with a welcome desk facing the street, glass doors to the workout area on the left, and locker rooms and Juha's office to the rear.

The gigantic picture of Juha at his heaviest had been mounted on the wall since the last time Greene had visited. Next to it hung an equally large picture of the current fit version of Juha. It seemed not to have been touched up in any way—the age lines on Juha's face remained, as did the loose skin on his neck from his extreme weight loss. Nonetheless, he looked great for a man of forty-five.

Greene felt surprise at how few people he saw in the building, and he wondered whether business was struggling or if he'd just come during off-peak hours. Possibly the latter if Juha was so readily available.

Juha Karjalainen leaned over the front desk, talking to his younger sister Satu. Juha wore sweaty workout clothes, and his hair hung loose to his shoulder blades.

"No, I don't want to hire Vince," he said to Satu. "I don't want to interview Vince. I don't even want to speak to Vince. Vince is a terrible fucking coach."

"He's extremely good looking, though," Satu said.

Juha shrugged. "How else do you think he got this far in life? Maybe he can stand in the corner and hand out towels, then. I don't want him so much as talking to any of my clients."

"Why?"

"In the first place, he is an irredeemable nutritional despot if ever I've seen one, which is compounded by the fact that he doesn't know what the fuck he's doing. Literally fuck all. For example, do you know that he took a 140-kilo client, morbidly obese, had never set foot in a gym before, and put him directly on a super-low-calorie protein-only diet, trying to get him to lose two kilos a week? He told me this, smug and proud, and I said to him, 'Just imagine eating nothing but synthesized chicken breasts for six weeks and then trying to take a shit. It's inhumane. But more importantly, what on God's sin-cursed earth makes you think that this is not a horrific option filled with suffering for *anyone* just starting out, or even for ninety-nine percent of the population in general, or that this guy isn't going to gain every last bit of that weight right back the minute he stops engaging in your dietary self-flagellation?' He didn't have a real answer, some spew about willpower, as though you can't look around at the state of the world and see that the overwhelming majority of people aren't capable of willpowering their sorry asses out of a wet paper bag. Goddamn irresponsible nonsense is what it is."

Satu looked up and saw Green, and her eyes brightened. She straightened in her seat and adjusted her form-fitting tank top, which showed off her excellent muscle tone. "Hello, Green!"

"Hello, Satu," Greene said.

She thumped Juha on the arm. "You didn't tell me Green was coming."

"What am I, your secretary? Oh, that reminds me, you're leading the two o'clock class." Juha straightened and turned away from her indignant look. "Green, you're looking sharp. And you've got two hands again, good for you. Your wife have that baby yet?"

"Not yet," Greene said.

"Oh, good. You still have time to name it Juha, then."

"We're having a girl."

"Well, then— I actually don't know the feminine equivalent in Finnish. But don't let that stop you; nobody will know any better."

"Juha—"

Juha clapped his hands together. "Well, I'm sure you're in a hurry to talk, because you're always in a hurry to do everything, so let's step right into my office, shall we?"

The office behind the front desk was just as bare as it had been a month ago, containing only a desk, a chair, a loveseat, a mini-fridge, and a cabinet, with a couple of pictures of Juha and Satu on the walls.

"Anyway, sit down." Juha massaged his forehead. "God, I have got a headache." He opened the mini-fridge and took out a glass carafe. "Coffee?"

Greene sat down on the loveseat. "No thanks."

"No coffee? Must be serious." Juha brought the carafe to his lips and drank half its contents in one draught.

Greene waited for Juha to take the carafe to his desk and sit. He'd seen too many of the man's dietary antics to show a reaction.

Juha took a bottle of pills from his desk and tipped a few into his mouth. "I think I know why you're here," he said, chewing them.

"Do you?" Greene was happy to give Juha as much rope as he wanted.

"I do. The convention center, right? I heard about it."

Greene raised an eyebrow. To his knowledge, the media hadn't made the connections that seemed to be implicit between them. "How?"

Juha waved a hand languidly. "You know me. I have a lot of connections."

"Connections?"

"Yeah. Connections. Like you."

"But I—"

"Look, this obviously isn't a social visit." Juha put his feet up on the desk. "It's not like you come visit me for fun. It's been a month since we killed your dick boss and you haven't so much as texted."

Greene felt a flush of guilt. "I've been really busy with everything. I'm sorry. You know how it is."

"That's lame, Green. But it's all right. I'm not mad. It's true, isn't it? I didn't text you either, did I? Everybody's busy. So let's not beat around the bush here."

Greene nodded. "Fine. Where were you this morning?"

Juha looked surprised. "Straight there, huh? I respect that. Does Xiong think I did it? Blew up your tech show? Do you believe that I've turned to a life of crime? Are you here to wreak corporate vengeance?"

Greene chose his words carefully. "The investigation is ongoing, but Xiong does not currently have a reason to consider you the prime suspect."

"Oh, that's very reassuring." Juha raised the carafe. "Cheers."

"But we also need to talk about the Crestridge business." Greene's eyes narrowed. "You know about that also."

"Yes," Juha said innocently. "Connections, you know. Are they coming for me too?"

Not only was Juha unreadable, but Greene would have sworn the man was doing this on purpose.

Greene took a deep breath, trying to keep emotion off his face. "I don't know, but I don't know why they were after you in the first place." Greene chose not to qualify this remark.

Juha studied Greene's face a moment, then shrugged. "Might be good to find out."

"I've got to be honest with you," Greene said. "If you knew about it already, I'm a little surprised to find you here. I saw you, or whoever was allegedly impersonating you. And Ojukwu saw you."

Juha smiled up at the ceiling. "Oh yes, Perseverance Ojukwu. What a blast from the past. Turns out she's Crestridge's new chief of security. Who knew? Man, I hate that lady."

This caught Greene by surprise. "Why?"

"Because she hates me," Juha said matter-of-factly.

"I know you two had your differences, but that seems like a very dramatic overstatement."

"You were a young man at the time, very green, as it were. I tried to shield you from some of what happened. It's not good for mom and dad to fight in front of the kids, you know."

So there was more backstory here than Greene knew. His curiosity burned inside him, but right now, he had to stay on task.

"Juha—"

"Just a minute. You say you saw me, or an impersonator. Am I coasting by on good faith here?"

"I work for a hologram company," Greene said. "There's very little I take at face value these days."

"Good for you. That's the beginning of wisdom, that is."

"Still, if Crestridge comes after you—"

"What do you think I should do, Green?" Juha put his feet down and sat up straight. "So whether it was me or not at your thing today, you think I should ... what? Run away and hide like a guilty person?"

Greene chuckled in spite of himself. "Touché. But still, you're kind of exposed here."

"Not to belabor the point, but again, do you want me to hide out? For how long? I have a life in the first place, and I couldn't outlast a company like Crestridge in the second place even if I wanted to make the attempt."

Juha said all this very conversationally—he certainly didn't look or sound worried. Then again, he never did.

"How long?" Greene repeated. "Until all of this gets resolved." As he said it, he realized that he didn't have the slightest clue what "all of this"—or even *any* of this—was about.

Juha smiled. "Then how fortunate for me that I have you here to resolve it. I'm grateful, Green, I really am."

Greene sighed, suddenly feeling very tired. "I'll help you however I can, really, but that's not primarily why I'm here."

"Oh?" For the first time, Juha looked genuinely curious. Perhaps to mask his expression, he drained the rest of the coffee.

"Is that caffeinated?" Greene asked.

"Of course. Why?"

Greene shook his head. "Are you up for a job?"

"Does it pay?"

"Yes. But it shouldn't take more than two hours."

"Mm hm. Right now?"

"Right now." Greene decided to pull the string—he so rarely got the opportunity. "My boss suggested that you might be of use and explicitly told me that your help would be appreciated."

Juha traced his finger along the outside of the empty carafe, making a line in the condensation. "Oh yes, a new boss. You and your corporate masters. Is it another mercenary psychopath, like your old one? Or have they gone for a different variety of psychopath to mix things up?"

"It's Marlena Ranga Rao."

This time, Juha failed completely to keep the surprise off his face. "Huh. Interesting. Well ... I suppose I could clear my afternoon. Seeing as you're paying and all. Is it dangerous?"

Greene fought back a smile. "I hope not."

"You *hope* not." Juha opened a desk drawer, rummaged around, then laid his pistol on the desk. "Got it. So what are we doing?"

"Shepherd was dealing Xiong tech behind all of our backs, as you know. He got away with it for so long because he had some technology we hadn't seen before. We've been through his house, his apartment, his yacht—we've gone through all of his assets and we still don't know where he got it. But we've just identified a safehouse that belonged to him. We hope it might contain some of his tech, or at least some leads on where it came from. But we're afraid there might be some holographic defenses."

Juha gathered his long hair and tied it up in a ponytail on top of his head. "So let me get this straight. That man shot me in my goddamned kidney, and you're telling me I have a chance to fuck him over one last time beyond the grave?"

"Uh, sure."

"Damn, son, you should have led with that." Juha slapped both hands down on the table. "I'm in, let's do it. While you transfer my fee, I'm going to go change and see about the class schedule. Give me five minutes and then we'll go have some good times."

FIVE

Greene fed the safehouse address into his car's computer and engaged the autodrive.

Juha was unexpectedly non-conversational, spending the bulk of the ride on his phone—contacting clients, he said. Greene wasn't certain what to make of it. However, the silence enabled Greene to spend most of the trip reviewing the safehouse floor plans.

There didn't seem to be much to the place. The safehouse was just a small apartment—a kitchen-and-living area with a tiny bedroom and bathroom—in an immense building. It wasn't Shepherd's style at all, which was likely why it had gone undetected for so long.

"Huh," Juha said, and Greene looked up. "Not what I was expecting. Here I thought you were going to take me someplace classy."

Greene glanced at Juha's jeans and leather jacket, but said nothing.

The car had brought them to the Foundry District, a poorer area on the outskirts of the city cramped with high-density tenements. Greene noted the cracked, trash-lined streets. A surprising number of people were outside, many of them sitting on the curb or leaning against these ugly concrete buildings, seemingly just watching. The scene contrasted sharply with Portsmith's pristine city center.

This road had no parking lane, but the car nevertheless pulled up behind an unmarked van that Greene's Spec-Trons informed him belonged to Xiong. The team had already gone inside.

Greene stretched as he got out of the car, wishing he had thought to bring another dose of Pain-Kill.

"Well, this is some kind of shithole," Juha said. "Are you sure you want to leave the car? Is it going to be here when we get back?"

Greene looked around. They were attracting a lot of attention.

"Logos on, credentials on," Greene said, and glowing blue Xiong Holonautics emblems appeared on the hood and doors.

Juha yawned theatrically, lifting a hand to his mouth and deliberately revealing the shoulder holster under his jacket. "You know, if someone's desperate enough, that might be an enticement rather than a deterrent."

Greene sighed. Juha was right. "Security countermeasures on."

The car produced a crackle of electricity, followed by a steady hum, and the emblems changed from blue to bright yellow.

"Be sure to remind me to turn that off before you try to get back in," Greene said.

Juha laughed. "If I didn't know you better, I would have thought you were making a joke."

"Stop staring down the vagrants and let's go," Greene said, making for the front door.

The sunny, pleasant weather outside only amplified the smothering atmosphere of the dark, tiny lobby, which smelled faintly of urine. When Greene's eyes adjusted, he saw weak yellowish light on checkered vinyl flooring and wallpaper that would have been ghastly even when it was new.

The lone elevator was out.

Juha had already reached the stairs. "How high are we going?"
"Seventeen."
"Oh, is that all?"

Greene said nothing on the way up, his efforts focused on keeping up with Juha.

At the eighth floor, Juha motioned at a particularly large stain on the landing that was probably blood. "It must really have galled Shepherd to set foot in this place. He was a fancy motherfucker, you know."

When they reached seventeen, Greene motioned for Juha to stop. It wouldn't do for his team to see him out of breath and sweating. Juha, in contrast, looked as though he had put forth no exertion whatsoever, and Greene, not for the first time, found himself experiencing cardiovascular jealousy.

Greene was mollified by the fact that it took him less than sixty seconds to compose himself. His legs weren't burning nearly as much as he'd feared. He'd improved a lot in the last month. Maybe Juha was a good influence on him after all.

They stepped into the seventeenth-floor corridor. The Xiong team waited for them outside a unit about halfway down. Greene's Spec-Trons gave him their names before he could identify them properly: Sonnenschein, Reeves, Sandow, Cadine, and Krylov from Security, plus Banon, a slim tech of indeterminate gender, who was concentrating intently on a scanner set up at the base of the door.

As they neared, Greene saw that all the Security staff were equipped with carbines. Marlena wasn't taking any chances.

"Only five armed?" Juha muttered under his breath. "No, this isn't dangerous at all."

"Hello, Chief," Sonnenschein said. "We've secured the floor." She indicated a pile of gear near the door of the unit. "We were waiting on you to go inside."

"Very good, Sunny," Greene said. "There are no other entrances to the apartment, correct?"

She nodded, her purple pigtails bouncing. "Correct. There's one external window, but there's no balcony. We sent a drone up, but the window was blacked out and we didn't want to breach before you got here."

"Good. Have you checked for traps?"

"We've been here long enough to run a scan and use the snake camera. We didn't find anything. Ordinarily, I would tell you confidently that we're clear. But, you know ... *Shepherd. Holograms.*"

"I know."

"In addition," Sonnenschein said, "this door has a metal core and a reinforced frame, which I'm guessing is not remotely standard for this building."

"Surely you aren't telling me we can't breach it."

Sonnenschein shook her head. "No, of course not. I'm asking if you're sure you want to given the possibility of traps we can't detect and how much of a ruckus you want to raise."

Juha had leaned against the wall with his arms crossed. "Since when does Xiong Holonautics care about ruckus?"

"He's right," Greene said. "Hand me that breaching hammer, please."

Cadine handed him the hammer, a smile on his face.

Greene hefted it. "Please stand back."

"Sir!" Sonnenschein looked as alarmed as she sounded. "That door is reinforced! You're not going to be able to just—"

Greene swung the hammer at the wall a meter from the door. The drywall put up no resistance to his strike, disintegrating into tiny particles and releasing a cloud of dust.

After several more blows, Greene dropped the hammer and stepped back, coughing and wiping dust from his eyes.

Sonnenschein gaped at the person-sized hole in the wall. "Well, that's one approach. Sir."

Greene futilely brushed at the dust covering his suit, wishing he'd worn his tactical uniform like the rest of the team. It was easier to clean.

"Shepherd," he said. "Never quite as smart as he thought he was. Or maybe the rest of us aren't quite as stupid as he thought we were."

Juha laughed. "Well said. I hope the Big X pays your dry cleaning bills."

"They do."

Greene left the Security team posted outside the apartment, and as the thick cloud of dust settled, he, Juha, and Banon entered through the hole into a small living area with a kitchen. The lights inside were already on.

The interior of the apartment was not at all what Greene had expected, but *very* Shepherd. In garish contrast to the rest of the tenement, the apartment was opulent: bright, clean, and ornate, with pristine white walls and dark herringbone hardwood flooring.

"This is all holograms," Juha said. "Even most of the furniture. Look, you don't even need me to tell you."

Greene followed his gaze and felt a brief wave of disorientation. The hole he had just made was gone—he saw only a clean, undamaged wall. But he also saw the pile of rubble on the floor.

Holograms, indeed.

"Can we shut them down?" Greene asked.

The tech, Banon, was moving around the room with a scanner. "The source is shielded. We'll have to find it and shut it down first."

Juha yawned. "I guess that's why I'm here. All right, let's make it happen."

"Right," Greene said. "And be careful what you touch. Shepherd could have left other traps. Oh, and Banon—" He motioned for the tech to follow him back out to the corridor. "Set up a mobile hologram emitter and cover this hole, will you? We're attracting enough attention as it is."

"Sure thing, Chief."

Down the hall, an older woman emerged from her residence and stared at the Xiong team with wide eyes. Greene met her gaze, and she held it for several long seconds, disdain creeping onto her face. Finally, she locked her door, turned, and went down the stairs.

Sonnenschein appeared at his side. "Is there a problem, Chief?"

"No, I—" His phone buzzed, and *Incoming Call: Nisha Greene* appeared on his Spec-Trons' display. "Give me a minute. Go keep an eye on Juha, will you?"

"On it."

Greene walked several meters down the hall for privacy before answering. "Hey. How are you?"

"I'm fine. *We're* fine." Nisha's voice was strong and warm.

Greene felt relief flow through him. "Nothing is wrong?"

"Just a little sore and stiff."

"Where are you now?"

"I just left the doctor and I'm on my way home, where I'm sure that your mother will practically if not literally chain me to the bed."

Greene smiled at this. "I'm sure she will. Do you want me to make you an appointment with the masseuse?"

"Hm ... No, not right now. Maybe tomorrow. I just want to rest, honestly."

"All right," Greene said. "Are you sure you're fine?"

Nisha laughed. "All those times you went out and got shot up and punched while I was stuck at home and couldn't do anything— Maybe now you know a little bit of how it feels. But yes, I'm fine. Stay in your lane and let your mom handle the worrying. God knows I get too much of that as it is."

"Fair enough," Greene said. "I'll try to be home at a decent hour tonight."

"All right."

It was an empty pledge and they both knew it. Greene would be subject to the dictates of the day, as always—whatever The Bear required.

Greene got off the phone and returned to the apartment, feeling with his hand to find the hole in the wall. Xiong really did do good work.

As Greene entered the living area, Sonnenschein waved to him from the doorway to the bedroom.

"Hey, Chief. They're working in here. There literally isn't room for anyone else."

Greene nodded. "Any progress?"

"Hang on," Juha said from the bedroom. "Let's see what this does."

"No, *wait*–" Banon said, and the apartment went completely dark.

Greene's Spec-Trons tried to adjust, but there was no light at all. "What happened?" he demanded.

"Huh," Juha said. "Looks like the lights were all holographic, too."

Greene activated his phone light and found the switch near the front door. He flipped it, and a sickly fluorescent bulb came on, illuminating stained wallpaper and a dingy linoleum floor.

Sonnenschein's eyes widened. "Holy shit, Chief, look at that!"

He followed her gaze to the apartment's front door. "My God." Greene wasn't a demolitions expert, but he could tell the bomb affixed there was big enough to wipe out the whole team.

"It's a plasma charge, too," Sonnenschein said, indicating a greenish cylinder at the bottom of the device. "It would have been a bad day for everyone if we'd tried to come in that way. We didn't see that *at all*."

Greene shook his head. Holograms. Detection methods were falling farther and farther behind the advances.

"My guess is that the intention was to destroy not only any intruders but also whatever's inside this apartment," he said.

Sonnenschein walked over to take a better look. "That much plasma would destroy not only this unit but the ones on either side, and would also collapse the ceiling and the floor. Probably a lot of fatalities no matter what time of day it happened."

"Shepherd wouldn't have cared about that," Greene said.

"Oh ho!" Juha cried from the other room. "What's this? You sneaky bastard!"

Greene turned toward the tiny bedroom. "What have you got?"

Banon emerged, holding a black case about the size of a shoebox. "It was in a hollow compartment under the floor, masked from underneath by a small secondary projector with its own power source. Without your friend here, there's a good chance we would have missed it."

Juha followed just behind him. "You're welcome."

Greene took the case and placed it on the scuffed table in the center of the living area. "Let's have this scanned, please."

"Right away, Chief." Sonnenschein stepped through the hole in the wall and into the corridor.

Juha elbowed Greene in the side. "Pretty good, huh?"

Greene nodded. "Thank you."

"No, thank *you*. For the easy paycheck *and* for the opportunity to once again prove my superiority over your asshole boss. Thus always to assholes."

Sonnenschein returned with the scanner and went to work. "Looks good," she said after a moment.

"Thanks," Greene said. "Please take Juha outside. I'll join you in a minute."

Juha peered at him a moment, then grinned. "You don't want me to see what's in the box! Wow! Look at you, on the fast track to becoming a soulless corporate pawn. I'm proud of you, Green, I am." He winked, then stepped out through the hole.

"Oh, Sunny," Greene said, before she could follow. He motioned toward the trapped front door. "We can't leave this here."

She nodded. "I'll have Cadine get to work on it. He's got more demo cred than I do."

"Thanks." Greene sat down at the small table, took a deep breath, and opened the case.

Inside he found two hard drives, a creased packet filled with handwritten notes and ledgers, and a heavy cloth bag. He picked up the bag, undid the drawstring, and pulled out a metal and plastic ring about the size of a saucer.

Greene turned it over. It bore no manufacturer's imprint. The ring was about four centimeters thick, with a clasp on one side and a hinge on the other. The rest of it was studded with tiny electronic devices. It was hard to tell in this bad light, but Greene thought that perhaps they looked like the smallest hologram projectors he'd ever seen.

He sucked in a sharp breath as realization dawned. This was a facial projection collar, like the one Shepherd had used to impersonate Dr. Ranga Rao. It had to be.

Greene scrounged in his memory for the details. Xiong was working on one of these, Garcinia had told him, but it wasn't remotely close to ready.

The implications were considerable.

Cadine entered the apartment through the hole, his broad shoulders scraping the edges, leaving streaks of white dust on his black uniform and tool bag.

"Bomb disposal, Chief? Here I thought we were about ready to go home. You don't want to leave it for the cops?"

Greene shook his head. Who knew how long it would take them to get here and deal with it, especially in this part of town, if they even came at all. And scavengers would be all over this unit the minute the Xiong team left.

Greene placed the collar back into the bag and closed the case. "File it under corporate social responsibility," he said. "The PR people will tell you: Xiong being a good neighbor is good for business."

Cadine raised an eyebrow.

Greene sighed and stood. "If you don't want to do it for the ten thousand people who live in this building, do it for your stock options."

Cadine laughed. "Whatever you say, boss."

As Greene stepped into the corridor, Sonnenschein flagged him down.

"Trouble?" Greene asked.

She tapped her ear. "Just got word from the van. There are armed multiple contacts at the front door."

Greene held out his hand, and she pulled out her earpiece and gave it to him. He wiped it on the inside of his jacket, then stuck it in his ear. "This is Greene. What have we got? Is it a gang?"

"Sir, this is Ng, in the van. They're wearing tactical gear. My guess is they're corporate."

"Are you guys safe down there?"

"Yes, sir, we relocated as soon as we saw them. Watching them on drone now. They've just gone inside."

"Are they at the front stairs?"

"Looks like it, yes."

Greene turned to his team. "Sunny, stay with Cadine until he's done." He handed her the case. "Then get this out the back way. The rest of you are with me. We're going to go deal with these people."

Ng was in his ear again. "Sorry, Chief, but it looks like they've got another squad at the back. Not coming up, just holding the exit. Six more. Definitely corporate. The colors are Crestridge."

"So penned in but not outnumbered on any one front," Greene muttered. "All right, never mind about the back. We'll have to handle them here."

Juha came alongside him. "Are there any other exits?"

Greene shook his head. "Just those two."

"God, what a deathtrap. I'm excited to see how you get us out of this."

"Call the tower," Greene told Ng. "Have them send reinforcements, but with enough space on the autocopter for the rest of us. Sunny, take that stuff upstairs and find the roof access. Banon, go with them."

Sonnenschein looked apprehensive. "Sir, reinforcements will take fifteen minutes to get here at minimum. By then ..."

"I'm hoping we won't need them," Greene said. "But if we do, we'll buy you the time. Now get going."

"So where do you want to take these guys?" Juha asked. "In the apartment? We could turn the holograms back on and confuse them. They'd be easy targets. Or, hell, is that bomb still on the door? Maybe just let them kick the door in and let nature run its course."

"We're not going to shoot our way out of this if I can help it," Greene said.

Juha nodded. "I figured. That's admirable, but you realize it's not entirely up to you."

"I know that. All right, weapons ready. Let's take position on the stairwell landing."

Carbines in hand, the Xiong team followed Greene to the landing and took their places with gratifying efficiency.

Juha took out his pistol and looked it over. "It's good to know 'not dangerous' still has the same meaning for you as it ever did."

Greene put a hand on his gun but didn't draw it.

"Oh, God, not the heat ray again," Juha said. "Please tell me you have a real gun."

"I have both. It's a new heat ray, though. It's better."

Juha snorted. "It can't be worse. Your old one couldn't reheat coffee."

"I'm hoping I won't need either of them. We're going to talk to these people if possible, understand? You don't shoot first unless I say so, got it? Actually, Juha, it might be better if you went back around the corner and stayed out of this."

Juha shook his head, his topknot bouncing. "No way, man. I'm helping."

Greene rolled his eyes. "Fine. But you're going to let me handle it."

"Sure thing. Just don't get me shot."

Greene sighed. "I'll do my best."

He heard heavy footsteps on the stairs below them, a number of people. Surely the Crestridge squad. He looked back at his team, all of whom had their guns lowered but ready, precisely as they should.

Greene took a deep breath, let it out slowly, and held out his hands at his sides, palms open. "Oh, God, please," he murmured.

There were six of them, all carrying the standard-issue Crestridge submachine gun, all wearing orange body armor over deep green jumpsuits. In the lead came Perseverance Ojukwu.

"That's far enough, please," Greene said when they'd reached the half landing below.

Ojukwu stopped, but she raised her weapon, and her squad followed suit. Greene heard movement behind him as well, surely his team raising their guns.

"Hold!" he said.

"Oh, it's Ojukwu," Juha said quietly. "She's going to shoot me. Maybe you too, but definitely me."

"Ojukwu," Greene said, acutely aware that her gun was pointed directly at him and that he was the only one here not holding a weapon.

"Greene," she said, her voice as hard as the expression on her face.

Be calm, Greene told himself. Be cool. Be *Xiong*. But be reasonable.

"What are you here for?" he asked.

She snorted. "What am *I* here for? You're standing right there with Karjalainen behind you and you're asking me what I'm here for? If that isn't the typical Xiong hubris. Standing there all smug and not bothering to hide it. I expected better from you, Greene. I guess I shouldn't have."

Greene took a deep breath while he pushed down the sting of her words. "I'm just trying to understand what's happening, that's all."

Without shifting her aim, she took a hand off her SMG and pushed her smartglasses up the bridge of her nose. "Understand? You want to understand? Understand that this looks a *lot* like Juha Karjalainen, who brazenly robbed our company this morning, is working for Xiong Holonautics. Do you want me to connect the rest of the dots for you, or can you figure it out yourself? You *used* to be a detective—before you became a thug."

Greene fought to keep the surprise off his face. There were still too many pieces missing from this puzzle for him to get even the vague outline.

He turned and glanced back at Juha, who only shrugged, his face blank.

Greene sighed and turned back to Ojukwu. "I must admit that this is a bad look. Wait just a minute— You were watching Juha at the gym and you followed us here, didn't you? But if you were after him, you could have taken him at any time."

"She could have *tried*," Juha piped up from the back.

Greene resisted the urge to give him a dirty look. "Why?" he asked Ojukwu.

She curled her lip. "I'm just trying to understand, is all."

"I don't suppose you'd believe me if I told you that this isn't what it looks like."

Ojukwu laughed. "Not at all."

Greene looked back at his team. They were holding their positions, alert but not twitchy. Good people, well trained. And even Juha was mostly behaving.

He turned back to Ojukwu, who still had her gun pointed at him. It was time for a change of tack. If shooting started, he wasn't going to make it out in any case.

Still holding his hands palms-up, he said, "Can I sit down? I'm going to sit down."

Without waiting for her to respond, he did so, using slow and exaggerated movements. He planted his feet two dirty steps down, leaned forward, and put his elbows on his knees.

Ojukwu didn't move except to adjust her aim, and neither did her squad.

"All right," Greene said. "There are a lot of guns pointed at a lot of people, so why don't you tell me what you're here for?"

She shook her head. "What are *you* here for?"

"Xiong business completely unrelated to Crestridge or anything that happened this morning."

"Bullshit."

Greene felt his exasperation growing. "It's the truth."

She tilted her head and her eyes narrowed.

"Ojukwu, you know me," he said.

"I *did*. But you're Xiong now."

This lit a fire in Greene, small but hot. He realized that he'd squeezed his hands into fists.

"No, actually," Juha said from behind him. "I mean, I totally get why you'd think that, but I promise, he's the same old boy scout, somehow."

Now she moved, pivoting to aim her weapon at Juha. "All right, let's talk about why *you're* here."

"I'm helping," Juha said, as casually as he said everything. "I've done consulting work for the Big X before. You probably heard about it."

She studied him. "Yes. Shepherd. Your house devours itself."

Juha shrugged again. "Look, you can say what you want about Xiong Holonautics, and it's probably true, but Greene here deserves some credit for trying to singlehandedly rehabilitate the corporate culture and reputation of a multi-billion-gigayuan scumbag company. I mean, he's *really* trying. It's actually very impressive. Like trying to empty Reclamation Bay with a teaspoon, maybe, but he hasn't given up."

Greene put a hand to his forehead. "Please stop talking."

"Yes," Ojukwu said. "Please do."

Greene still couldn't figure where Ojukwu was coming from with all of this, and his diplomatic approach didn't seem to be making much progress.

He tried to view the situation from her perspective. She was brand new in her role, new to the corporate world. She was in the same boat he'd been in when he'd started with Xiong—and was still in, if he was honest with himself. Under tremendous pressure to perform and enthusiastic to do so, but under even more to not screw up. She was ready for a fight, but she wasn't here to start one—she couldn't be.

So what was the best way to handle her?

As soon as he thought it, he knew. Challenge. Bluff. Confront. To her, he was Xiong, with all that entailed. Fine—he would give her Xiong.

"All right," Greene said to her. "How about this. Does Crestridge want a war with Xiong?"

She blinked. "What?"

Greene took off his Spec-Trons, blew dust off the lenses, and put them back on. He felt much more comfortable now, more in control.

"Does Crestridge want an all-out war with Xiong Holonautics? Because if you start shooting here, that's exactly what's going to happen."

She stared at him, trying to read him. "We have more guns downstairs."

"And we have more on the way. Maybe you do, too. But this isn't about today. This is about tomorrow, the next day, the next month, the next year. If you fire a single shot here today, you are declaring war on Xiong Holonautics."

Greene closed his mouth, hoping that Juha would keep quiet. He waited for his words to sink in. There was no need to twist the knife, or to point out that Crestridge was running a distant third in the battle for holographic supremacy in Portsmith. Ojukwu was smart. She would have no trouble getting there.

Ojukwu chewed on her lip for a moment, then lowered her gun.

Relief washed over Greene in spite of himself. He turned to his people and held up a hand, and they all lowered their guns.

Ojukwu motioned for her squad to do the same. "Fine," she said. "What happens now?"

Greene made himself smile. "Now, I would like to cordially invite you to come to my office tomorrow morning—"

She opened her mouth to protest, but Greene didn't stop.

"—where I will present you with what is at least a plausible explanation for why Juha Karjalainen may not be responsible for whatever it is you think he did. And we can discuss, openly and honestly, any other matters that you care to. *Any.*"

As she thought about this, Greene suddenly felt glad that he had worn a suit instead of his Xiong tactical uniform.

He dismissed this as an irrational thought. Had it mattered?

Ojukwu still looked uncertain.

Greene stood up and brushed himself off. "Look, you know what happened to us today at the convention center. You've got problems and I've got problems. Maybe we can work together to solve some of them."

She finally nodded. "Fine. But I want the usual safeguards and provisions in writing before I set one foot through your door."

"Done."

"Then I will see you tomorrow morning at eight o'clock."

"Nine," Greene said.

She cocked her head. "Eight."

Greene decided to be magnanimous in victory and accept the disruption to his schedule. "Fine."

Ojukwu nodded curtly, turned, and went down the stairs, her team in tow.

Greene felt all the muscles in his body relax.

One of his people, Reeves, clapped him on the arm. "Nice job, boss."

"Well done, everyone," Greene said. "See if Cadine is done with that bomb, and then let's get packed up and get out of here."

His phone rang. It was Sonnenschein.

"Chief, the autocopter is on the roof and the gear is secure. And Ng says the corporates have withdrawn from the back entrance."

"Thanks, Sunny. I think everything's under control now. Go on and head back to the tower. We'll see you there."

"Understood," she said, and disconnected.

As the Xiong team dispersed, Juha draped an arm across Greene's shoulders. "Good work, high fives all around.

Although, you know, you could have just shot her and saved yourself a lot of hassle."

Greene shrugged him off. "I also could have just given you to her and saved myself even more hassle."

Juha put a hand to his chest. "Oh no, my feelings."

"You're a lot more trouble than you're worth sometimes, you know that?"

Juha shrugged. "It's true. But that's what's so great about you, Green—you love me anyway."

"If that were the case—which I am by no means acknowledging or agreeing to—it is something that you have never failed to capitalize on any time it might benefit you."

Juha chuckled at this. "I'm impressed, though, really. Brinksmanship? You? Who knew?"

Greene frowned. "Not how I would have preferred to handle it."

"You're never happy, are you? Even when everything works out. Nobody got shot. What more do you want? All's well that ends well, I say."

"I suppose. Come on." Greene headed down the stairs. "Listen, after everything that's happened, do you want a guard for the night? Do you want to stay in the tower?"

"Nah," Juha said. "I'm good, thanks."

"Are you sure?"

"Your concern is touching. But the last time I was in your tower, you got your arm chopped off and I almost got blown up with a plasma grenade."

"*You* were the one holding that plasma grenade, but fine, have it your way." Greene felt too tired to argue the point.

Juha stroked his chin, obviously recollecting. "Ah, but we had fun, didn't we?"

SIX

Greene's phone alarm yanked him from sleep, and his first feeling was disorientation. He opened his eyes, saw an elephant, and questioned his lucidity.

His alarm continued chirping.

Bewildered, he made himself sit up, and everything slowly fell into place. He was on his couch, in the living room of his apartment, in the middle of the peaceful Kerala backwaters, near a family of elephants drinking from a green river choked with water hyacinth. A grand two-story houseboat floated downstream. The entire panorama was eerily silent.

Mother had turned on her holograms.

Greene fumbled for his phone and switched off the alarm. "Turn off the living room program," he told it, and the lush scenery vanished, replaced by white walls and simple simulated daylight.

Getting up took a concerted effort. All of his medications had worn off overnight, and he was stiff from the waist down. He wished he'd soaked in the tub last night, but he'd been too tired and had too much on his mind to think of it.

He stumbled to the bedroom, trying to be quiet. Nisha was still in bed.

When he came in, she hauled herself into a sitting position and switched on the lamp. "Good morning."

He sat on the bed and held her hand. "Sorry, I didn't mean to wake you."

"You didn't." She patted her belly. "*She* did. What time did you finally get home last night?"

"I don't know. Late. After eleven. I didn't want to bother you."

She nodded. "How was work?"

"A mess." He related the events of the previous day, omitting the encounter with Crestridge. He had no need for her to know how many guns he'd had pointed at him. Or *any* guns, for that matter. "Anyway, based on the reports they sent me last night, it's looking increasingly like the projector was blown up on purpose."

"Is that better or worse than the alternative?"

He shrugged. "Better for the company's image. Worse for me, because I have to figure out who did it, and why. But what about you? Are you okay?"

"Yes, I already told you that. What's the matter?"

He turned one palm up. "You were in an explosion and I didn't even get to see you the entire day." He felt an unexpected surge of emotion in his chest, and he frowned. "I'm sorry. I'm sorry I can't be here. I'm doing my best. It's not good enough, and I'm sorry it's not good enough."

She patted his hand. "You're doing fine. Except there's one more thing I need from you."

"What's that?"

"I need you to not run yourself into the ground figuring this out."

"I won't."

Nisha let out an exasperated grunt. "You always say that. And you always do."

"I have to do my job," Greene said.

Now she looked genuinely annoyed. "That's what you always say."

"Because it's always true. What do you want me to do? This isn't exactly a job I can half-ass."

She made a fist and thumped him in the chest hard enough to be irritating. "And I'm trying to have a baby here, damn it. *Your* baby. For God's sake, you're no good to me dead."

Greene realized she was worried about him, somehow as much or more than he was worried about her. If he said the things that came naturally to his mind, she would get angry, they would fight, and everything would be worse.

Instead, he said, "Don't be like that. The life insurance is all paid up."

She stared at him for a moment. Then she laughed, and the tension broke.

Greene kissed her forehead, then rose and went into the bathroom. He opened the medicine cabinet, grabbed the bottle of pain medicine, and swallowed two capsules without water.

"Can you get some Pain-Kill when you do the shopping order?" he called. "We're almost out."

"Again?" Nisha said, her tone combative. "You're taking too much of that stuff."

"I have to get to an early meeting. I'd be happy to discuss that with you later," Greene said, having absolutely no intention of doing so. Conflict with Nisha was to be avoided at all costs. He could put Pain-Kill on the list himself, or better yet, just pick some up after work.

Greene showered, dressed, and emerged from the bedroom to find Nisha and his mother sitting down to breakfast. The pleasant scent of steamed rice flour cakes and coconut filled the dining room.

His mother accosted him immediately. "Green-kutty! Don't you sleep in your own bed anymore?"

"I came in pretty late," Greene said. "I didn't want to disturb Nisha."

By her expression, she approved of this excuse. "Yes, it's terrible, people just blowing things up everywhere. Sit down and have food."

"I can't. I have to be at work in twenty minutes. I'm just going to grab some coffee."

Nisha, holding a mug of tea in both hands, gave his mother a knowing look. "I told you."

"Yes. I don't know how you think you're going to save the world on an empty stomach. All right, wait here." His mother disappeared into the kitchen, then returned with a plastic container, which she forced into his hands.

"Thanks, Mom," Greene said.

She patted his hand. "Be safe, Pacha."

When he had kissed them both goodbye, he took out his phone and summoned his car to the front of the building, then headed for the elevator.

Greene reached the ground floor and found his car waiting for him. He got in, fastened his seatbelt, and instructed the car to take him to Xiong Tower, maximum traffic diversion.

Almost immediately, he found himself scratching absently at his reattached forearm, his thoughts fixed in a tight loop as he tried, probably in vain, to guess how his meeting with Ojukwu would go. It had been a long time since he'd seen her. He was in the position of advantage, but he also wanted to impress.

He opened the container his mother had given him, and the fragrance of the contents filled the car. Six discs of noolappam and a cup of coconut chutney. His stomach growled, and when he had eaten the food, he felt better prepared to face the day.

Greene arrived at Xiong Tower at ten minutes to eight. "Park and charge," he told the car.

The sun warm on his face, Greene looked up at the black facing and gold leaf of the massive Art Deco building, an anachronism amidst the taller, sleeker steel-and-glass skyscrapers that filled downtown Portsmith. The holographic golden bear that endlessly roamed the sky above the tower came into view, looking down, seemingly directly at him.

"I am Xiong Holonautics," Greene reminded himself.

He entered the building and was met at check-in by Rich Lather, Xiong Security's hulking first impression.

"Morning, Chief," Lather said as Greene badged in at the executive scanner.

"Morning, Rich. Is my guest here yet?"

"She came through about fifteen minutes ago. We screened her, got her cleared, and sent her upstairs."

That was conspicuously early.

"Good. Any issues?"

The big man shook his head. "No, sir. Just her attitude."

"Right. Thanks for the warning."

After passing through check-in, Greene paused to take in the sight of the five-story Xiong lobby: the geometric designs in the tiles and on the walls, the magnificent stained glass windows, the huge splashing fountains, all of it absurdly intricate, all of it done in gold and black, all of it opulent without being pretentious.

Ojukwu had to be impressed. Had she been in this building before? Greene didn't know. But he'd seen this sight several hundred times and was still impressed.

Greene headed for the elevators at the far end of the lobby, half-expecting to be accosted by Max Fill or one of the members of his PR team, as was typical the morning after a newsworthy event for the company.

But Max Fill had been severely injured in the explosion at the convention center and was lying in Medical, clinging to life. Greene didn't particularly care for Max's personality, but this sobering thought sucked the positive feelings he'd scraped together right out of him.

He got onto the elevator, informed it of his destination, and spent the duration of the short ride taking deep breaths and reminding himself to project calm, secure strength.

By the time the doors opened onto the Security floor, he'd almost convinced himself.

Perseverance Ojukwu stood in front of the waiting area desk, wearing her green and orange Crestridge uniform, her jet-black hair wrapped around her head in a crown braid. Not sitting in one of the numerous available chairs, not pacing, not using her phone—just standing there, still, her arms crossed, a lithe, imposing goddess.

As Greene approached, she gave him a disapproving look. The time on his Spec-Trons' HUD was 7:59, so it couldn't have been tardiness. Then again, he reflected, at no point in the past day had he seen a substantially different expression on her face.

Greene hoped his smile looked sincere. "Welcome," he said, extending his hand.

Ojukwu hesitated a moment before taking it. Her grip was firm, challenging.

He held her eye contact and his smile even though she was crushing his pinkie against his ring finger. "Would you care to step into my office?"

She nodded, released his hand, and followed him.

Greene's door opened upon his retina scan, and he beckoned her through into the darkened room.

As they entered, the tint on the plate-glass wall lightened to full transparency, flooding the room with the morning sun.

Greene closed the door behind him. Before he could invite Ojukwu to sit, she occupied one of the chairs in front of his desk. Greene removed his suit jacket, tossed it onto the couch in the corner, and sat at the desk.

He opened a drawer and pulled out a blockbox, which he placed on the desk. He removed his Spec-Trons and placed them inside, then motioned for her to do the same with her smartglasses. Once she had, he closed the lid and sealed it.

"That's a good show," Ojukwu said. "I'm supposed to believe you don't have any other recording devices in here?"

Her voice, her accent, and her face brought back a flood of memories from his police days. He dismissed them all, forcing himself to focus on the present.

"As a matter of fact, I don't," he said pleasantly.

Her eyes narrowed. Then she shrugged. He knew what she was thinking—either he was telling the truth or he wasn't, and she had nothing to gain by pressing the issue.

"Shall we get down to it then?" Greene asked.

Ojukwu looked around at the décor covering his walls and shelves: family pictures, police awards, certificates in recognition of professional achievements.

"You seem pretty well moved in here," she said. "But you must know that this isn't a position known for longevity."

It was the complete truth.

"Maybe," Greene said. "But as long as I'm here, I'm going to *be* here." Making the office his own helped him manage his own insecurities in that regard, but he didn't need to tell her that.

Ojukwu leaned forward in her chair. "Greene, how did you get one of the best security jobs in Portsmith?"

Greene opened his mouth, then paused. Unbidden, more memories flashed through his mind. How he'd initially applied for the deputy position, Burg's job, and not even with any expectation of getting it; his shock and pride upon being named Xiong's newest chief of security; the gut punch of learning that Shepherd had hired him as a patsy and set him up to fail. He couldn't possibly explain these things to her.

"Just lucky, I guess," he said.

"I guess," Ojukwu said, frowning. "You know, in a way, I have you to thank for my job. At least in part." She glanced at the blockbox on the desk. "It's not a secret that Crestridge has been something of a ... follower in the industry lately. We're third behind you and Algary. Everyone knows it. After you took down Shepherd, Crestridge decided to follow the trend and go out and find somebody with a clean record, a conscience, someone who wasn't ... brutal."

She seemed uncomfortable assigning positive qualities to herself.

"Someone honorable?" Greene said.

She seemed to consider this descriptor, then shrugged. "Perhaps."

"Well, congratulations. You're well qualified. You were a good captain, a good cop, and a good boss."

"Thank you."

"I wish it were under different circumstances, but it's good to see you. It's been, what? Three years? When we wrapped up the Pascal case. That was the last straw, I guess."

She nodded. "It really was."

"I've never fully understood it," Greene said. "Juha carried that investigation on his back. And it resulted in five convictions. We never would have solved the case without the leads he found."

"Yes, he was absolutely invaluable. Right up until the point that he nearly blew everything with his freelancing."

"I remember. You had us transferred to the Silver Cove Precinct for that."

"I had *Karjalainen* transferred, not you," Ojukwu said. "He's a man of many talents, but he's also a buffoon, and he's been getting by his whole career on the fact that his positive qualities marginally outweigh his considerable negative ones. He was exhausting to work with, even on routine cases."

Greene nodded. "I know."

"Not to mention that he singlehandedly cost me at least one promotion with his fuckups. Probably two." Ojukwu pointed a finger at Greene. "But *you* were a good officer. I never had any problems with you. You know that."

Greene processed this. "I thought— I always figured you kicked us out as a package. What happened with me, then?"

"I assume that Karjalainen used whatever clout he'd accumulated to take you with him. I didn't look into it. I was sorry you left, but those were busy days, and I had bigger fires to put out."

"I see."

Juha had done it? The thought had never crossed Greene's mind. For Juha to have gone to that trouble ...

Ojukwu leaned back in her chair and crossed her arms. "Greene, as much as I might love to spend the day here reminiscing, I have many pressing matters to attend to. And I'm sure you do also."

Greene made himself smile at her. "You're absolutely right, of course." He felt that his efforts to get her to warm up to him had been at least somewhat successful.

"You had a bombing yesterday, yes?" she said.

"Yes."

"We had a theft. At precisely the same time. I think it's unlikely to be a coincidence."

"Tell me what happened."

"I was on the floor of the convention center, overseeing the installation of our displays. We had a room up in the hotel where we were keeping the vital components and new technology. Full sensors and alarms, guards, holographic defenses, and a force field on the door. It was very discreet, totally secure. Or so we thought."

"That sounds by the book," Greene said.

"I received a call that the door had been breached. I got there as fast as I could—it took about two minutes to get over to the hotel and up. As I got there, he rushed out, and I went after him."

"He?" Greene asked, although he already knew what she was going to say.

"Karjalainen. He had taken out four of my people."

Greene frowned. "Killed?"

"No. Unconscious. He used a stunstick."

"Go on. Would you like some coffee or tea?"

"No, thank you. Anyway, I chased him. He went down the stairwell to the lobby and cut across to the convention center. He found another set of stairs going up and tried to lose me on the administration floors, and then he came back down—it was a lot of stairs—and that's where we ran into you."

"I guess you didn't catch him."

She shook her head. "He was too fast. Too elusive."

"What was taken?" Greene asked. "The man you were chasing wasn't carrying anything in his hands. Whatever he took couldn't have been anything larger than would fit in a pocket."

She scowled at him. "The man I was chasing? Greene, I know you're naïve, but you never used to be stupid. It was Juha Karjalainen. I saw him and you saw him. Juha Karjalainen, who can recognize holograms with his naked eye, broke into our room and got past all our holographic defenses."

"Just a minute—"

She jerked a finger in the air with such force that he closed his mouth. "*Never mind* that he was with you on a company operation yesterday. *Never mind* that he was with you when you took down Shepherd. He works for Xiong, and he attacked and robbed us."

"He does not work for Xiong," Greene said, as calmly as he could.

She rose up in her seat, seething with furious energy. "How can you sit there and say that to me?"

"We have engaged him as an independent contractor precisely twice. That is all."

She crossed her arms. "Xiong chips all its people, doesn't it? That's industry standard. Is he chipped?"

"He's not chipped. He doesn't work for us."

"But you trust him to do work for you."

"I trust him as a friend and as a colleague."

Ojukwu raised an eyebrow. "Why?"

"Among other reasons, he's saved my life numerous times."

"When you were police officers. And you saved his once or twice back then. I know about that."

"And he saved my life again last month with Shepherd," Greene said.

She shrugged. "Here's what I know: ultimately, Karjalainen is for Karjalainen. Everything he does is for his own ends."

"I understand why you say that," Greene said. "Believe me, I do. But I have decided to trust him and I am going to continue to trust him until he gives me a reason not to."

"He killed his wife. Is that not a reason?"

"You don't know that."

She clucked her tongue. "Oh, come on, Greene, take your head out of the sand. Your loyalty to this man—"

Greene shook his head. "The evidence isn't there, or they would have charged him."

"I know that. I was there the same as you. But it doesn't change the fact that you and I both know he did it, don't we?"

Greene held up a hand. "I think we're getting off topic. What was taken from your room?"

Her eyes were burning slits. "I suppose if Xiong took it, you would know the answer to that question already. It was a prototype lens for light blurring— no, light bending, that's what they told me. It has stealth applications. That's all I can say."

Greene stroked his chin and realized he'd forgotten to shave. "Stealth ..."

Ojukwu rapped a hand twice on the desk. "All right, Greene. I've showed you mine, now you show me yours. Let's say I believe you when you tell me to my face that Xiong didn't do it. Why shouldn't I believe it wasn't Karjalainen? You said he doesn't work for you. He could be working for anybody."

"That's fair," Greene said. "You heard about the business with Shepherd. But you probably don't know that Shepherd had tech that could perfectly simulate another person's face. It's how he got away with half the things he did. But it's not our tech. We haven't figured out where he got it from."

Ojukwu's curiosity showed on her face. "You've seen this tech in person? This isn't hype?"

Greene recalled his encounter with the "resurrected" Dr. Ranga Rao, who had turned out to be Shepherd. "It's true to life. There's no lag, no blur."

Ojukwu nodded. "Sounds like it could be Algary tech."

Greene tried to contain his sudden excitement. She'd said it so matter-of-factly. "How do you know?"

Her chin dropped and she looked away. "Recently, Crestridge has had several cases of unauthorized computer access. Each time, we checked the security logs, and no one was ever in there who wasn't supposed to be. Finally, from the security footage, we figured out who it was, and the next time it happened, we followed him. Straight back to Algary Applications. But at the same time, this employee had an alibi—video evidence of being out at the baseball stadium at the time the breach happened. So we figured impersonation of some kind, but we couldn't work out the particulars."

"Did you catch whoever did it?" Greene asked.

"No. Either we weren't as discreet as we thought and we tipped our hand, or else he got what he was after and hasn't come back."

"When was this?"

"Two weeks ago. Right after I came on board."

"The tech I'm talking about would be ideal for what you're describing," Greene said.

"It would. And you're suggesting that someone used it to impersonate Karjalainen yesterday, and that he may therefore be innocent. But why would anybody impersonate *him*? Who is Karjalainen to Algary, or to any other company?"

"I'm still trying to figure that out. To implicate him, maybe, although I don't know why Algary would want to do that any more than you do. Perhaps to implicate Xiong by proxy. Maybe to start a war between Xiong and Crestridge. I mean, look at us."

Ojukwu nodded. "That's certainly something Algary would do."

"And our projector didn't blow up on its own," Greene said. "It was sabotaged. Which is also something that Algary would do. And these things happened at the same time? Of course I don't think that's a coincidence. Maybe one was meant to be cover for the other, but even if not, it's tough to believe that the two occurrences aren't related in some way."

"I concur."

That was a relief. "Listen," Greene said, "I know you don't trust Xiong on this, and I understand all the reasons why. But if Algary *is* looking to start a conflict, it would be great if we could work together."

Ojukwu grunted. "Xiong and Crestridge working together? You expect me to be able to sell that to my bosses?"

Greene shook his head. "I'm not proposing anything so formal. Just you and me, comparing notes, like we're doing right now."

She leaned back and put a finger to her temple. Then, after a moment of thought, she nodded and got to her feet. "All right. But I want you to know that I'm only agreeing to this because it's *you*."

Greene also stood. "You don't owe me anything for the past."

She snorted. "I know that. But if there's an honest person in this city, it's you."

"Thank you." He opened the blockbox, and she retrieved her smartglasses. "If I turn up anything related to any of this, I'll let you know."

"Fine." As she placed the glasses on her face, one side of her mouth turned up in what might have been a smile. "It *is* good to see you again, Greene."

"Likewise," he said diplomatically. "Can I walk you out?"

"You may."

He led her out to the elevators.

As they waited, she peered at him, tapping her chin with one finger. "You know what? Something's been bothering me this whole time, and I've just figured it out."

Greene's eyebrows narrowed. "What's that?"

"I think I liked you better with the mustache."

Well, Greene thought, it was progress.

SEVEN

Greene arrived at Marlena's office and found Burg already there, which put him slightly on edge. As he entered, the two women broke off their conversation so abruptly that his mind itched to know what they'd been discussing.

Marlena smiled at him. "Chief. Please, have a seat. I was told you were in an important meeting, but I didn't get the details."

"Yes, ma'am." Greene sat in the nearest of the black leather chairs and related his conversation with Ojukwu.

"You did the right thing," Marlena said when he'd finished. "If it *is* Algary that's behind this, stopping them is our highest priority. It's not a good time to get into any trouble with Crestridge."

Burg set her tablet on Marlena's desk, pushed up one short sleeve of her uniform, and absently massaged her sizable bicep. "How do we stop them, though? All right, most likely, it *was* Algary, but we don't know for sure. And on top of that, we don't know what they're after, besides spreading mayhem."

One of the doors opened behind them. Greene turned to see Garcinia enter, carrying her own ever-present tablet.

"Sorry I'm late, dears," she said. "I wanted to be absolutely sure before I told you. And now I am."

"Sit down, please," Marlena said. "Let's have it."

Garcinia took the seat between Greene and Burg. "In my professional opinion, there is a zero percent chance that the projector exploded through accident, flaw, or failure. It was sabotaged. I would bet my life on it."

This was not a surprise, but her certainty hit Greene with force. "So what happened?" he asked.

"The power regulator was removed. Completely and deliberately. That was a fast and clever step on the path to wiring it to blow, I must say."

"How do you know?" Burg asked. "The whole thing was blasted all to hell. There was hardly anything left."

"True," Garcinia said. "But we found the power regulator casing, or most of it. And it was sufficiently intact that there should have been remnants of it left inside. No, I think they stole it. Whoever 'they' is."

"Stole it?" Green and Burg said at the same time.

Marlena loosened and retightened her rib brace. "It fits. If it was Algary, the power regulator could well have been the target. Dropping a bomb on us would have been icing on the cake."

"Just a second," Greene said. "Why would they want the power regulator?"

"It's new tech," Garcinia said. "Much improved over the previous model. More stability under greater loads. But it's not the sort of thing one shows off to the public. Not very shiny, you know. Doesn't fire the customer's imagination."

Burg threw up her hands. "When did they steal it, and how? The implications of what you're saying ... We reviewed all the security footage from the convention center. The only people fiddling with the gizmo from the moment we took it off the truck were our people. All right, maybe one of them sold out to Algary, but they'd be damned stupid to do it so blatantly. And everyone who worked yesterday—and *lived*," she added bitterly, "is here in the tower today." She held up her tablet. "I can have them rounded up in five minutes."

"Go ahead," Greene said. "Do it. Sequester them. Run their chips. Deep-dive their finances. But I don't think it's that simple. You're right, it would be idiotic to do that and then show up for work the next day. What Garcinia is describing isn't something we weren't going to figure out eventually. You're going to do something like that and then show up for work like normal to get taken down for murder? What's worth that? No matter what Algary pays, you can't spend it when you're dead."

Burg was tapping away at her tablet. "I agree, but do you have a better idea?"

Greene held up one finger. "The collar. The holographic collar. Garcinia said that Algary was ahead of us on that tech. If everything that happened *was* Algary, then it all makes sense. Algary could have impersonated Juha to steal from Crestridge, and they could have impersonated one of our technicians to get access to our projector." He turned to Garcinia. "What you think happened— How long would it take, do you think?"

"Oh, if you knew what you were doing and came prepared, only a couple of minutes."

"I'm afraid you're on the right track," Marlena said, her face creased with concern. "It's frightening to think about. Based on what you're saying, we could have Algary people in the building right now, undetected, getting into whatever they please?"

"Now, now. It isn't nearly so dire." Garcinia reached over and patted Greene on the arm. "Our security is a fair bit better than that. We have biometric screening. Everyone is chipped. With the collar alone, certainly, you could get into the building, but you couldn't access any sensitive areas. At the convention, though, we had a lot of coming and going. We weren't screening our people there. It wouldn't have been hard for an impostor to wait until one of them went to the restroom or stepped out of the area to duplicate them."

Marlena drummed her fingers on the desk, frowning. "Then clearly we need to beef up our public demonstration protocols immediately. Chief, I want you to— Green, I'm talking to you!"

Greene blinked. "Sorry, I was thinking. I—" He turned toward Burg. "Don't we have some biometric data on a couple of Algary people?"

She went to work on her tablet, and he took out his phone and pulled up the data on his Spec-Trons.

"Looks like we've got a few," Burg said. "Why?"

Greene felt excitement rising inside him, and he looked at Garcinia. "That collar we found yesterday—can we use it?"

She considered this. "I'm sure we could get it working well enough. There's only the matter of the interface, and—"

"Chief?" Marlena said. "What are you—"

Greene spun back around toward Marlena, suddenly overflowing with energy. "We could send somebody in!"

"In?" Marlena repeated. "In where?"

"Into *Algary*."

Marlena's mouth dropped open. "Into Algary? Chief, are you out of your— Wait." She looked at Garcinia. "Can we?"

Garcinia clapped her hands together. "If we can't, I won't be the reason why, I can promise you that. What do you have in mind, Chief?"

"Through the course of various security operations, we have accumulated biometric data for a number of Algary employees," Greene said. "If we can use the collar to impersonate one of them, we might be able to get into their systems and poke around and maybe get some insight into what this is all about."

Marlena held up a hand. "Hold on. You just said that getting into our systems wasn't that simple. This is just a reverse of that situation."

"Well ..."

"On top of that, what you're proposing— How do we know that someone won't—or hasn't—done the same thing to us with one of our people's biometrics?"

"We don't," Greene admitted. "But if someone had, and they'd gotten into any sensitive areas, they would have left a trail. Just like we would surely leave a trail at Algary. It would be a one-shot."

Marlena nodded. "All right. You might be onto something. But what about the chip? Algary chips their people too. They would catch that right away. Can we spoof a chip?"

Greene looked at Burg, and then they both looked at Garcinia.

The elderly woman looked crestfallen. "Probably not, I'm afraid. At least, I wouldn't want to stake anyone's life on it."

"So that's that, then," Marlena said.

Burg shook her head. "We could pick a promising target. Anyone we wanted, really. Grab him off the street or at home, cut the chip out, get the biometrics, and hold him until we've got what we want."

Greene opened his mouth to protest, but Marlena was already shaking her head.

"That's a bit more brute force than I'm willing to use," she said. "We're building on a foundation of guesswork and not a lot of evidence. If there's going to be a war with Algary, we're not going to be the one who starts it."

"Let's look at this from the other side," Greene said. "Not everyone who comes into our building has a chip. Assuming that we could program the collar with multiple faces, it would be a lot easier to get into their building as a guest or a vendor and then to switch over to the employee."

"That could work," Garcinia said.

Marlena was still frowning. "Even if it did, you're obviously not going to be able to walk in there as any old employee and just grab what we're looking for."

"No, that's true," Greene said. "And I don't think it's reasonable to expect that we'd be able to determine what their master plan is in any case; that would be too high up. But if my hypothesis is correct, they stole a part from us and a part from Crestridge on the same day. If we could get into their R&D systems, we might be able to find out what they're working on, maybe even what they're using those parts for. Wouldn't that be worth it?"

"It might," Marlena said.

Greene turned to Garcinia. "Ours was a power regulator and Crestridge's was a light-bending lens. Correct me if I'm wrong: that tech is good, of course, but none of it is game-changing on its own, is it? It's not going to put Algary over the top?"

"I'd have to see the lens," Garcinia replied. "But that's probably fair to say."

"What they've done feels like too big a play for that sort of tech," Greene said. "You can't go running around grabbing up every piece of technology with bombings and violence. That's not a sustainable business model. You'd draw way too much heat. All the other corporations would band together against you out of necessity, and as soon as word of it got out, your stock would crater."

Garcinia stroked her chin. "You're suggesting that they want those pieces for something specific."

"Something big," Marlena said.

Greene shrugged. "Could be."

Burg looked up from her tablet. "If we have to limit ourselves to what we've already got, I have a candidate. Ernest Hart. Works in Algary's R&D. He fell asleep on the metro about a month ago and had his briefcase stolen. We later acquired it. There wasn't anything particularly good inside, but you know we keep everything." She sent the information on Hart to Marlena's wall screen.

Greene nodded. "That looks promising. What else have we got for him?"

"We have a good handprint from the briefcase," Burg said. "We would probably also want retina, which would be easy enough to get when we scan for the facial model. Let's see ... He's single and lives alone. It shouldn't take much more than twenty-four hours to surveil him and get it." She paused as Marlena gave her a pointed look. "In a *non-brute-force* way."

"How?" Marlena asked.

Burg crossed her legs. "There are lots of ways, most of the easiest of which simply involve getting into his apartment. A scanner on his bathroom mirror, hidden by a hologram, for example. Then we just need his schedule. It shouldn't be hard to get that."

Marlena steepled her fingers. "All right, let's say you get what you need from him undetected. And let's say you can get into R&D with it. What about passwords?"

Greene shook his head. "We'd have to rely on our breaker software."

"That's not ideal."

"Again, we could just grab him," Burg said. "I'll bet we could get some passwords out of him one way or another."

Marlena shook her head. "That's even less ideal. And you can't be sure."

Greene bit down his frustration. "What's the alternative, then? Sit and wait for them to blow something else up, or steal another of our innovations, or just attack us outright?"

Marlena took a deep breath, winced, and put a hand to her ribs. "No, that's not an option."

"Then we can send someone?"

"Yes," Marlena said. "We'll send someone. You."

Greene thought perhaps he had misheard. "I'm sorry?"

"*You*, Chief. This is a job for you."

Greene shook his head. "I was thinking we need somebody with computer skills. Somebody with R&D experience. Somebody with the knowhow to react on the fly to overcome technical obstructions. That's not my skillset at all."

"No, it's not," Marlena said. "But it's no good if I send in a computer tech and they end up captured or dead. I want someone with situational awareness, undercover experience, countless hours in the field, and the ability to think on his feet and adapt. That's *you*. Do you disagree?"

It was a question with only one answer.

"No," he said.

"Good."

He glanced at Burg, who looked ... amused.

"What about my hands?" Greene asked. "The collar will reproduce his face, but Hart's skin is lighter than mine."

"That's no trouble, dear," Garcinia said. "We'll print up synthetic gloves that will cover your entire hands. Thin, very natural-looking, don't worry. You'll barely know they're there. They'll change your fingerprints, too."

"Hand condoms," Burg said.

Garcinia frowned at her. "When you put it that way ..."

"Hm," Greene said. He was out of objections.

"I believe in you, Green," Marlena said. "Don't worry, we'll have somebody in your ear the entire time. Somebody with the technical insight that you need."

"Fine," he said, with substantially less enthusiasm than he was going for.

"All right, get going on the surveillance," Marlena said. "And in the meantime, I want all three of you to work on ways to tighten our security so that they can't do to us what we're about to do to them."

EIGHT

The unmarked Xiong car parked down the block from the Algary building, and Greene got out.

"I've arrived," he said.

"We read you," came Burg's voice in his ear.

"Don't forget the facial projector, dear," Garcinia said right behind her.

"I didn't."

"Vendor mode, not Hart mode."

"Got it."

"And don't forget to switch it once you get inside."

"I know."

Greene had been briefed—in fact, they'd all been at the briefing together. Garcinia was extremely concerned about this operation, he figured, and this was her way of showing it.

"I'm going now," he said, and began walking toward Algary.

"I'm here, sorry." Now it was Marlena's voice in his ear. "I got held up in a meeting. Where are we?"

"Just underway," Burg said.

Three voices on his comm simultaneously. That was a first. Greene remembered his Greek mythology—these three women were the Fates, sending him to his destiny.

"Oh, dear, I do wish we'd managed a voice modulator, though," Garcinia said. "I apologize for that."

"I'll make it work," Greene said, unsure of how exactly he might do that beyond avoiding anyone who knew Hart personally.

The Algary building captured his attention the moment it came into view. An enormous structure, at least twice the height of Xiong Tower, it erupted from the earth as if trying to escape into the heavens. The building dazzled in the sunlight, all silver metal and blue glass, a twisting, sinuous edifice with no flat surfaces and no hard edges. The design gave Greene the vague impression of silver tentacles reaching skyward to drag the central tower back down into the ground. At the very top, Algary's serpentine silver dragon flew perpetually in its holographic courses.

The building greeted visitors with an immaculately landscaped plaza featuring winding paths that led between arrangements of trees and shrubs up to the main entrance.

As he neared the doors, Greene's reflection in the blinding glass gave him pause. Jeans, a polo shirt, tennis shoes, and a light jacket, worn by a stranger with fairer skin, hair a lighter shade of brown, and more prominent cheekbones. He grimaced, and the reflection grimaced back at him in perfect time. He approached to get a closer look at his face. The collar was working perfectly, and doing a fine job of concealing the earpiece he wore.

He reached the front doors and paused. He'd been in this building once before, briefly, almost a year ago, when he'd interviewed for a position on their security staff. Not a leadership position; just staff. He'd been told then that he "wasn't what they were looking for." At the time, he'd been hurt, but in retrospect, knowing what he did about Algary, he wondered whether he shouldn't have taken it as a compliment.

Then again, he was here to commit crimes against them, so maybe everybody was wrong.

"I'm going in," he announced to the Fates.

There wasn't much traffic in and out of the building on a Sunday afternoon. He went through the automatic doors and approached the security checkpoint, which looked much like Xiong's.

Greene took a deep breath and let it out slowly, making sure that his pulse was normal. He didn't want to do anything that would attract the attention of the biometric scanners.

The security people all wore the standard blue and silver Algary jumpsuits. Their weapons were quite a bit more conspicuous than Green was used to seeing, though. The staff working the desk and scanner had pistols, as was standard, but a number of additional security personnel standing against the wall were holding rifles, seemingly not doing anything beyond making an impression.

Greene took a little tray from the stack and emptied his pockets into it: a forged commerce card, a burner phone full of dummy information, a small external drive, and a credentials card. He reached for his Spec-Trons, remembered he wasn't wearing them because they interfered with the signal from the collar, and recalled that Garcinia had instructed him not to touch his face in any case.

As he put the tray onto the scanner belt, a burly guard motioned him into the body scanner, barely looking at him.

Greene tensed, resisting the urge to bring his hand to his jacket pocket. If the jamming device that Garcinia had given him didn't work, the holographic collar would set off the metal detector and show up on the scanner.

The big guard stared at his screen for a moment, then waved Greene through.

On the other side, another guard picked up his credentials card from the tray and scanned it. "What's the reason for your visit?" she asked.

"I'm updating the operator permits for the vending machines," Greene replied.

She looked him over. "Don't you need a tablet for that? Or at least a clipboard? Some stickers?"

"Nah," Greene said. "It's all on the phone now."

"Figures." She began to slide the tray toward him, then paused, a calculating expression on her face.

In spite of himself, Greene began to feel nervous. His palms itched, and he fought the urge to scratch them. Garcinia had said that doing so could damage his synthesized palm prints.

"You've got some control over the machines, right?" the guard asked, her hands still on the tray. "Listen, none of the soda machines on this floor have any Paleocola in them. You know that one?"

Greene did indeed know that one. It was the kind his mom had always bought when he was a kid even though he'd told her it wasn't sweet enough and had a cough medicine aftertaste. To her, that somehow meant it was healthier than other sodas, and to this day, she liked its heavy acidic bite because it "melted everything down in your stomach after you've eaten too much."

"Of course," Greene said to the security woman. "Paleocola: 'The soda your ancestors drank!' Right?"

"Ha, that's the one! I mean, they don't even have a slot for them. It's a real problem. Is that something you can help me with? It doesn't need to be all the machines. Just one or two. Preferably the one in the security lounge."

Greene smiled at her. "I'll see what I can do."

She nodded and gave him his tray. "Thanks, partner."

Greene pocketed his belongings and entered the Algary lobby. It was a wide-open space, bright with natural light, filled with trees and with water features that filled the air with soothing ambient splashing.

"I'm through security," Greene murmured. "I'm going to go find a place to change."

"Copy that," Burg said.

Greene found the nearest restroom. He pretended to use a urinal until the other occupant left, then checked under the stall doors to be sure.

But there was a security camera mounted on the ceiling in the corner.

Greene went into a stall, closed the door, and switched his collar projector program to Hart. Then he used his phone's front-facing camera to make sure that everything was as it should be. Yet another face: the same light skin of the vendor persona, but with a thinner nose, rounder chin, and blond hair.

He didn't want to go out and show his face to the Algary cameras. That would be too obvious of a trail, although he supposed Algary would figure it out soon enough once they got this far.

Quickly, with his head down, Greene left the stall and went out the restroom door, keeping his face angled away from the camera. He wondered if there was another camera he'd missed, perhaps one hidden by holograms.

"We don't have hidden cameras in our bathrooms in the tower, do we?" he asked.

"No," Burg said.

Greene headed for the elevators. "I didn't think so."

"Put that on the list of potential new security measures, though," Marlena said.

"I'm heading up," Greene said.

"Ninety-eighth floor," Burg reminded him.

Greene was well aware, but he didn't respond. "Ninety-eight," he told the elevator.

The elevator car was covered in mirrors—walls, floor, and ceiling. Everywhere Greene looked, he saw Hart. It was unnerving. But the lady who was in the car with him didn't give Greene a second look—she seemed to be engrossed in whatever was happening on her Spec-Trons.

A moment later, the doors opened, and Greene exited. "I'm on ninety-eight."

"To your right," Burg said.

Greene knew that too, but told himself not to take it personally. Better to be sure than to be lost.

The corridor was empty, and the entrance to this section of R&D was quiet.

Greene followed the blue and silver designs on the walls to the access terminal, where the handprint scanner illuminated. He pressed his synthetic palm to the scanner, and after a long moment, the light changed from white to green.

"Present for retina scan," the terminal said.

Greene took a deep breath. This was the moment of truth— Well, one of many today. He had to drop his facial projection for an instant for the scan.

He reached into his shirt and pulled the gaiter he wore free, then glanced around again to make sure there was no one else nearby. Hoping that the special contact lenses he wore were up to the task that the collar was not, he pulled the gaiter over his nose and mouth, put his face right up to the scanner, and dropped the projection of Hart.

"Access granted," the terminal said, and the lock on the door snapped back.

Greene turned Hart's face back on, tucked the gaiter away, and entered R&D 98, not knowing precisely what to expect.

"Here be dragons," he said. "I'm in."

"Let us know what you find, and we'll help if we can," Marlena said.

Greene gazed upon a vast field of cubicles, each divided from its neighbors by shoulder-high transparent glass. The huge room was quiet, but not to the extent that he was convinced that he was alone.

"It's a cube farm," Greene murmured. "There must be five hundred. I don't suppose I can use just any of the computers?"

"I'm afraid not, dear," Garcinia said. "At least, I doubt it. That's not how *we* do it. For security, you know."

"That's reassuring," Greene said. "I don't suppose you have any tips on finding Hart's area?"

"I'm afraid not."

Greene didn't see a directory of any kind. "I guess I'll just wander around until I find it."

At least the cubicles had nameplates.

Greene grew increasingly nervous as he made his way up and down the aisles. If someone was watching the security feed, he would look very suspicious—he was having to go too slowly, pay attention to too much to pass convincingly as a desk jockey stretching his legs.

"Ernest!" It was a woman's voice. "Hey, Ernest, are you lost?"

It took Greene an instant to realize he was being spoken to.

"Oh no," he muttered. He'd known that the odds of running into one of Hart's coworkers were quite a bit higher than zero, but why did it have to be one of the extroverted ones?

Greene stopped and turned. The speaker was a middle-aged woman in the cubicle he'd just passed.

She leaned forward in her chair, eyes wide, biting her bottom lip.

Well, great, he thought. Not only did Greene not have a voice modulator, he had no prayer of imitating Hart's voice to someone who knew the man.

He decided to pretend to be sick.

"Oh, hey," Greene said in a raspy voice.

Her plaque read *Teighyiahah Thompson*. She and Hart were on a first-name basis, apparently, but he had no idea how to pronounce hers and was afraid to make the attempt.

Teighyiahah was still holding eye contact. "Wow, you sound like shit. What are you doing here, anyway?"

"Yeah, I'm sick," Greene said. "Still have to get caught up on a couple things, though. You know how it is."

A burly woman wearing a flannel shirt and carrying a cup of coffee came down the aisle between them. "Hey, Ernest. Hey, Tia," she said without slowing.

Greene nodded to her, and Teighyiahah gave her a wave.

Tia? Greene looked again at Teighyiahah's plaque. "Huh," he said.

"Yes, Ernest, I *do* know," Teighyiahah said, turning back to him, her face all sympathy. "Would you like me to get you some soup from the machine?"

"That's very kind of you, Teighyiahah, but no, thank you," Greene said, forcing himself to smile. "I'm hoping to be in and out pretty quickly today."

Her face fell. "Oh. Well. See you around, I guess."

"See you," Greene said.

"Just a minute!" She stood up. "You're looking a little short from here."

Greene fought down his internal screaming. He was six centimeters shorter than the real Hart. Nothing major, nothing he'd thought would be readily apparent. But of course this lady who was hot for Hart would notice.

"Uh ... Maybe it's the shoes," Greene said hoarsely. "Different pair today."

Her disappointment was obvious. "You wear elevator shoes? I wonder what else about you is an *exaggeration*."

He gave her a sheepish look. "Don't tell anyone, okay?"

Teighyiahah crossed her arms. "Sure, Hart. Feel better." She sat down and turned to her console, presenting him with her back.

Greene continued down the aisle.

"Well, you've ruined Hart's romantic prospects," Burg said in his ear. "Nice going. That's going to be all over the office by Monday."

At the moment, Greene couldn't think of anything he cared about less.

At last, he found Hart's cubicle. It was sparsely decorated: a few certificates in frames and a small trophy, all for work-related achievements, and a couple of photos of work teams.

Greene sat in Hart's chair and switched on the computer. The facial recognition scanner activated, approved him, booted up the system, and prompted him for a password.

He dug in his pocket for the external drive and connected it. "I'm hooked up," he told the Fates.

"Just give it a moment," Garcinia said. "This will definitely get you in. Probably. Truthfully, the real question is whether it will trip their security when it does."

Greene fought the urge to put a hand to his forehead. "Are you serious?"

She clucked her tongue. "Trust me, dear, I'm good at my job."

"If it does trip, will I know on this end?"

"Hm, that's a good question. Maybe?"

While Greene waited for Garcinia's drive to access the system, his eyes fell on a framed photo of Hart with a man he recognized: Victor Carandini, Algary's President. They were at some sort of corporate event. Hart wore a huge grin, clearly delighted to be in the presence of the big boss, whose disinterested face showed the fatigue of what surely must have been dozens if not hundreds of photo ops with the drones in his employ.

At last, after an eternal two minutes, Garcinia's drive accomplished its mission and granted Greene access to the system.

"All right, I'm in," he said. "What am I looking for?"

"Run a search for the name of our stolen part," Garcinia said. "It's a N-19 Fluxer."

Greene did so, and a number of files came up.

"They've done a lot with this already," Greene said. "It looks like they're working on it as we speak. In the labs."

"I'm sure," Marlena said. "It'll cut months off their catch-up time."

"Run a simultaneous search for the stolen Crestridge part, the J-26 Capitor," Garcinia said. "See if there's any overlap, if any project is using both parts."

The Algary machine took its sweet time.

"There's one," Greene announced.

"What is it?" Marlena demanded.

"I don't know. Give me a minute. The file name is a bunch of gibberish. Okay, let's see. It's a report. Highly technical. Well above my paygrade, sorry. Uh ... it looks like some kind of cloaking technology."

He heard a grunt that was probably from Marlena. "What's it called?" she asked eagerly. "What's the name of the project?"

Greene inflated his lungs so that he could get it out in one breath. "'Full-Body Real-Time Three-Dimensional Continuously Multidirectional Broadband Light Deflection Garment.'"

"Oh, shit," Marlena said.

"Oh, my," Garcinia said at the same time.

Greene looked at the report and saw jargon-filled sentences about angles and lenses and paraxial rays. He got the gist of the principle but not the application.

"So what is it exactly?" he asked.

"It's a stealth suit," Marlena said.

"I'm sorry, a what?"

"A stealth suit, dear," Garcinia said.

"You mean a full cloaking suit? Like an ... an invisibility suit?"

"It very well could be," Marlena said. "That would certainly be big enough of an accomplishment to justify what Algary has done. Copy all of the related files, Chief."

"This is absolutely fascinating," Garcinia said. "Very exciting! You know, we aren't remotely close on this."

"I know," Marlena said, her voice gravelly.

"Sorry, I'm not finding any other files," Greene said. "And this is just an overview. Could it still be in the theoretical stage?"

"Doubtful," Garcinia said. "If they're raiding us for parts, I'm guessing they're well along in development. Far enough to have hit some dead ends."

"Maybe this Hart guy doesn't have clearance to access the rest of it," Burg said.

Greene quickly scanned the rest of the file. "Wait. It looks like they're doing something with it offsite."

"Offsite? Where?" Marlena demanded.

"There's just a site codename. 'The Preserve.'"

"You're sure it's offsite and not in another department?" Marlena asked. "Another level of security?"

Greene turned his palms up, a gesture none of the women could see. "I'm not sure about anything. I'm just telling you what it says."

"He's done what he can," Garcinia said. "Chief, please copy all of the files related to both pieces of tech before you leave."

"Wait a minute, Chief," Marlena said. "This is an unprecedented opportunity to loot their R&D. Don't you concur?"

"Well, yes ..." The reluctance in Garcinia's voice was obvious. "But ..."

"Chief, I want you to copy everything to the drive," Marlena said.

Greene raised an eyebrow. "Everything?"

"As much as you can get."

Greene obediently began to copy files. "It could take thirty minutes, an hour, or longer to get all of this."

"Ma'am, this can't be worth it," Burg said. "The number one priority is to get him out safe and undetected, isn't't?"

"Of course it is," Marlena said. "Chief, do you feel that you're in any immediate danger?"

Greene glanced around. The cube farm was still quiet and nearly empty. "Not that I can *see*."

"Then please proceed until you do. By all means, clear out if you even *suspect* that you're in danger. But remember that what you bring back could be worth an untold fortune to the company in time and tech. And it might include other keys to what Algary is working on."

"Understood."

Greene shook his head. Marlena had put it completely onto him. Very clever of her. Aborting this mission was now his responsibility alone. And she had a pretty good sense of what decision he would make.

He slumped in Hart's chair as thousands of files copied, trying to stave off the anxiety he felt creeping in at the edges of his mind.

Estimated time: 39 minutes, the computer screen read. *38 minutes.*

"This collar isn't going to run out of power, is it?" he asked. "There's a good chance I'm going to need it to get out."

"You should be in good shape for about another hour," Garcinia said.

Greene did not find this reassuring. He swiveled back and forth in the chair and tried not to think about how idiotic he thought this all was, or how much he might regret coming up with the idea.

Estimated time: 33 minutes.

He needed to use the restroom, but he didn't want to leave the drive unattended. Never mind that it might take him the better part of the remaining copy time to find Hart's cubicle again.

In his ear, Marlena and Garcinia were going on to one another about the technical aspects of a stealth suit. He didn't understand most of it.

Estimated time: 28 minutes.

A rough hand fell on Greene's shoulder. "Excuse me, you're in my— Hey! What the hell do you think you're doing on my terminal?"

Greene jumped, then turned in his chair, using the scratchy voice again. "Oh, I'm just getting caught up on some—"

He broke off as he looked up into the face of Ernest Hart.

NINE

Hart's eyes went wide as Greene turned to face him.

"Oh no," Greene murmured.

"What is it?" Marlena said in his ear. "What's happening?"

Hart's mouth fell open, and Greene could see the gears turning in his head.

Greene held up a hand. "Listen—"

"Help!" Hart shrieked, his voice cracking. "Security!"

"Oh, for God's sake." Greene grabbed the external drive from the desk, yanked it free of the computer, and bashed Hart in the face with it as he stood up.

Hart staggered back into the aisle, giving Greene room to escape the cubicle. Hart clutched his bleeding nose but continued screaming, his voice piercing and astonishingly loud.

"Chief!" one of the Fates said.

Greene punched Hart in the side of the head, just behind the ear, and the man went down in a heap, mercifully silent.

"Unlucky," Greene muttered.

He oriented himself and headed briskly for the exit. A number of heads had popped up around the cube farm, including the woman he'd talked with earlier, but none of them seemed to be paying attention to him specifically.

"Chief, *what* is happening?" Burg asked.

"Apparently Hart works on Sundays sometimes," Greene said.

"Oh, shit," Burg said. "Sorry."

"I'm getting out."

"Go." It was Marlena this time.

Greene's heart sank as he saw an Algary security man heading toward him at a jog.

"You, there, stop!" said the man. "Who's screaming?"

Daniels, read the man's nametag.

"Oh, thank God, there you are," Greene said. "There's a guy back there, I think he's having a seizure. He hit his head. He needs some help."

"Where?" Daniels wrapped a beefy hand around Greene's arm. "You come and show me."

Daniels was bigger than Greene, and more muscular. But he was also off his guard.

"Yes, absolutely," Greene said, motioning back toward Hart's cubicle.

As soon as Daniels took a step in that direction, Greene dropped behind him and struck him on the base of the skull. Daniels grunted and stumbled to one knee but didn't fall.

Greene turned and ran, trying to locate the exit.

As he turned at an intersection, he heard gunfire and glass shattering nearby.

Adrenaline jittered through his body. "Stupid transparent cubicles," he muttered.

He spotted the exit and sprinted toward it.

Behind him, someone said, "Intruder at my position. In pursuit. Request support. Shut down the doors!"

Greene reached the door. It wanted a retina scan.

There was no sense worrying about his identity if he was dead, Greene thought. He dropped the projection of Hart, scanned out, and hurtled through the door the moment the lock retracted.

"Damn it, I said shut down the doors!" he heard from behind him. "Now shut down the elevators!"

Stairs, Greene thought, trying to remember the floor plan. Where were the stairs? Close enough to the elevator to keep going that way.

He was busy reactivating his Hart face and didn't see the woman in front of him until he had plowed her to the ground.

"Sorry," he muttered as he ran past.

He saw a metal door with a crash bar just past the elevators. That had to be it.

Greene bulled his way through the door and found himself in the stairwell. He hurled himself down the stairs as fast as he could go, flight after flight, his heart racing and his pulse pounding in his head.

"Chief, what the *hell* is going on?" someone said in his ear.

Greene paused and realized that the stairwell was silent except for his thundering pulse. He was alone. No one was chasing him.

And why should they? He had fifty-odd more flights to go, and by the time he reached the bottom, they'd have the entire building locked down.

He realized he was still clutching the hard drive in a white-knuckled fist, and he tucked it into his inner jacket pocket.

"The whole place will be looking for me now," he said.

"No, Chief," Marlena said. "They're not looking for you, they're looking for Hart. Switch your face back to the vendor."

"Right." Greene made himself take a deep breath and tried to focus. He should have thought of that himself. He ducked his head, switched the hologram, and continued down the stairs.

Greene found it difficult to force himself to go at a casual, unsuspicious pace, and it seemed like an eternity before he reached the ground floor. He felt as though he'd been in this stairwell for hours, surrounded by bare gray walls and dull lighting, the faint odor of dust tickling his nostrils. At last, his descent ended at a blue metal door with a silver G painted on it.

The brightness of the Algary lobby made him squint, and the splashing of the water features mingled with the murmurings of the mass of people now present produced a considerable level of sound. After a hundred flights in the concrete womb of the stairwell, it nearly overloaded his senses.

He didn't seem to have the attention of anyone in a security uniform, so he took a moment to get his bearings.

Security was everywhere. The sheer number of them could only mean a lockdown. A mob of perhaps fifty other people, some wearing expressions of concern, others of worry, pressed around the security station.

"I'm downstairs, but they're not letting anybody out," Greene murmured.

"The car is waiting for you down the block," Marlena said in his ear.

Greene walked casually to the crowd at Security. No one appeared to give him a second look. He edged into the throng and pushed his way to the front.

He waved down the nearest security man. "Excuse me, sir. I'm sorry, I need to get through."

The security man barely glanced at him. "We're in a lockdown. You'll have to wait."

Greene tried his best to look subservient. "I'm sorry, I don't know what all this is about. I don't work here. I just take care of the vending machines. I have another job I have to get to."

Now the guard looked at him, and Greene could see that he was nothing more than an annoyance to the man. "We're locked down. You have to wait."

Greene nodded. "Yes, I understand that, I'm sorry. But I'm going to be late if I can't get through. If you could just—"

The security man jabbed a finger into Greene's chest hard enough to be painful. "I said *wait*. Now if you want to keep being a problem for me, I can be a problem for you."

"Sorry," Greene muttered, and faded back into the crowd.

"What's your situation, Chief?" Burg asked in his ear.

Greene wandered over to the fountains, where there were fewer people. "There's too much security. Maybe twenty, all armed. Even if the doors are unlocked, which I doubt, there's no chance I'm getting out this way." There was a sudden hush in the lobby, and Greene glanced up. "Hang on a minute. Something's happening."

Victor Carandini emerged from the elevators, flanked by two bodyguards. He stalked toward the security station, glaring fury. He stood a head taller than anyone in the crowd, and they all gave way to him silently. He began an animated conversation with the man Greene had just spoken with, but in hushed tones that Greene couldn't make out.

"Now the company president is here," Greene murmured. "It's getting worse, not better, at the security desk. I need another option."

"There are other exits," Burg said.

"Yes, but they'll also be locked down and defended."

"Probably not as many guards, though."

Greene shrugged helplessly, a gesture she couldn't see. "I don't have *anything*, Burg. I don't have my Spec-Trons. I don't have a gun. What do you want me to do?"

"I'm afraid you can't rely on the collar to outlast a lockdown," Garcinia said. "I suggest you make a move before they figure out what's going on."

He sighed. "I had a feeling you were going to tell me that."

"Good luck, dear," she said cheerfully.

Fighting down desperation, Greene glanced around the lobby again, considering the growing horde of people. Their murmuring had subsided—they had accepted their situation, and many had turned their attention to their phones and devices as they waited.

The army of security staff had grown as well. The exit was becoming more unassailable by the minute. There was no way out here—Greene would be shot thirty times before he got two steps out the front door.

Greene's gaze wandered outside, to the trees, shrubs, and walkways in the plaza just on the other side of the plate glass windows. Freedom was so close, so unreachable.

He tapped his fingers rhythmically on his leg and said, "I've just had a terrible idea."

He turned around and made his way back to the stairwell, where Algary employees had continued to emerge sporadically in ones and twos, everyone taking in the situation in a general way and no one paying attention to him.

He slipped through the door and began to climb the stairs. Only one person, a woman staring at her phone, passed him as he climbed the several flights to the landing of the next floor.

The door was locked on this side.

"Of course it is," Greene muttered.

He glanced through the narrow window in the door and saw, to his relief, someone heading in his direction. He turned away from the door and went up several steps. When he heard the door open, he came down, heading casually for it, reaching for the handle.

"Just a minute," said the security women who emerged, and Greene tensed. "Where are you going?"

Be cool, Greene told himself. Be stupid.

"Do you know what's going on?" he asked. "I've been checking vending machines all afternoon. I've got one floor left but now the whole place is going crazy. You sure have a lot of people working on a Sunday. You know, I've got to get over to the Maneki Neko Bingo Palladium by five. Please, they don't like it when I—"

The security woman raised a hand to cut him off. "All right." Her face made it clear that she wanted nothing more in this moment than for him to stop talking. "I don't know if you're going to make it to your next appointment. You stay on this floor until the lockdown is over, do you understand? Go sit in one of the conference rooms. The security staff inside will show you where."

"Thank you very much," Greene said, and went through the door as she headed down the stairs to join her compatriots in the lobby.

At the end of the hall, another security staff member corralled an employee and directed him into a conference room. When she looked the other way, Greene ducked down an aisle of cubicles to his left.

No clamor ensued, so he took a moment to orient himself. As best he could tell, the building's front entrance was down this aisle, then over two or three to the left.

Staying low, he made his way in that direction and reached the windowed offices that ringed this floor without incident.

The first office door he tried was locked, naturally, but the second opened to his touch. He slipped inside and closed the door behind him.

The office was unoccupied. He crept to the window and looked out. The plaza lay below—far below, at least ten meters. It was too far to drop, and he didn't see any way to let himself down more easily, but there *was* a tree perhaps six meters tall that looked robust enough to support him—if he could reach it.

"Okay." Greene took a deep breath and let it out slowly. "Looks like I'm going to have to jump."

The window spanned the entire exterior wall from floor to ceiling—there was nothing to open.

Greene scanned the room. On a shelf above the desk stood a large trophy with a substantial marble base. He picked it up. The plaque read 2nd *Place – Algary Company Picnic – Plant-Based Egg Toss.*

It was heavy enough for his purpose, anyway. He turned and slammed the base of the trophy against the glass with all his might.

The sound of the blow was flat and underwhelming. Beneath his hand appeared a crack about the size of his fingernail.

Of course it was security glass. Still ...

He hit the window a second time, and the crack spider-webbed out about a centimeter in multiple directions. He struck again and again, until the trophy broke off the base, but to no avail—he couldn't break this glass.

Now what?

Greene dropped the broken trophy and ran a hand through his hair. "Are there any drones in the car?" he asked.

"There should be a surveillance drone," Burg said in his ear. "That's the only one. There's nothing with ordnance; we can't blast you out."

"Is it the infiltration model?" he asked, hardly daring to hope. "Does it have a laser cutter?"

"One sec ..." The pause seemed interminable. "Yep, that's the one."

"Excellent. Can you send it up to my position and have it cut this glass?"

"I'm on it," Burg said. "Hold tight."

Greene crouched behind the desk and waited impatiently for perhaps two minutes.

Finally, Burg said, "All right, look out and tell me if I'm in the right place. I can't see in."

Greene crept closer to the window. "I don't see— Wait, there you are. Yes, right there." The fist-sized quadcopter drone hovered just outside. Its neutral-tan frame made it difficult to pick up against the surrounding buildings, but once he saw it, it was easy to stay focused on.

"Got it. How big a hole do you want?"

"About my height and width, if it won't take too long. Bigger is better." The last thing he wanted was to launch himself into the void without room to keep his balance.

"Stand by." The drone moved near his feet. "Here?"

"About two centimeters higher. Right there."

A thin red line, incredibly bright, appeared between the drone and the window. Greene watched, transfixed, as it slowly etched his deliverance into the glass.

Its pace was much too slow for Greene's liking. God only knew what was happening downstairs. At some point, probably sooner rather than later, Algary would decide to systematically sweep the building. And what if somebody spotted the drone?

But there was nothing to be done but hunker down where he couldn't be seen from outside the office and wait. He'd never been particularly good at waiting.

The drone finished its horizontal cut and began to move upward.

"How are you getting along?" Marlena asked.

"Fine," Greene said. "Assuming this works."

"I'm sorry this happened, but this is exactly why we sent you. Your incredible resourcefulness."

As much as he didn't want to, Greene found he had to concede the point.

Finally, the drone finished its work: a rectangle about the size of a man had been carved into the window.

"I'm backing off the drone," Burg said. "Give that a good kick and it should come right out. Just make sure you don't tumble out headlong after it."

"Right," Greene said. One more thing to worry about. "Thanks."

"The car's ready to go. See you soon."

He stood, went to the window, and kicked the cut panel as hard as he dared. Burg had done her job perfectly: the top tipped out first, and then the whole piece fell outward, toppling end over end. The clang it made when it hit the concrete below reverberated throughout the plaza.

As Greene braced himself in the window, he heard the office door open behind him. "You! Come away from there!" someone shouted.

Oh well; at least he wouldn't have the luxury of lingering and overthinking the jump.

Greene leapt.

In the first moment of freefall, panic electrified his entire body. What was he *doing* with his life?

He hit the top of the tree harder than he'd expected. Thin branches scratched at his face and hands as he plummeted through them, desperately grabbing for anything big enough to stop his descent.

The tree's springy limbs pushed back against him as he fell, and for an instant, he thought he might land headfirst on the pavement after all. At last, though, he hooked an elbow over a branch thick enough to slow him. But his momentum twisted him around—he lost his grip and dropped the rest of the way.

Greene landed side-first on a shrub that gouged his torso and ear. But he was down, and he was intact.

"I guess that could have been worse," he muttered.

Greene struggled to his feet, gasping for breath. As he lurched toward the sidewalk, he heard two gunshots, and pain bit through his left arm.

He grunted and stumbled, tearing a palm raw on the pavement as he caught himself and nearly bowled over a preoccupied pedestrian.

But no more shots were forthcoming. Like any good corporate citizen, Algary cared about public, demonstrable collateral damage.

Greene spared a glance behind him. At least four blue uniforms, probably more, had emerged from Algary's main entrance and were sprinting after him.

He broke into a run, pushing past the people on the sidewalk, trying to generate as much momentum as he could. Every breath hurt his side where he'd hit the ground.

"We see you, Chief," Burg said in his ear. "The car's right where you left it. Do you want me to bring it to you?"

"No, I can get there!" he gasped through clenched teeth. He had enough distractions without trying to track it on a busy street. "Just be ready to get me out of here the second I get in."

"Copy that."

Greene kept running. There hadn't seemed to have been as much foot traffic when he'd gotten here. And he hadn't parked quite so far away, had he?

"They're closing, Chief," Burg said. "Looks like they sent the track team after you."

As fine an incentive as this information provided, Greene was already giving his maximum effort.

Greene spotted the Xiong car. It had pulled out of its parking spot and was idling in the nearest lane, blocking traffic, its bulletproof black body promising safety. He sprinted for it, feeling the Algary guards breathing down his neck, not daring to spare another look.

With no time to slow down, he slammed against the side of the car. Multiple gunshots cut through the air as he grabbed for the door handle, and bullets ricocheted off the metal centimeters from his hand. He dropped to the ground and dove behind the car as more shots followed.

"Chief, get in the damned car!" Burg shouted.

"I can't! Pop the trunk and I'll get in there!"

The trunk released almost immediately. As Green braced to hurl himself inside, multiple rounds hit the nearest back tire, and he heard more strike another part of the car he couldn't see.

"The tire's gone," Greene said.

"Just get in," Burg said. "It'll reinflate in a minute."

Indecision seized Greene. He wasn't sure he *had* a minute. Yes, the car was armored, but the thought of being sealed inside, helpless, while an entire squad of Algary security worked to literally or figuratively crowbar him out—while further immobilizing the car, certainly—was not appealing.

All of these thoughts flashed through his mind in an instant, and he decided.

"Going to need a Plan B," Greene said, and jumped to his feet.

Staying as low as he could, he sprinted away from the car, toward an area with relatively heavy foot traffic, wagering that Algary's love of its public image and stock value would prevent indiscriminate fire.

"Damn it, Chief, what the hell are you doing?" Burg bellowed in his ear.

Living, maybe, he thought.

A car braked sharply in front of him as he darted across the street. He bounced off the side and pressed on, the momentum of the impact carrying him forward.

Several people behind him were shouting, but he heard no shots.

"I'm moving," Greene gasped as he ran on. "They're right behind me. I need options."

"We have other pieces moving toward you, but in the short term, you're going to have to lose them yourself," Burg said. Her tone had become completely businesslike—she was engrossed in doing her job now; the criticism of his strategic decisions would wait for later.

"Understood." Greene had no idea which direction he was running. The world had become a blur of cars and pedestrians and blinding glass towers, and he longed again for his Spec-Trons.

"Okay, there's a metro station half a block down the way you're headed," Burg said. "That's probably your best bet, especially once they get drones airborne after you."

"Got it." His lungs had started to burn, and he inwardly admonished them to suck it up. He didn't have his Power-Through inhaler.

He reached a brief stretch of pavement with no other foot traffic. Gunshots rang out immediately, and he felt a sting in his shoulder.

So much for that, he thought. Still, he was fortunate not to be riddled with bullets by now. Then he was back amongst pedestrians, thick enough that he had to dodge around them.

The metro entrance lay just ahead. He flung himself down the crowded staircase, shoving people aside and leaping over others.

"Sorry, sorry," he muttered reflexively to no one in particular.

When he reached the landing and turned, he spared a glance back and spotted at least two Algary people at the top of the stairs. Renewing his efforts, he leapt down the remaining steps, landing painfully on a trio of suit-clad businessmen and sending them all sprawling.

"Excuse me," Greene said in response to their outraged cries.

He hissed in pain as he climbed to his feet: he'd rolled his ankle.

Greene lurched toward the turnstiles, peripherally aware that everyone on the concourse was looking at him.

He half-jumped, half-climbed over the nearest turnstile, triggering a red light and a shrill alarm.

"Hey!" shouted someone behind him.

Greene made for the platform without another look back.

A train was just arriving.

"Oh, thank God," he murmured. "A break, finally."

He bumped his way through the crowd, muttering apologies no one could hear, and pushed his way onto the packed train.

"Chief, report!" In the chaos, he wasn't sure whether the voice in his ear was Burg's or Marlena's.

"I've made it onto a train," he said, as more passengers pressed up against him.

"Which one?"

"I've got no clue."

The doors seemed to be taking forever to close even though the train was at if not beyond maximum capacity. They wouldn't hold an entire train for one turnstile jumper, would they?

Blue Algary uniforms appeared on the platform, and the crowd there gave way to them.

"Close, close!" Greene commanded the obstinate doors.

There were two of them—no, three—coming right toward him.

Greene felt his entire body tense. "For God's sake, *close*!"

The doors continued to ignore him.

The first member of the Algary security team, a short, lean man with slicked-over hair, reached the doors and lunged aboard.

Greene dropped his uninjured shoulder and bulled him back out. When the man tried again to push his way onto the train, Greene gave him a quick palm strike to the nose.

As the first Algary man fell back, a second, this one bigger and broader, leapt over him, knocking Greene into and through the passengers pressed around him.

Greene's back impacted the rough, dirty floor of the train car with a jolt, but his head was spared the same by someone's shoe.

Through a forest of legs, Greene saw the train doors belatedly close. The train rumbled into motion beneath him.

Then the Algary man was on top of him, pressing a knee into Greene's chest and grabbing for his wrists.

Greene managed to roll a quarter-turn sideways and was promptly stepped on by at least three people who had nowhere else to go.

"Chief, what's happening?" one of the Fates said in his ear.

But the floor of the train was hot and suffocating, and Greene had neither the time nor the oxygen to respond.

The Algary man was on him again, trying to grapple, to use his size advantage to pin Greene. The man's weight was smothering, his grip on Greene's wounded shoulder excruciating.

Greene's adrenaline had already been running high, but the heat, the pain, the lack of air, and the crush of humanity created in him a surge of desperate energy.

He had precious little room to maneuver, but Greene had his hands free, and he managed three weak jabs to the Algary man's throat.

The weight on Greene's torso lessened slightly, and he bucked upward, shoving the man back. Gasping for air, Greene got a knee planted on the floor and slammed his fist into the man's temple.

The mass of passengers let the Algary man fall as they had Greene, and he hit his head on the floor of the train car.

Greene was on top of his assailant in an instant, one hand digging into the man's throat and the other feeling for his sidearm.

"When I get off, you stay here," Greene barked. "Do you understand?"

The man, clearly dazed, didn't respond.

Greene didn't trust it. It wasn't enough.

He held the pistol where the man could see it. "Handcuffs. Zip ties. I know you've got something."

"Pocket," the man gasped, indicating with his eyes.

Without lessening his pressure on the man's throat, Greene tucked the pistol into his jacket pocket and dipped his free hand into the pocket the man had indicated.

Handcuffs.

"That's good," Greene said. "For you. Flip over if you know what's good for you."

The man allowed Greene to roll him over, and Greene released his hold on the man's throat. Greene cuffed his hands behind his back as he gasped for air.

Better.

Greene stood, keeping a foot on the man's back, and gratefully took a deep breath of recirculated train air, ripe with sweat and body odor.

The passengers around him looked conspicuously away, lest they inadvertently get involved.

Greene took another deep breath and scanned the train car, then froze. A pang of terror shot through him as he spotted another blue Algary uniform at the far end of the car, by the other set of doors.

Greene ducked his head quickly and switched his collar back to Hart's face. It might buy him a few seconds, anyway.

But the Algary woman at the far end wasn't moving toward him. Was it possible that his altercation had escaped her notice? The fight had been brief, and the train car was crowded, but he had no confidence in that degree of good fortune.

He became aware that the Fates had been talking in his ear nearly the entire time.

"I'm on a train," he said to them in an undertone. "I don't know where it's headed, but I need to get off. I need you to come get me."

"Never fear, dear," Garcinia said. "We've been tracking your chip movement the entire time."

"You're headed toward the New Causeway Bay Retail District," Burg said. "Get off at the next stop. We're on the way. We'll be there in twenty minutes."

"All right."

Greene felt himself relax a bit. A plan. Reinforcements. Escape. And only one Algary security woman in his way.

Greene looked up at her, and as he did, she turned her head away. But he could have sworn she'd been looking directly at him. Nevertheless, she was staying put at her end of the car, and that was what mattered.

Everyone else on the train continued pointedly to *not* look at him, so he had to take it on faith that his facial projector was still working.

He became aware of a warm stickiness down his right arm, just beneath the gash in his jacket sleeve, but he was sore in so many places that it was hard to dwell on any one spot. He tried to focus on taking deep, slow breaths.

"Arriving, New Causeway Bay Station," the train's automated system announced.

At last. Greene felt like he'd been stuck in this smothering metal box for hours. More likely, it had been about fifteen minutes.

The train stopped, the doors hissed open, and Greene squeezed his way out, eager for the sun and the comparatively fresh Portsmith air.

He glanced sideways and saw that the Algary woman had disembarked as well. He didn't like that, not one bit. Still, it didn't necessarily mean that she was onto him—and, for whatever it was worth, she wasn't looking at him, or even in his direction.

Making sure the pistol was secure in his jacket pocket, Greene headed up the metro steps. His task was the same regardless.

"The car is ten minutes away," Burg said in his ear.

"Understood."

Evade one guard for ten minutes? That would be no problem at all.

Greene reached the surface and shaded his eyes from the noonday sun until they adjusted.

He was outside the city center, surrounded by more modest buildings, most of them four or five stories tall. Many featured residences above and businesses beneath—tiny but high-end condos targeted to up-and-coming business types, gimmicky restaurants, and shops for those who wanted to be seen engaging in consumption more than they valued the convenience of the Net.

He looked back at the sparkling spires of downtown Portsmith. He couldn't make out Xiong Tower from here.

A large crowd had departed the metro station and was beginning to dissipate, and he let it carry him along. It would be straightforward enough to lose himself and lie low until the cavalry arrived.

But unease knotted his stomach.

Maybe it was because he'd nearly been killed, or captured. Then again, he'd been in and out of bad scrapes before.

Or maybe it was because he'd been too deep into the unseemly side of corporate business today. Certainly, everything he'd done had been at his employer's behest and, broadly, within his job responsibilities, but a good deal of it was indisputably unscrupulous, unethical, and illegal. If he hadn't been under the aegis of a supremely powerful megacorporation … well, then he wouldn't have been in this position in the first place, would he?

Nevertheless—

Greene's thoughts were jolted from his mind as though a door had been slammed in his face.

A shiny blue Algary autocopter hovered over the parking garage across the street from Greene. Its door opened and eight blue-clad figures rappelled down.

"Oh no," Greene muttered.

"What is it, Chief?" Marlena asked.

"Algary's already here." He touched his wounded shoulder, remembered the sting, and understood. "They're tracking me."

TEN

Greene bit his lip as his whole body tensed. Suddenly, ten minutes seemed like an eternity, and the pistol in his pocket felt useless.

He glanced behind him. The Algary woman was there, walking some twenty meters back, not closing—just keeping him fenced in.

Greene continued down the street, trying to stick with the crowd that had departed the metro, but it had thinned out too much.

"You've got to get that tracker out," Burg said in his ear.

"I know." He touched the device in his jacket pocket. "This jammer thing you gave me can't block it?"

"I'm afraid that's an entirely different sort of signal," Garcinia said. "At best, it might keep them from pinpointing you precisely, but likely not in a large enough radius to be useful."

"Too bad," Greene said.

Resisting the urge to run, he accelerated to a brisk walk, and his sprained ankle protested immediately. If he ran—if he was even *capable* of running—he'd push Algary to move on him even faster, and then he'd be even more tired when they did so.

The shops on this street all projected holographic signage and advertising into the air above the sidewalks.

He passed a hologram boutique—that would have been an ideal place to hide if they hadn't been tracking him. A ritzy clothing store. A teahouse. A coffee shop. Another teahouse. A takeaway place holographically projecting glistening delicacies that Juha Karjalainen would surely have railed against. None of it helpful for his purposes.

Greene heard a minor commotion and looked behind him.

Some distance back, the Algary troops from the parking garage had hit the street. They headed toward him at a jog, displacing pedestrians, making no attempt to be discreet.

The autocopter had taken off and was hovering low enough to emphasize its presence even if it wasn't posing a direct threat.

Greene's pulse began to race again. He didn't have long.

Across the street in front of him, a particularly garish hologram flashed. An immense, blindingly yellow shopping cart became a blindingly yellow hammer, then a refrigerator, then a pot of flowers.

A big-box hardware store.

It was his best chance.

He ran, gritting his teeth against the pain in his ankle, willing it not to give out. Dodging traffic—or rather, triggering the auto-driven cars around him to stop by dashing in front of them—he made it across the busy street.

The automatic doors fronting the street slid open before him, allowing him to dash inside the store without breaking stride.

But he didn't see the store's greeterbot in time.

"Welcome to the House Station," it was saying. "What can I help you—"

Green plowed into the rolling silver cylinder and knocked it over.

As it thunked on the floor, the stylized face on its display panel changed from a smile to a frown, and its lights flipped from yellow to red.

"Error," it said. "Contacting live personnel. Please wait for assistance."

Greene quickly hoisted the thing back upright—it was lighter than it looked—and its display returned to normal.

"Sorry, I'm really in a hurry," Greene told it. "What aisle are the knives on? Utility knives."

"Aisle seventeen," the greeterbot said. "How else may I assist you today?"

"Nothing," Greene said absently as he scanned the aisle numbers. He was out of time. Algary couldn't be more than a minute behind him. "No, wait! There are some people behind me. They have guns. They're going to try to rob the store. You should lock the place down and let your security people know."

"Please wait," the greeterbot said. "Contacting manager."

Greene threw up his hands. "You don't have any security?"

"Valued customer, your safety is our primary concern," the greeterbot said. "That's why the House Station puts our own personal touch on—"

"Ugh, forget it," Greene said, and ran for aisle seventeen.

He didn't see any other customers—that was fortunate.

He wasn't completely surprised at the lack of securitybots, though—armed and unsupervised bots tended to have more than their share of mishaps. Shootings were bad for business.

Greene turned down the aisle the greeterbot had indicated and quickly scanned the pegs.

A commotion—the sound of an impact on metal followed by breaking glass—came from the direction of the store entrance. Greene could just hear the greeterbot's voice.

"Welcome to the House Station. Please, weapons are not permitted in the store."

Algary had arrived.

Greene snatched the smallest utility knife he could find off its peg and ran down the aisle away from the entrance, yanking at the knife's plastic clamshell package. It didn't open.

He turned at the end of the aisle, saw the sign for the restroom, and headed that way, dodging the occasional customer, still grunting and straining against the packaging.

"Chief, what's going on?" said Burg in his ear. "Are you fighting? Have you engaged?"

"Wrap rage," Greene said through clenched teeth.

"Huh?"

"For God's sake, I thought we lived in the future," he muttered, tearing futilely at the plastic.

He reached the restroom, yanked the door open, and was relieved to find it vacant.

"Attention, customer. Merchandise is not permitted in the restroom."

Greene started. The voice had come from an automated sensor eye on the wall.

"I'll pay for it." Greene gripped the hang hole of the knife packaging with both hands, dug in with his nails, and pulled with desperate strength.

The plastic sheared open, launching the utility knife into the air. It clattered into the nearest sink.

"Please wait," the sensor eye said. "Summoning manager."

The sight of Hart's face in the mirror instead of his own startled him. But there was no time to think.

Greene pulled off his jacket and dropped it on the floor, then jerked his arm out of his sleeve and slid his shirt up. He grabbed the knife, extended the blade, and jammed it into the red gash in his shoulder.

The pain was awful. The sight of the blood welling from the chunk of flesh he was carving out was worse. But he had to be thorough, to get it right the first time. He had to cut deep.

Blood streamed down his arm, running all over his clothes, the sink, and the floor.

He clenched his teeth, widened his eyes, and growled against the pain as he sliced into the muscle.

"God, Jesus, come on," he muttered, doing his best to hold in a scream.

In his ear, the Fates were inquiring about his well-being.

At last, a thumb-sized hunk of flesh dropped into the sink, where it sat in a broad splash of blood, an outrage, a testament to the absurdity of the events of the last hour.

Greene turned away from the infuriating sight and shrugged back into his shirt, his knees buckling from the pain of the fabric against the gaping rawness of his wound. Blood soaked through immediately. Greene picked up his jacket and struggled back into it, and it too was immediately bloody.

His eyes watering, Greene yanked open the restroom door and lunged out.

Two Algary men were there, guns drawn, one in the act of reaching for the door.

Greene leapt at the nearest, tackling him. Scrambling on top, he raised his bloody utility knife and brought it down just below the man's clavicle.

The knife bounced off hard body armor, and Greene used the momentum to direct the knife toward the man's shoulder. This time, it went in.

The guard yelled and thrashed, but Greene clung on with one bloody hand like a bronco rider, his shoulder screaming.

"Move, Whitley, I don't have a shot!" the other one shouted.

Greene slammed both fists into the ears of the man he was on, then rolled into the legs of the other, throwing him off balance.

Greene struck wildly and managed to knock the guard down. As he fell, Greene jumped up and gave him a hard kick, then limped down the nearest aisle.

"How long?" he demanded.

"Five minutes," Burg said.

"I'm in a store. Algary is here already. They'll be guarding the doors."

"See if you can get out, Chief," Marlena said. "We have three plainclothes staff in the car. They're armed but not equipped for a prolonged firefight. More support is a little farther off."

Only three. Well, it didn't matter if there were fifty if he didn't survive until they arrived.

Greene reached the end of the aisle and turned. This whole place was wide aisles and long lines of sight, no good for hiding or stalling.

He ducked between two stacks of plywood to get his breath. The store's ubiquitous odor of dust was particularly strong here, and he choked out a painful sneeze.

"What about a back door?" he said. "What about receiving?"

"We don't have a visual on the store yet, but we've got the floor plan," Burg said. "There are four exits. How many units are you looking at?"

"I counted nine when I got here. They've probably got more on the way."

"Nine's pretty thin to cover four exits and sweep for you," Burg said. "Are you up to making a move?"

Greene sighed. What choice did he have? "Just meet me out front."

"Understood."

Greene switched his facial projector back to the vendor once again, for all the good it would do—the bloody trail he was leaving on the polished concrete floor would be difficult to miss.

He made his way to the front of the store, frightening customers, at one point having to dive back around a corner to avoid the two guards he'd just attacked. When he was reasonably confident no one was watching, he lunged across the main aisle and ducked behind the nearest register.

"Greetings," the cashierbot said. "Are you ready to check out?"

Greene waved a hand at the thing. "Shut up!"

"I'm sorry, I didn't understand that. Please repeat."

"Stop talking to me! I mean, uh, no, I'm still looking."

The manager was probably the only human employee in the store, and if he knew what was good for him, he was back in the vault, waiting for all of this to blow over. It was just as well.

Greene peeked out at the front door, a stone's throw away. Two Algary men stood guard there, both wearing that same heavy body armor. He wasn't going to get past them with just his pistol. But he didn't have time to wait, either.

His heat ray sure would have come in handy right now, he thought. But maybe there was something else he could use.

"Robot," Greene said softly. "I'm ... disabled. Can you bring me a pack of fire starters? The ones that are just down the way on that display in the main aisle?"

"I cannot leave the register," the cashierbot said, and Greene realized that it was actually mounted on the counter and had no legs. "However, another associate will be happy to bring them to you momentarily."

"Thanks," Greene said. "Wait, make it three packs."

"Affirmative."

Greene squatted behind the checkout counter and contemplated. He needed something else, but he couldn't very well wait for these robots to fetch things from all over the store. He didn't even know if the robot would bring him what he'd asked for in a timely manner.

He grabbed a lighter from the rack by the register and crept back to the main aisle, scanning the racks on the off chance something would be of use.

Greene could scarcely believe his good luck. The endcap nearest him was stocked with Real Orange Magic Zesty All-Natural Pure Organic Air Freshener. He picked up a bottle and scanned the label to make sure. He read, *Contains d-limonene. Extremely flammable. Extreme risk of explosion by fire, shock, or other sources of ignition.*

He stuck it into his jacket pocket, then grabbed a full tray, twelve big bottles, and returned to his spot behind the register.

"Here you are, sir," said a voice behind him, making him jump.

A vaguely humanoid retailbot had rolled up with the fire starters in its pincers. God, he might have a chance after all.

"Thanks," Greene said, taking them. "Very fast. Five stars."

"Thank you, sir. Will there be anything else?"

"No."

Greene grabbed the plastic wastebasket from under the register and dumped the contents onto the floor. Then he opened a box of fire starters and lit them all. When he had the package burning nicely, he placed into the wastebasket, then dumped the other two boxes on top of it.

"Please do not open merchandise before purchase," the retailbot said, still standing right next to him.

"Yeah, sorry, I'm going to buy it right now. Listen, those gentlemen up at the front of the store were looking for you. They wanted to hear about applying for a House Station credit card."

"Very good," the bot said, and rolled away.

Maybe the contraption would buy him even a second of distraction.

Greene jammed the entire tray of citrus air freshener, cardboard and all, into the burning wastebasket. He had to be quick, before the bottom of the bin melted out.

The retailbot had almost reached the front doors, and the Algary men's attention was on it. Greene stepped into the aisle, took several steps to build up some speed, and slung the burning trashcan toward them along the smooth concrete floor with all the power his good arm had in it.

Greene immediately dropped to one knee, drew his pistol, and fired four shots at the skidding wastebasket.

The liquid from the punctured bottles ignited immediately. The Algary men saw it now, spitting out jets of fire as it spun toward them. Just before it reached them, it detonated in a ball of fire with a short but deafening bang.

The blast knocked Greene on his rear end. One of the Algary men fell on his back, and the other was spun around. The retailbot had been closest to the blast, and now it lay facedown in a tangle of potted plants by the exit.

Greene jumped to his feet and charged, commanding his ankle to hold. The fire was already burning out. Still, he thought, it had certainly been as zesty as he'd hoped.

Could he get out the front door before these men realized what was happening? No—the one still on his feet was already turning toward him, pistol in both hands.

Greene felt his ankle buckle as he neared the door, and he threw himself along with it, dropping into a feet-first slide and taking out the Algary man's legs. They went down in a heap together.

He shoved wildly, trying to get free, to at least get the man's weight off his mangled shoulder. As they struggled, the Algary man's pistol went off, and white-hot pain punched through Greene's thigh.

Greene couldn't bring his own gun to bear. He pushed back with whatever muscles would respond, and for his efforts, he got an elbow right below his eye that made his vision flash white.

He lashed out blindly, desperately, with his good arm and connected with the man's ear. Greene grabbed it and pulled, the man bellowing in rage.

Greene managed to shove the man sideways and get free. He hurled himself on top and went for the throat, pressing, squeezing. When the man stopped thrashing, Greene released him immediately, and the man lay still on his back, his breathing ragged.

With some difficulty, Greene climbed to his feet, gasping for breath, and took in a lungful of burned orange air. A pistol lay at his feet, and he kicked it away.

The other Algary man had sat up and was shakily attempting to stand. Greene took the can of air freshener out of his pocket, removed the lid, and sprayed the man in the face. The man shrieked and put both hands to his eyes, and Greene left him there.

Greene tossed the can away, clamped a hand over the bloody wound in his thigh, and limped for the front entrance. He wasn't sure how bad he was hit, but every step sent pain through his entire body.

He stepped out into the Portsmith evening, welcoming the cool air on his face, grateful to see the setting sun again.

"I'm outside," he said.

A plain black car with dark windows pulled up and stopped in the nearest traffic lane.

"At last," Greene muttered. He staggered toward it.

"Good news," Burg said in his ear. "They're just a block away. One more minute."

Greene froze.

The car's rear window slid down, and Algary President Victor Carandini smiled up at him. "Good day."

Two Algary people jumped out of the car on the opposite side and pointed pistols at Greene.

Carandini opened his door, then slid to the far end of the seat, making room. "If you please," he said, beckoning.

Greene didn't move. "Carandini," he muttered under his breath for the benefit of the Fates.

"I'm a busy man. Get in or be shot," Carandini said, still smiling, looking for all the world like a kindly grandfather.

Greene had thoughts of trying to stall until the Xiong car arrived, but now more Algary troops had appeared. They shoved him roughly into the car.

"Chief, we can see you now," Burg said in his ear. "Don't get in that car, it's the wrong—"

The nearest Algary man slammed the car door closed behind him, and his comm signal cut out.

So close, Greene thought, as the cumulative trauma of the past hour rushed in on him. He'd been so very close.

ELEVEN

Greene considered his situation. Beside him sat Carandini, elderly and, apparently, unarmed. In the front of the car were two security men, both of whom had twisted around in their seats so that they could point their pistols at Greene.

Not great odds to try something even if he hadn't been exhausted and wounded. Greene contemplated the alternative.

"All units accounted for," the security man in the driver's seat said. "Numerous injuries. No fatalities."

Carandini's eyebrows rose. "Remarkable. Very good. Well, let us be on our way."

The doors locked and the car pulled out, diverting the traffic around it, heading swiftly toward the city center. Toward the Algary building, no doubt.

Carandini turned to Greene, and his voice was calm and pleasant. "You, sir, have managed to take down a good number of my people while making a considerable mess halfway across the city, all without killing anyone. That's very impressive. In fact, I would venture to guess that you intended it to be so. Extremely wise. I trust that you will find that this is to the good of all parties concerned."

Greene said nothing. He was on his own. Xiong wouldn't attack this car—not in public, and not as long as Greene was alive. At most, they might try a blockade, but surely Algary would establish a protective convoy to prevent such a move. Xiong didn't want an all-out war in the streets, and Greene hoped he hadn't just given Algary cause for one.

Carandini clasped his hands together. "Now then. As I said, I'm a busy man, and I don't wish to keep you, but we do have a bit of business. First of all, empty your pockets."

Greene sighed, then reached into his pockets and pulled out his forged commerce card, his burner phone, his Algary credentials, and Garcinia's jamming device, placing all of it on the seat between them.

Carandini picked up the jamming device and inspected it with keen interest. But as he put it back on the seat, his eyes narrowed and his jaw tightened.

"You seem to be laboring under the misapprehension that I am a fool," he said. "What follows will be precisely as difficult as you choose to make it."

Greene weighed his options. He had none. He reached into his jacket pocket and handed over the drive with the Algary data.

"There, you see how easy this can be when we're honest with one another?" Carandini turned the drive over in his hands. "I suspect, given your frantic pace, that you have not yet transmitted this data." He passed the drive up to the security men in the front.

It wasn't a question, and Greene didn't answer. At least the pain of his wounds prevented him from dwelling fully on the catastrophic scope of his failure.

His back was stiffening, and he twisted to get more comfortable, realizing as he did so that he was smearing blood all over the seat.

Oh, well, he thought. It was the least he could do.

"Goodness me, where are my manners?" Carandini said. "You must be parched after the ordeal you've just put yourself through." He reached under the seat in front of him, pulled out a bottle of water, and offered it to Greene.

Greene eyed it with suspicion and made no move to take it.

Carandini laughed. "Poison? Serum? A tracking device? All of Algary around you, and this is what you fear. You are indeed an amusing fellow."

Greene realized just how thirsty he was. Bloody and beaten, he had no pride left to salvage here. He accepted the bottle, twisted it open, and drank the water greedily.

When he'd finished, he looked out the window. They were still headed toward the city center, but whether toward the Algary building or somewhere else, he couldn't say.

"You're putting forth quite a lot of blood," Carandini said. "You don't suppose you're bleeding out, do you?"

Greene took stock of his injuries. The gaping wound in his shoulder. The gunshot wound in the meat of his thigh. His throbbing ankle. Several dozen assorted bumps and bruises.

He shook his head.

"Very good," Carandini said. "Nevertheless, I'm sure you'll be wanting to have yourself looked at, and I don't want to hold you up. So tell me: do you know who I am?"

Greene nodded.

Carandini smiled. "Of course. And *I* know who *you* are."

A chill shot through Greene. He hadn't expected this. But it was only a matter of time, he supposed.

"Yes indeed," Carandini said. "*You* are Xiong Holonautics."

Greene struggled to keep a straight face and wished the collar's holographic facial expressions didn't mirror his own quite so faithfully.

"Yes. You are either Xiong's golden boy, Green Greene, or someone who works for him. No, don't bother to deny it. Look how you've bled all over my car. It would be no trouble at all to take a sample, but it really doesn't matter. You are *Xiong*."

Greene said nothing.

"Furthermore, you are wearing one of our holographic collars," Carandini said. "It's an older model, and I confess to a certain curiosity as to how you came by it. But that is neither here nor there. Undoubtedly your engineers have already copied the technology. You may keep the one you're wearing. Consider it a trade for this." He patted the jamming device.

Greene looked away. The security man in the seat in front of him was still looking straight at him, still pointing the gun at him, the hint of a smile on his face.

"Do you know," Carandini said, "that Algary and Xiong have been rivals, not only here in Portsmith but around the world, for three generations?"

Greene just listened. He knew the broad strokes and didn't see the relevance of the particulars.

"Since my grandfather founded Algary, many competitors have arisen, and challenged, and some have even dominated—for a time. But only Xiong has endured. And I respect that. But this struggle has spanned *decades*: The Dragon versus The Bear. Do not think that your collar or a few bits of stolen data will turn the tide in your favor. Far from it. You may move a few grains of sand from my side of the scales to yours, but that is all."

Greene thought about this, then decided to speak for the first time since entering the car.

"Why are we having this conversation?"

Carandini nodded. "Straight to the point. Spoken like a true security man. Very well, here it is. You have trespassed on Algary grounds. You did so cautiously, delicately, even, to try to spare your corporation from culpability and wrath. Yet I have every right to kill you for it, as you know. No one understands the parameters of this contest better than I, because no one has been playing it as long as I have—with the possible exception of Mr. Xiong himself."

The mysterious Mr. Xiong—whom neither Greene nor anyone he knew had ever seen. A tiny part of Greene was dying to ask Carandini what he knew, but there would never be a right time or place for that question.

Carandini stroked his beard. "Your actions today suggest that Xiong does not seek and is therefore, I believe, unprepared for all-out war with Algary. Neither does Algary want war with Xiong. But there must be recompense. This is why you are being spared: to inform your superiors that there will be reprisals commensurate with Xiong's offense. Swift and harsh, but commensurate. Ah. We have arrived."

Greene looked out the window and was surprised to see the familiar black granite and gold doorways of Xiong Tower.

"Goodbye," Carandini said. "I hope you will reflect well on today's events. Many lessons can be learned from them."

The lock on the door released with a click, and it took Greene a moment to process what was happening. They were letting him go.

He opened the door and eased out of the car. His legs had gone stiff, and standing was difficult. The instant he'd gotten clear, the car door shut behind him.

Finding himself surprised and grateful to be alive, Greene limped toward the main entrance. There was no sense in pretending he belonged anywhere else.

Burg's voice in his ear made him jump. "We've got him again. He's ... *here?*"

"Chief, report!" Marlena said.

Greene willed his heart to stop racing. "I'm just outside."

As he entered the building, a new wave of exhaustion swept over him, fogging his brain.

The nearest guard at the security checkpoint was looking at him suspiciously, one hand on his sidearm.

For a moment, Greene felt confused. Then he realized he still had the holographic collar active. He couldn't seem to recall how to turn it off.

"I need a medic," he said, and collapsed.

TWELVE

Greene awoke with no idea where he was. He felt floaty and numb, and his extremities didn't seem to be responding properly. The lights on the ceiling above him were dim enough that they didn't hurt his eyes, which he appreciated.

He lay on his back, propped up, in a bed—the most comfortable bed he'd ever been in, or so it felt.

He managed to get his neck to work, looked around at familiar white walls, and realized he was in Xiong Medical. Several bags of fluid hung from an infusion stand beside the bed, connected by tubes to his arm. He still wore his bloody clothes, but his sleeves had been cut off.

The sound of snapping bubblegum from outside the open door helped him focus his concentration.

"Mainprize?" he said, his voice unexpectedly raspy.

A moment later, the small, trim woman appeared in the doorway, brushing lint from her many-pocketed white medical suit. "Hey there, Chief. How are you feeling?"

He didn't really know how to answer that concisely, so he said, "What time is it?"

"Evening. Don't try to get up." She entered the room and studied the instrument panel next to the bed. "Good, good. Coming along nicely. We got the first rounds of bioprinting done while you were out. I'll start flushing the meds out of you, so you should be able to walk out of here in one piece in half an hour or so."

"Thanks. Can I have some water?"

"Sure. Can you handle visitors? Mrs. Ranga Rao wanted to know when you were up."

Greene nodded. "Call her."

Mainprize nodded, left, and returned a minute later with a large lidded cup of water. His hands shook, and she helped him guide the bendable straw to his mouth. "Mrs. Ranga Rao says she's on her way down."

Greene grunted acknowledgment as he guzzled the water.

"Take it easy," Mainprize said. "Don't rush it."

"Thanks," he said when he'd finished.

"Let me know if you need anything else," Mainprize said, and left the room.

Greene's head was beginning to clear, and his thoughts swarmed unrelentingly around one topic like insects around a streetlight.

The mission had failed spectacularly. It was bad enough that he hadn't brought the data home, but to be captured and identified as Xiong—that was disastrous.

He found that he was less concerned about losing his job over this debacle—although, he suspected, it would have been a different matter if Shepherd were still in charge—than about where the investigation went from here, and what Algary might do.

Marlena appeared in the doorway, immaculate, free of the rib brace, with Burg right behind her.

"Chief!" Marlena said. Her smile upon seeing him lit up her whole face. "Thank God you're all right." She came and sat in the chair next to the bed and put one hand on top of his. "Thank God you made it back."

Burg leaned against the wall and crossed her beefy arms. She said nothing, but her eyes clearly stated that she too was glad to see him.

"I'm sorry," Greene said. "I—"

Marlena shook her head. "Nobody else could have done better. You got back here alive, and that's what matters most."

"Algary knows it was us," Greene said.

"What they know and what they can sell to their board and their shareholders may turn out to be two different things. Chief, I know you've been through hell today, but I need to know everything that happened."

Greene related the day's events in as much detail as he could recall, feeling the sting of failure all over again. By the time he finished, both women wore concerned expressions.

Marlena leaned forward and rested her chin on one hand. "Hm. 'Swift and harsh reprisals.'"

"What does that even mean?" Burg said, scorn in her voice. "He didn't kill any of theirs. So what's Algary going to do? The Corporate Code is confusing. And stupid."

"We aren't talking about killing people," Marlena said. "Algary doesn't want war either, or they would have killed Greene—or kept him."

"What are we talking about, then?" Burg asked.

Marlena took a deep breath and blew it out. "We're talking about corporate espionage—and sabotage."

"Sabotage," Burg repeated. "If they've really got stealth suits, there's no telling what damage they could do."

Marlena turned to face her. "Priority one, the two of you are going to work with Garcinia on ways to neutralize that technology. And to prevent them from doing to us what Greene did to them today."

Burg nodded her approval.

Greene tried to sit up but was stymied by a rush of lightheadedness.

"No, Chief." Marlena turned back to him. "You rest. This is mostly on the tech side to start with. Garcinia's team is working on it now. I want you to take a break. But be ready to go through it first thing tomorrow morning. I don't want to overlook *anything*."

"All right," he said, surrendering. He was too tired to do otherwise.

Marlena patted his hand and rose from her chair. "Good work today, Chief. I mean that. Now, if you'll excuse me, a lot of people need my attention right now."

"Sure," Greene said.

She gave him another smile, then turned and left.

Burg remained, still standing against the wall. "You're all right, Chief."

He wasn't sure if it was a question or a judgment. "I'll heal," he said.

"You're not mad?"

Greene raised an eyebrow. "Mad about what?"

Burg glanced into the hall, pulled the door closed, then sat in the chair Marlena had just vacated.

"It's bullshit," she said. "She shouldn't have left you there to grab all that other data. She got greedy."

Greene shrugged, or tried to. "It's the job."

"Nevertheless, it was irresponsible."

Greene agreed completely but didn't say so.

"She didn't even apologize to you," Burg said.

"We both know she doesn't have to. And we have to get to work regardless."

Burg shook her head. "You heard the boss. You have to rest. I'll take care of it for now."

Greene's eyes narrowed. "When was the last time you went home?"

She had to think for a moment. "Day before yesterday."

"What? You're not serious."

"I slept," she said defiantly. "I have a couch in my office."

Greene shook his head. "God, Burg, you're still after my job."

The tiniest smile crept onto her face. "Maybe I've decided I don't want your job. I get to stay here, deal with logistics, and drink coffee while you chase halfway across the city, running around and getting shot at everywhere you go. It sounds exhausting. I'm not as fond of either cardio or bullets as you seem to be."

Greene laughed, and it felt like the first time in a long time. "You do make it sound glamorous ..."

"Although," Burg said, "I haven't figured out whether it's the job itself or just your natural way with people."

Greene snorted.

Burg stood up and jabbed a finger at him. "You go home and rest. I'm going to keep working on this thing, and I'll hand it over to you when you come in in the morning, and then *I'll* go home. Maybe."

Greene surrendered to her also. "Fine. But be sure you check in with Kingjack. If the Armory's not secure, nothing's secure."

She gave him a little play salute on her way out the door. "That's my first stop."

Greene mustered his energy and sat up. He swung his legs off the bed and discovered that the legs of his pants had been removed mid-thigh. He peeled up the bandage on his leg and saw that the wound there had been bioprinted extensively. He expected to see the same when he got a chance to look at his shoulder.

He planted his feet and got himself half-standing. The position was less painful than he'd expected—Mainprize did good work.

"Doc," he called. "Can I get out of here?"

In a moment, she appeared in the doorway. "I don't know, can you?"

Greene sighed.

Mainprize looked him over, then inspected her instruments. "You could do with another round of bioprinting, but your vitals are fine and you shouldn't have to worry about bleeding." She deftly removed the tubes from his arm, pulled a bandage out of one of her many pockets, and stuck it over the tiny holes in his skin. "How are you doing for walkies?"

Greene staggered across the room as Mainprize looked on disapprovingly.

"Not great," she said.

"No," he admitted.

"You can stay here as long as you want," Mainprize said. "I don't need the bed—Max Fill left this morning, so I've got no overnight guests at all. Or I can take you up to your office. Or we can call your car and send you home."

"Max is doing all right?"

"He is. Fortunately, we got to the point where we were bioprinting faster than he was deteriorating, and pretty quickly. Fairly smooth sailing after that. I was glad to send him home; he wouldn't stop talking there toward the end. Anyway, what'll it be?"

Greene absolutely did not want to stay in Medical, and he wasn't about to go straight home so his wife and his mother could see him in these bloody rags. "Can you give me something so I can walk like a normal person?"

Mainprize shrugged. "Sure. What have you got? Pain? Stiffness? Weakness? We gave you the standard pain cocktail while you were out; you should be good for another hour or so."

"Dizziness, mostly. And I'm feeling a little stiff."

"Gotcha. Stay put. I'll be right back. Don't fall over."

Greene sat back down on the bed. In a few minutes, Mainprize returned with a syringe. She swabbed his uninjured shoulder with a disinfectant pad and then jabbed him.

Whatever the needle had contained kicked in almost immediately. Greene's limbs warmed, his sense of balance returned, and his mind sharpened.

"Thanks." Greene found he was able to stand up straight and walk in a straight line with ease. He could barely feel the pain in his ankle.

Mainprize nodded. "You good, then?"

"Yes. I—" He paused. "I'm going to feel like garbage tomorrow, though, aren't I? Can you give me something for the morning?"

"You will, and I can."

"Thank you."

"You know," Mainprize said, "with the caveat that I'm just your doctor and not some sort of holistic shamanic practitioner, I feel compelled to point out that the best way to get you back to one hundred percent is going to be for you to lay off the chems and rest your body the traditional way."

"Tomorrow is going to be a demanding day," Greene said. "But when I have time, I will."

"Your call. My job is to keep you going, but I don't get paid by the injection. And if you can make the time, come by for your last rounds of bioprinting. You'll feel better after that."

"I'll try. Thanks, Doc."

Greene left Medical and took the elevator up to his office, feeling thankful for his own personal shower. He wasn't sure it made up for getting shot, but it was a nice perk nonetheless.

He threw his tattered clothing into the trashcan, then got into the shower and stood under the hottest water he could stand, letting his mind drift into blankness for a few glorious minutes.

He got out, toweled off, and surveyed the contents of his closet. He wasn't in the mood for a suit, and he found that his shoulder mobility was limited despite the meds, so he grabbed a black and gold Xiong Security jumpsuit and pulled it on. In clean clothes, he almost felt normal.

Greene combed his hair, glad to see his own face in the mirror, bruised though it was. On top of a reddened, swollen eye that would be black tomorrow, he had an abrasion under his other eye, plus a gash on his cheek that he didn't remember getting. All told, he admitted to himself, he was a disaster.

He suddenly realized that he didn't want to go home. He didn't want Nisha to see him like this, didn't want to be an emotional burden to her. She would worry even if she didn't say anything—but she probably *would* say something.

He went to his desk and called her.

"You're going to be late, aren't you?" Nisha said upon picking up.

At least she made it easy. "Yes. I'm sorry."

"Is everything okay?"

"Yeah. I'm fine. Just a lot of work things."

"I miss you."

A pang of guilt made his heart spasm. Or maybe it was all the meds. "I miss you too."

"Your mother is complaining that you're never here for meals."

Greene forced warmth into his voice. "You're the real hero for dealing with her."

"That's true," Nisha said. "Well, go on and get your work settled and pay our bills. But if you miss the birth of this baby, I will kill you personally unless your mother beats me to it."

"Fair enough," Greene said. "Are we close?"

"Nothing to report, Chief," she said, affecting a formal tone.

He sighed. "You know I don't like it when you call me that."

"And I don't like it when we only see each other for twenty minutes a day, but there you have it."

"I love you," he said.

"As well you should," she said, and Greene smiled in spite of himself.

When he hung up, he reflected that he would save a lot of time if he only called when he *wasn't* going to be late.

Greene sat down at the desk and activated his console. Then he recalled Marlena's admonition to take the night off and realized he didn't actually have the mental energy to sift through the minutiae of this part of his job.

He didn't want to stay in Xiong Tower and he didn't want to go home, but he needed to process his thoughts. Things he couldn't grasp firmly tumbled around in his mind.

Greene tapped his phone. "My car to the front."

He found it waiting for him when he got downstairs.

Greene got in, sank into the seat, and took a deep breath. "Take me to FatAss," he said.

THIRTEEN

The sun had set by the time Greene arrived at FatAss, but the holographic décor from the many businesses around the gym lit the sky as bright as day. The burger place across the street, Morbid O'Beefity's Triple Bypass, had a line out the door and down the block.

Greene was a little surprised that Satu wasn't at the desk, but he supposed she couldn't work *all* the hours this place was open.

In her stead was a humanoid bot, an older skinned model with unsettlingly not-quite-human features.

"Welcome to FatAss," it said. "How may I help you?"

Greene realized he hadn't called first. Juha could be at home or anywhere else.

"Is Juha here?"

The deskbot stared at him with dull eyes. "Please clarify your request."

Greene fought down the urge to snap at the stupid machine. "I'm here to see Juha Karjalainen."

"Mr. Karjalainen is teaching a class right now," the deskbot said.

"When does it end?"

"This class has an average termination time of 8:17 p.m."

Greene glanced at the clock on the wall. Twenty minutes. "I'll wait."

"Thank you for your patronage," the deskbot said.

Greene sat down in a chair in the lobby, rested his head against the wall, and promptly dozed off.

The next thing he knew, Juha was kicking him repeatedly in the foot.

"Wake up," Juha said. "No loitering."

It took Greene a moment to get his bearings. Immediately in front of him, Juha, profoundly sweaty, was wiping himself down with a towel. Behind him, fifteen or so attractive middle-aged ladies in tight workout clothes milled around the lobby, slowly making their way out.

Classic Juha.

"Hello," Greene said.

"Always nice to see you, but shit, man, you look like you've had a day. Do you have another job for me or are you having a personal crisis?"

"I'm sorry I didn't call. Do you have time to talk?"

"That was my last class." Juha let down his sweaty topknot, shook out his hair, and retied it. "Once these valued customers clear out, it'll be just you, me, and the bot there. I hate that damned thing. But Satu complained about having to sit there for seventy hours a week. Can you imagine? The ingratitude. This is just a short-term fix, of course; that ugly piece of shit isn't good for business. I've got to have some muscles or some tits behind the desk. Preferably both at once. You know, a personal touch. First impressions. Anyway, let me lock up and I'll meet you in my office."

"Thanks."

Greene entered the austere office and passed the time by studying the few pictures on the wall: Juha in front of FatAss with a *Grand Opening!* sign, Satu deadlifting an impressive number of plates, Juha and Satu side by side on a blue tennis court, holding a small trophy between them.

Juha arrived sooner than Greene had expected. "Have a seat. You want a drink?"

Greene found that he wanted one very much. "Yes, please."

Juha opened a cabinet. "Okay, I've got vodka, baijiu, gin, rye, scotch, Irish whiskey, Estados whiskey—"

"Rye, please. You've got a full bar in a gym?"

Juha poured him a tall glass. "I like to be prepared. You can't underestimate the importance of hospitality in this business. Ice?"

Greene shook his head.

"Good man, I don't have any anyway." Juha handed him the glass.

"Thanks." Greene sat down on the loveseat and took a big drink, letting the liquid rest in his mouth before swallowing. It was a good rye—sharp, spicy, peppery—and it went down smooth.

He took a deep breath and exhaled slowly, feeling every muscle relax a bit. He wondered idly if alcohol had any interactions with any of the meds he was on, then made the executive decision that it was probably fine.

Juha poured himself a quarter of what he'd given Greene, then sat down and propped his feet up on the desk. He swirled his drink around his glass, then stuck his nose in it.

"I had some protestors today, you know that? It's always some damn thing in this business."

"Protestors?" Greene took a sip of his drink. "What are you doing for people to protest about?"

"I had that same thought myself. Well, they enlightened me. It turns out I shouldn't be telling people that they should lose weight in the first place, never mind actively help them to do it, that's what they said. They called me a colonialist, whatever the hell that means. Three or four of them, very heavy, obese by every medical definition—they rolled in the front door on their electric scooters like a panzer battalion. I wasn't even mad, honestly; at least they're getting out and about."

"And what did you say to them?"

"I told them that their health was the most valuable thing they possessed. I told them that the best way to love yourself is to care for your body. I told them that we had a very beginner-friendly and sustainable low-intensity weight-loss program and that I would give them twenty percent off if they wanted to sign up. And then the leader called me a microaggressor who was spiritually crippled by internalized fatphobia, and then they left."

Greene wasn't sure he understood half of what he'd just heard. "You certainly have a way with people," he said.

"I certainly do. Hey, do you remember the time we investigated that case where that sex robot got hacked and then killed three people?"

"It was two people," Greene said. "The third one was only ... mutilated."

"Right, right. And then when we finally tracked that guy down and got him cornered, he took eight doses of Power-Through, and then he punched you right in the face four or five times while I was busy trying not to get my balls—among other things—crushed by Trixxxie the Robo-Whore, and then he was so out of his head that he peed on you? Man, that was a hell of a time."

Greene sighed. "Why are you bringing this up?"

"I thought of it just now. Your face looked similarly the next day to how it looks now. Ah, we had some fun times."

Greene reflexively touched his cheek, which was becoming tender.

"So was it Ojukwu who did this to you, or someone else? Algary?"

"Algary."

Juha nodded. "I'm sorry to hear that. Did you deserve it?"

Greene scowled. "What does that mean?"

Juha shrugged. "You know how it is. They dick with you, you dick with them, they dick with you a little harder, things gradually escalate, a few people get killed, the press gets hold of it, the stock tanks, a couple of high-but-not-too-high-level people get fired, and then things more or less go back to normal. Tale as old as time. Is that what you're in the middle of right now?"

Greene took another deep drink of his rye. "I'm trying not to be."

"Yeah, that's what everybody says. No, no, don't get upset. I believe you. Really, I do. It's everyone else I'm worried about."

Greene frowned. "Are you worried about me being here? Are you worried that I'm going to drag you into the middle of this?"

Juha ran a finger around the rim of his glass, a strange smile on his face. "No, I wouldn't say that. Not the *middle*, no. I'd like to think I can always count on you to bring me over to your side. You know I'm always glad to take your money."

A thought crystallized unexpectedly. "Can I ask you a question?" Greene said.

"I assume that's what you came here for."

"The Crestridge break-in at the expo. The chase with Ojukwu." He pieced it together as he spoke. "I got tackled by— That wasn't an impostor. There wasn't a holographic collar. It was *you*."

Juha raised an eyebrow. "Did you figure that out, or are you guessing?"

The truth was somewhere in between.

"It makes too much sense," Greene said. "Crestridge was using holographic defenses. Who better than you to get past them?"

"That's a fair point."

How casually he admitted it! An unexpected rage welled up from deep within Greene. "You actually did it! I can't believe it. I trusted you, and you—"

Juha held up a hand. "Let me stop you right there. You *trusted* me? Trusted me for what? You didn't even *ask* me. I never lied to you. And I don't work for your company, Green. I can take a job with Xiong if I want. I can take a job with Algary if I want. But I didn't have anything to do with that bomb, and that's the truth."

"A *job?*" Greene set his drink on the floor because he was afraid he might throw it otherwise. "*Algary?* Breaking and entering? Theft? That's the kind of job you're doing now?"

Juha now held up both hands, palms out. But his face remained placid. "In my defense, that's not what they told me."

Greene crossed his arms, waiting.

"What actually happened was not what I signed up for," Juha said. "You can believe it or not. This is the truth. Algary told me they were conducting a test of some new holographic camouflage. They wanted to see how long it would take me to get through it. They told me it was their hotel room and their people."

Greene massaged the bridge of his nose. "That is incredibly thin. You aren't nearly so stupid as to have taken all that at face value."

"Well ... no. That's true. But a paycheck is a paycheck. And anyway, nobody got hurt by it."

Greene picked up his glass and drained it. "I'm eager to see whether you can stick the landing on this mental gymnastics routine."

"Man, you are spicy tonight. Did you get shot or something today? All right, fine. Look, Green, I've always been straight with you."

Greene wasn't sure that was true, but he chose not to contest the assertion.

"To be honest," Juha said, "I've been having some financial difficulties lately."

This was surprising. By all accounts, Juha had plenty of money from his tour of duty on the Mars colony, and the gym seemed to be doing well enough.

"What sort of trouble?" Greene asked.

"You remember how a while ago, I told you that when I was coming back from Mars, I had an opportunity to get into the illegal zombie safari operations that they've got going on in Florida, over in Los Estados?"

"Vaguely. You didn't take it."

"Correct. And not a day has gone by that I haven't regretted it. Especially when I saw the numbers some of those guys were pulling down. Guys I knew. Guys who weren't as good as me."

"All right," Greene said, because he had no clue where this story was going.

"But then, a couple of weeks after you helped me save your company, I got another opportunity through some of my connections. By then, of course, I was fully established here with

FatAss, so I wasn't about to pull up the stakes. But I was able to make a considerable investment in a successful, reputable operation over there. Well, you can figure what happened next."

"I have no idea what happened next."

Juha raised an eyebrow. "You don't watch the news?"

Greene shrugged. "I guess not."

Juha swirled his drink around his glass and held it under his nose. "Can't blame you for that. Nothing but assholes on the news."

Greene waited.

Juha put his legs down, then leaned forward and propped one elbow on the table. "Two weeks. Not two weeks later, Los Estados announced a crackdown on the safari trade, making some noise about trying to reclaim that land sooner rather than later, although in my opinion, the government is just trying to keep the riffraff out so they can take over the industry themselves. Why else would those corrupt bastards go to all the expense if not to get a monopoly on hunting the Florida Men? They tripled coastal patrols. They increased security on the panhandle wall. They're even doing regular aerial surveillance over the entire area, for God's sake."

"That's a lot," Greene said dutifully.

"A *lot*. A month later, the company had been the target of three busts, the costs to evade all this security were going up, and they'd lost two thirds of their paying customers. They're now on the verge of getting out entirely. It's been a complete disaster. Nearly everything I've put in, I've lost. And it's ... let's just say that it's a considerable amount."

"You never mentioned any of this before."

"Because it's all illegal," Juha said. "Obviously. You're the world's moral compass; I didn't want to get you out of sorts."

Greene sighed. "So how bad is it?"

Juha looked down, chewing his lip. "Well, that may depend on Algary."

"Why?" Greene's eyes narrowed at a sudden thought. "You didn't sign on with them, did you?"

"No, no, nothing like that. But ... do you by any chance know why they wanted that part that I apparently stole so badly?"

Greene deliberated whether to tell him. Finally, he sighed, wondering why he kept being so open with Juha. "They're working on a stealth suit. Full-body cloaking."

Juha processed this. "Shit, it was a test after all. Just a different kind than I thought."

Greene didn't follow. "What are you talking about?"

Juha thought for a moment. Finally, he said, "Your wife still hasn't had that kid?"

Greene was taken aback by the non sequitur. "Not yet. Soon. A few more days."

Juha rummaged around in a desk drawer. "A girl, right?" He pulled out a small object and tossed it to Greene. "Maybe you can give this to her."

The thing squished in Greene's hand as he caught it. It was a little soft toy with beanbag pellets in its bottom, a floppy humanoid form with greenish skin and tattered clothes.

"This is a ... zombie? It's—"

"That's an authentic Florida Man beanie plush," Juha said. "Authentic, man. First generation. Not mint, but it's still got the tag on it."

Greene turned it over. The seam down the toy's back had been torn, then stitched by someone who had never been formally taught to sew. He inspected the crumpled heart-shaped tag.

Tracker

This little zombie will follow you
All through the day and all night too
Don't be afraid if he's crawling with bugs
Because, after all, he just wants hugs!

It *was* cute for a zombie, Greene had to admit. It had a kind face in spite of the wild eyes and missing teeth. Still, it wasn't on the list of the top one hundred things he would give a child to cuddle with.

"I picked it up that time I got lost in the Treasure Coast, so maybe it's lucky," Juha said. "Goddamn illegal zombie safaris. That's how they get you. Have I told you about that trip? No? Maybe another time. Anyway, take it."

"Thanks?" Greene said.

Juha nodded. "I know you'll take good care of it." He looked down, took a deep breath, then let it out slowly. "You take good care of everyone."

Greene was bewildered. What did that even mean? Why was Juha talking like this? He'd barely touched his drink. *But*, Greene realized, he *was* trying to change the subject. "Listen, I appreciate this. However—"

Glass shattered nearby, and they both sat up sharply.

Juha rose from his chair. "Well, fuck. I guess we're doing this now. That's what I was afraid of. I'm sorry you had to be here for it." He glanced at Greene. "But maybe that's *why* we're doing this today. Oh well, let's get it over and done with."

Greene put down the plush and his glass and got to his feet. "What's happening?"

Juha drained his drink in one gulp. "Algary is happening."

"What? Why?"

"That's too long a story to tell right now, although I think you know most of it already." Juha went to the cabinet in the corner and yanked it open, revealing a massive weapon that looked like the unholy drum-fed spawn of a combat shotgun and a grenade launcher.

"What is that?" Greene said, feeling more lost by the second.

"The Diplomat," Juha said, hefting it. "Armor piercing. Incendiary. All special order. This is no time to fuck around, after all. Come on. You got your shitty little heat ray? Maybe you can throw it at one of them."

Greene reached for his sidearm and remembered he wasn't wearing one.

Juha rolled his eyes, then handed Greene a pistol out of his desk. "Come on, Green, it's big boy pants time."

Greene accepted the gun, then checked the safety, the magazine, and the slide.

"All right, let's see what we're looking at." Juha tapped at his keyboard, then spun the screen around so Greene could see it. "Tactical analysis?"

The display showed closed-circuit footage of the FatAss lobby. Greene's heart sank. "There's a full squad. Algary colors, but no logos. Eight of them at least, with rifles. I'm guessing they're going to secure the entrance and then sweep the building."

"It's a lot," Juha agreed. "How convenient for me that this place is incredibly well insured. You know, this all might actually work out in the unlikely event that I live through it."

Greene shook his head. "Is there a back way out of here?"

"Escape?" Juha clucked his tongue. "That's a short-term fix, Green. Come on, we can take them."

Greene turned the monitor back. "They're in full body armor."

"You used to have a can-do attitude. What happened to that? Fine, *I* can take them. I've got a surprise or two up my sleeve anyway."

Greene opened his mouth to ask again about a back way out, but Juha was rummaging through the liquor cabinet.

"Where is the— Oh, this will work. No wait, where's the cheap stuff?"

"Juha!"

Juha pulled out a full bottle of whiskey and set it on the desk. "Fine. Stay behind me."

Without waiting for a response from Greene, Juha strode to the office door, kicked it open, and fired three booming shots into the lobby.

Greene immediately heard three small explosions, then, as Juha ducked back into the room, a shout and a hail of rifle fire.

"I think I got two," Juha said, as chips of plaster sprayed near his head. "Oh, good, these walls are cinderblock. I wasn't sure."

Greene came to the door and hunkered down next to Juha, then glanced at the monitor. Their assailants had moved up and were taking cover behind the main counter, where the deskbot sat inert.

Without leaning out, Juha blind-fired two more rounds through the doorway.

"They're still coming!" Greene said. He fired three shots of his own, if for no reason than to deter the assault team's progress for several seconds.

"Deskbot!" Juha shouted. "Welcome Protocol M-four-R-one-three-N-four!" He kicked the door shut. "You know, I'm going to miss this place. Get down."

"What?" said Greene. He was still watching the monitor, still wondering what use his handgun was going to be against a fully armored security force.

The deskbot exploded.

The blast shredded the welcome desk and dropped at least two of their attackers. Greene saw the burning remains of the deskbot's plastic and metal body scattered across the lobby, and then the monitor's view was obscured by dust and smoke.

The sprinklers kicked on in the office, quickly soaking them both.

"Masks!" someone shouted from outside the office.

"That's not good," Juha said, now back at the desk. He'd fashioned the bottle of whiskey and a strip of his sweat towel into a Molotov cocktail and managed to get it lit. He opened the door just far enough to lob it out.

When he slammed the door shut again, it had a dozen bullet holes in it.

"It's burning nicely, but I don't think it's slowing them down any," Juha said. "I've always wanted to use one, though."

"Breach!" a voice shouted.

"The desk," Greene said. "We can shove it up against the door, buy ourselves some time. The loveseat, too."

"I mean, the building's on fire now, but sure," Juha said. "Why not."

As Greene stood and lunged for the desk, he heard another boom. A plate-sized hole appeared in the doorway as he felt rather than heard debris and shot pass in front of his face.

"Jesus Christ," he muttered as he dove behind the desk.

Juha was firing his cannon through the new hole in the door.

"Help me!" Greene cried.

Finally, Juha dropped his spent weapon and turned to assist Greene with the desk.

They'd pushed it halfway there when a small cylindrical object bounced through the opening in the door and landed on the floor between them.

"Grenade!" Greene shouted.

"Shit." Juha stopped pulling on the desk and dropped behind his side. "I have a lot of regrets, you know that. Oh well. Green, I guess I'll see you lat—"

The instant he'd seen the grenade, Greene had fallen back, covering his head and diving for cover. Nevertheless, the concussive blast of the stun grenade flattened him, and his pistol flew from his hand as he slammed his nose on the floor.

He tried to get to his hands and knees, but he couldn't breathe—his sinuses were full of blood.

Algary was in the room now, too many of them, although Greene hadn't heard them enter. His senses wouldn't reply. The room had filled with people and smoke and water, and the tumult was too much for Greene's dazed mind to process. Gasping for air was all he could manage.

An Algary man pinned him to the ground, and Greene was unable to resist. However, no more abuse was forthcoming; the man seemed to be content to keep Greene immobile.

Greene watched as two others dragged Juha out from behind the desk. His face was cut and bloody, but he was conscious and alert as they bound his wrists behind him. Juha said something Greene couldn't make out, even though he was less than five meters away, and one of the Algary men smacked him.

Another produced a jet injector and pressed it to Juha's neck. A moment later, Juha slumped to the ground, motionless.

Greene understood: they weren't here to kill Juha; they were *taking* him.

The next thing Greene knew, a jet injector was being pressed into his own neck. And then he knew nothing at all.

FOURTEEN

Greene's consciousness returned, the smoky air, the damp carpet beneath him, and the continued shower of water from the sprinklers above testifying that he was still in Juha's office.

With some difficulty, Greene grabbed the arm of the loveseat and hauled himself upright. His head ached, his ears rang, and blood trickled down his throat. Coughing, he walked toward the office doorway and nearly pitched sideways. He grabbed the doorframe for support and peeked out into the lobby.

It was empty of people—even the Algary bodies were gone. The fire still burned around the remnants of the front desk, and the sprinklers still sprayed away to no effect. Greene realized that he couldn't hear them. If a fire alarm was going off, he couldn't hear that, either.

He returned to Juha's office. How long had he been out? It couldn't have been more than a few minutes, but long enough that Algary had been able to loot the place.

Juha's big weapon was gone, as was the pistol. Juha's computer and tablet had also been taken.

The little zombie plush still sat on the loveseat, sad and wet. Greene picked it up, turned the damp thing over in his hands, and tucked it into one of the thigh pockets of his uniform. Then he went out to the lobby.

The smoke was thinning now, and the sprinklers were washing away the spots of blood on the floor, red turning to pink that soon dissipated. Little bits of the deskbot littered the floor. Greene tried to be careful of his footing on the wet tile as he made his way toward the front door; even so, he nearly fell several times. His balance was wrong.

Through the smashed front windows, Greene saw a fire truck pull up, its flashing blue and red lights painful to look at. Surely its siren was blaring, but Greene couldn't hear it. He picked his way across the shattered glass carpeting the floor around the door and stepped outside.

It was a relief not to be rained on anymore, but the breeze on his wet uniform chilled him.

As if out of nowhere, an EMT appeared at his side, saying something that Greene couldn't make out.

"I'm fine," Greene said, his voice faint and far away. He didn't want to deal with these people; he just wanted to get back to Xiong Tower.

The EMT said something else, then motioned for Greene to sit down on the curb.

Greene shook his head. "I don't want to."

The EMT pointed at Greene's face, still talking, and put a hand on Greene's shoulder.

With a swell of anger, Greene jerked away more roughly than he'd intended. He tapped the Xiong insignia on the breast of his jumpsuit. "I'm declining treatment."

The EMT held up his hands and backed away.

More flashing lights appeared, and in a moment, a police car and a second fire truck pulled up behind the first.

Greene definitely didn't want to talk to the police. It would be difficult to get them off his case, especially without his hearing.

A crowd was gathering around the building, and the firefighters were busy inspecting the FatAss lobby, getting their hoses out, and keeping the crowd back. The chaos was more than sufficient to enable Greene to disappear.

He made for the crowd. A firm handed landed on his arm, and he shoved it away without looking, then pushed through the people.

When he had some separation, he ducked into an alley and waited a moment. As best he could tell, no one had followed him.

He pulled out his phone to summon his car and saw that he had a text message from an unlisted number.

Swift and harsh, Chief Greene.

His jaw tightened. Algary had taken Juha in retaliation for Greene's invasion of their offices. Except—

Something impacted Greene from behind, and pain, numbed by the medications he'd taken, pierced his upper back. He recognized the feeling, and as he stumbled forward, he knew in a flash: he'd been stabbed.

Algary? Again?

No—the blow was clumsy, too high to do any meaningful damage. Never mind that Algary had already passed up two golden opportunities to kill him today.

Greene spun around, the knife still in his back. The alley was darker than the streets but lit well enough that Greene could clearly make out the mugger in front of him. The man was weaponless now, but he was a bigger guy, with an unkempt beard and tattered clothing.

The man charged at Greene, going for a tackle, mouthing words that Greene didn't get.

The *audacity*. Greene couldn't catch a break. He might have laughed under other circumstances. Right now, it was an outrage.

He had no adrenaline rush now, just cold fury. Greene set his feet and tensed for action.

He sidestepped the tackle—almost. In his diminished state, Greene wasn't quite fast enough, and the mugger clipped him in the shoulder.

Greene spun into the blow, slammed his fist into the base of the bigger man's head, and kicked his legs out from under him.

As the mugger went down in a heap, Greene pounced, eyes wide with rage. He ground his knee into the man's spine and pressed his face against the asphalt with one hand. With the other, he reached up and yanked the knife out of his shoulder. Between his meds and his wrath, he barely felt it.

Greene leaned down close to the man's face, increasing his pressure, holding the knife where the man could see it.

"I could *kill* you for that," Greene spat. "By rights, I could. You're lucky it was *me* you went after. *Lucky*."

He jabbed the knife into the pavement near the mugger's face and the blade snapped, making the man start.

Greene gave his face a shove and dropped the knife handle. "This is you being *lucky*. Remember that."

If the man replied, Greene didn't hear it.

He rose, keeping a foot on the man's back, but there was no struggle.

Out on the street, Greene's car arrived.

He contemplated trying to haul the man back to the police, but he had more important things to do.

"Make better choices," Greene said. "Under other circumstances, you'd be dead now."

He strode quickly but not hurriedly to his car, got in, and shut the door. He took a deep breath as a feeling of cocooning safety washed over him. Outside, the mugger got slowly to his feet.

Greene felt suddenly disgusted with himself. He'd gone too far with that guy, way too far. And for what? The man wasn't going to learn anything from the encounter. He wasn't going to change his life. He was humiliated, hurt, and angry, and he'd take it out on the next person who came his way.

Exactly like Greene just had.

"What he does isn't your fault," he muttered to himself. Yet he found himself feeling responsible for events that hadn't occurred yet and that he would never find out about.

The car wasn't moving. Greene realized he hadn't heard the destination request.

"Take me to Xiong Holonautics."

The car pulled smoothly out into traffic, accelerating, signaling to the autodriven cars around it to yield.

Feeling spent, Greene sank back, his head pounding and his throat dry.

He scrounged under the seats and discovered a half-full bottle of stale water. He didn't care. He drank it all.

With drops trickling down his chin, he reflected on his day, his choices, his life. Apparently he had gotten to the point that it didn't even bother him when people tried to kill him. It was worse now than when he'd been a cop.

He stared out the front window, willing his headache to subside. The countless bright holograms and neon signs that lit Portsmith's night sky swept past in a hypnotic blur.

In the peace of the car, his thoughts turned to the incessant ringing in his ears. Losing his hearing was more inconvenient than losing a hand, he concluded. He wondered what tortures Xiong Medical had in store for him to get it back in a timely manner.

"Call Marlena Ranga Rao," he told the car. A moment later, he added, "Activate captioning."

The car's heads-up display illuminated, covering the front windshield. *Dialing* appeared, and was replaced a moment later by *Connected – Audio Only*.

"Yes, Chief?" Marlena's words appeared on the HUD.

"Algary attacked Juha's gym. They took him."

"What do you mean, they took him?"

"I don't know exactly. I was there when they attacked. They got us both, and when I came to, they were gone and he was gone."

There was a pause, then, "Where are you now?"

"On my way back to the tower. I need the medic." He pinched the bridge of his nose. "Again."

"Because of Algary," she said, and Greene wished he could hear her tone.

"Yes. 'Swift and harsh,' they said."

"Those bastards."

"But they weren't after me, they were after Juha," Greene said. "They had every chance to kill me."

"'Commensurate,'" Marlena said. "That's what Carandini said."

"But Juha—"

"Juha doesn't work for Xiong. Is not under the protection of Xiong."

"Well, they have him now. We have to do something."

"Do you have any idea where he is now? Where they might have taken him?"

Greene sighed. "No. But—"

"We'll talk it over when you get back. In the meantime, are you all right?"

"I suppose I will be. Eventually."

"Get yourself fixed up. Then get me a full report."

"Understood." He let Marlena end the call.

Greene shifted in his seat, feeling uncomfortably sticky from the knife wound in his back.

He opened the car's center console and found a bottle of Pain-Kill. His previous dose was still holding in all areas except his head, but it paid to be proactive. He itched, too, like he had ants crawling on his forearm and everywhere he'd had bioprinting done, but he didn't have anything for that.

He swallowed the pills and thought. He wasn't going home tonight, there was no chance.

"Join the queue for interior detailing," he told the car. "Blood on the driver's side. And have them put a full case of water in the backseat."

By the time he arrived at Xiong Tower, his headache had receded.

When he staggered into the lobby for the second time that day, he found Sonnenschein there to meet him.

She was talking, and he found that if he focused on her lips— her purple lipstick matched her hair perfectly—he could make out bits of it. Something about taking him up to Medical.

"I'm sorry," he said, indicating his ears. "I can't hear." At her expression of deepening concern, he added, "But I'll be all right. I'm not going to keel over."

She nodded but put a supportive hand on his elbow anyway. He didn't shrug it off.

On the elevator, Sonnenschein started talking again, and Greene found himself on the edge of losing his temper. It was exasperating and exhausting, being unable to communicate. If people quit trying to talk to him, it would save everyone involved a lot of aggravation.

He opened his mouth to rebuke her, but she held out a small case, which he accepted. His Spec-Trons.

"Thank you," he said, but she was still talking. He shook his head. "I can't—"

"*Turn! On! The! Captions!*" she bellowed, patience and amusement on her face.

Greene's widened in understanding. Why had he not thought of this? The idea had come to him quickly enough in the car.

He quickly took the Spec-Trons out of their case and put them on. As they booted up, he eagerly anticipated the comforting rush of information, but he immediately found it tiring and overstimulating. He took out his phone, enabled the captioning function, and disabled most of the rest.

"I'm sorry, Sunny," he said. "I shouldn't have been short with you."

She spoke, and her words blessedly appeared before his eyes.

"It's all right, Chief. You've been through a lot today, I've heard."

He felt every muscle in his body unclench. Communication. "Yes. I have. And you weren't responsible for any of it. So I'm sorry, and thank you for being here to look out for me."

She smiled. "Aw, Chief, we're a team. That's what we do. We help each other. Besides, if you fall over dead, then Burg will be in charge, and she's no fun at all."

Greene chuckled in spite of himself. "I'm no fun either, though."

"Maybe not, but at least you're nice about it."

When they arrived at Medical, they found Mainprize chomping her gum and clearly not doing anything other than waiting for them.

"You're still here?" Greene asked, surprised. "You don't usually work the night shift."

"No," Mainprize said, her face unreadable. "I was at home. I came back. Mrs. Ranga Rao told me to. She said you wrecked yourself again. Amazing swiftness, probably a record."

"Thanks. I hope you didn't have to interrupt anything too important on my account."

Her nostrils flared. "Does it matter? That's why they pay us the big bucks, right? But to answer your question, I was going to get laid tonight. So ... no. Nothing too important."

Sonnenschein tugged at one pigtail. "Doc, can I ask a question?"

"What?"

"When you do it, does the gum stay in?"

Mainprize's eyes went wide and her lips tightened. "Get out."

"Sure thing." Sonnenschein nodded at Greene. "See you later, Chief."

When she'd gone, Mainprize pushed Greene toward the same room he'd been earlier, but with a noticeably rougher touch than before. "So what did you do to yourself this time?"

"Stun grenade in a small room," he said. "I can't hear anything."

"All right, fine. Sit quietly on that exam table while I take a look."

Greene obeyed, sitting still as she affixed some sort of scanner to his forehead and then poked several instruments into his ears.

Finally, she said, "Doesn't look like a concussion, although I want to run an imaging test to be sure. Pretty significant hearing loss, though. Textbook tinnitus."

"Yes."

"I hope you have the good sense to shut yourself down once we're done here. Don't feel like you need to go for the hat trick on my account."

"Yes."

Mainprize sprayed something cold and tingly into his ears, and the ringing subsided from a high screech to a dull roar.

"Better?" she asked.

He nodded. "Is the hearing damage permanent?"

"Of course it's not permanent. Look at me, that's why I'm here. To make sure that none of the foolish things that you clowns go out and do to yourselves is permanent. But if you're asking if you need work done, we have to wait and see. Probably. There's a good chance you're going to need new eardrums."

Greene sighed. "How much bioprinting is that?"

"A lot. They're small but very intricate. I'll probably need you here for a full day."

Greene waved a hand. "I don't have time for that now."

Mainprize shrugged. "Meds and hearing aids it is, then."

He looked up in alarm. "Hearing aids?"

She fluttered a dismissive hand at him. "Oh, stop. What are you worried about? Social stigma? Fragile masculinity? You're falling apart—do you want to be cool, or do you want to hear?"

Greene opened his mouth, then closed it. He didn't have a practical objection, but he supposed he'd always thought of hearing aids as things that happened to other people. Much older people.

"Anyway, they're not so different from the earpieces you wear on missions," Mainprize said. "Just pretend."

"Okay, okay. Do you have them here?"

"No. That sort of item's not usually in demand, as you might imagine. I think I've only rebuilt two sets of eardrums my whole career. But I'll make some calls, and I should be able to get you set up with a pair first thing in the morning."

"Fine." Greene wasn't going anywhere. He had no leads, no idea where Juha was, and now he was exhausted all over again.

He'd absently taken the little beanie zombie out of his pocket and was turning it over and over in his fingers. Even damp from the FatAss sprinklers, it was soft, comforting, soothing. Maybe not such a stupid thing after all.

"Oh, that's cute," Mainprize said. "Shopping for your kid?"

"I guess." He didn't have the energy to explain, and she didn't care anyway. Figuring they were done, he stood.

"Chief!"

"What?"

Mainprize's eyes were accusatory, and he assumed her tone was as well. "There is *blood* on my exam table."

"Huh?" He looked and saw splotches of red on the blue surface. "Oh. Right. I got stabbed, too. I forgot."

"You *forgot*? Did you take more meds after you left here before? How much stuff are you on right now?"

"Yes. I don't know." It was hard to keep track. "A lot."

She gave him a stern look. "That's a problem for another day, but it *is* a problem. All right, while I clean this up, undress yourself so I can get at the wound."

He opened up his jumpsuit and pulled the top down, then lay face down on the table.

"So how'd you get this one?" Mainprize asked as she cleaned the wound. The disinfectant barely stung.

When he'd finished relating the encounter with the mugger, she laughed. "You've become quite the magnet for violence, haven't you?"

"I'm hardly in a position to disagree."

"All right, I'm going to put the autosuture on you, so hold still."

That wouldn't be a problem; he felt like he might fall asleep on the spot.

It only took a few minutes. "All right, we're done," Mainprize said, patting his leg.

"Thanks, Doc."

"Are you going home? Maybe you should get someone to go with you this time."

He shook his head. "I'm going to go to my office and work on my report for the boss."

Going home was not an option. It was bad enough having bruises on his face, but if he showed up with no hearing, there was no telling what his mother would do. And Nisha didn't need the stress, either. He would just send her a message and then spend the night in his office.

"Chief," Mainprize said.

"What?"

"I can give you drugs all day to keep you going, but I can't give you anything that can take the place of actual rest. If you aren't careful, you can run yourself straight into the ground, and you'll feel fine all the way down. I'm good at my job, but I can't fix dead."

"I'll rest. As soon as I get the report done."

She shook her head. "I don't just mean sleep, although God knows you Security types are bad enough about that. You don't impress me with all your macho bullshit. I mean *rest*. You have to give your body a break from all of this physical and mental stress and let it heal."

Rest certainly sounded appealing. And he *did* want to get his ears fixed. But Algary was out there, plotting who knew what, and now they had Juha.

Greene nodded. "As soon as I have a chance to do that, you'll be the first to know."

Mainprize rolled her eyes. "I've been a doctor long enough to know when a patient has no intention whatsoever of following my good, wise, and correct advice. And I know how this company works. It's fine. Destroy yourself. Just see if you can go twenty-four hours without needing me for something, eh?"

"I'll try," Greene said. "Thanks, Doc."

They understood each other. That was enough.

FIFTEEN

Greene was awakened to full alertness by someone shaking his arm. He started upright, still not fully cognizant of where he was, and received cramping pain in his back for his trouble.

He lay on his couch in his office. The lights were on. Burg loomed over him, her arms crossed.

Greene fumbled for his Spec-Trons and put them on. "What's happening?"

"I called you three times," she said.

He motioned at his still-ringing ears. "I didn't know, sorry."

"Oh, right. Your ears. I *heard* about that."

Greene blinked. He'd never known Burg to intend a pun.

Most of the functions of his Spec-Trons were still disabled, and his phone was over on the desk. "What time is it?" he asked.

"Nine-thirty. The boss wants us."

Greene felt like he would have easily slept a few more hours if left uninterrupted. He looked down at the T-shirt and gym shorts he was wearing. "Let me change and I'll be right up."

Burg nodded, and her expression softened a touch. "Are you all right?"

"It's nothing that Medical can't fix ... if I ever get the time to sit through it."

She nodded. "Good. You look like shit, by the way. I'll see you up there, then."

When she'd gone, he stood up and stretched carefully. He was stiff from head to toe, and sore.

He walked over to the desk and picked up his phone. He had missed calls from numerous Security staff, but at least none were from Nisha.

"Enable all Spec-Tron functions," he told the device. "And open the blinds." A moment later, the room filled with natural light. "Too much," he muttered. "Fifty percent tint." The plate-glass window darkened accordingly.

He put the Spec-Trons on his desk and headed to his bathroom, thinking about what Mainprize had said about rest and drugs. He contemplated taking a break from the meds, trying to get through the day without them.

No, there was too much to do. He had to be at his best. Xiong couldn't have any more failures on his account. Maybe tomorrow would be better.

After all, he thought as he swallowed a dose of Pain-Kill, he wasn't going to be taking this stuff forever.

He washed his face, gingerly dabbing at the many scrapes and bruises. The puffy purple-black skin around his left eye was too tender to touch, and he left it alone. He was getting used to seeing his face in this state, he realized. He needed a shave, too, but that wouldn't be remotely realistic for a couple of days.

Greene thought about putting on a suit, which he typically preferred when meeting with the boss, but chose a black and gold Security uniform instead. Today was a workday.

As soon as he stepped out of his office, Krylov waved him over to the Security lobby desk.

"Morning," Greene said.

"Mrs. Ranga Rao called down a few minutes ago," the massive man said. "She said you didn't answer your phone."

Greene winced. "I was getting dressed."

"She said she's changed the plan. She's coming down here instead."

Greene didn't try to hide his surprise. He couldn't imagine what this portended. "All right. I guess I'll be back in my office, then. Also, would you put in an order to the quartermaster for me? Have them send me a couple of new security uniforms. I've been going through them lately."

"Sure, Chief. Oh, one other thing." Krylov held out a tiny black box. "This arrived for you from Medical about an hour ago. They said it wasn't urgent, and I didn't want to disturb you."

"Thanks." Greene took the box and opened it. His hearing aids: small and black, designed to be completely in-ear. Mainprize had been right—they didn't look so different from the earpieces he wore in the field.

Nevertheless, he felt a wave of self-consciousness at the thought of inserting them in front of another person. He fought this sentiment down. He wouldn't be embarrassed about being seen with a bandage, brace, or sling—how was this any different?

He shook the devices out of the box and stuck them into his ears. To his surprise, as soon as they activated, the ringing in his ears decreased, replaced by much more pleasant white noise.

"Incredible," Greene muttered.

"Chief?" Krylov said, and Greene *heard* him.

The man's voice came through a bit fuzzier than normal, a bit farther away, but actually hearing it was nonetheless wonderful.

Greene smiled, warmed and energized by sincere happiness. "I'm fine. My compliments to the doctor."

"Do you want me to send a message down?"

Greene shook his head. "No, no, I'll tell her myself."

He returned to his office, still feeling good. He knew the sentiment would be short-lived, so he clung to it. He took out his phone and deactivated the captions on his Spec-Trons, then pulled a pair of chairs over to the desk.

Not more than two minutes later, there was a knock on the door.

"Come in," he called.

The door opened and Marlena entered, a fiery storm of bouncing red hair over a deep yellow dress suit. Behind her came Burg, followed by one of Marlena's assistants, who was pushing a service cart.

Greene's eyes widened. In addition to a giant pot of coffee, he saw six kinds of sweeteners, cream, milk, half and half, whipped cream, several varieties of pastries, and an assortment of protein bars. It was far too much for three.

"Who else is coming?" he asked. He might have to send out for more chairs.

"No one." Marlena came straight to Greene and took his face in one hand. When he winced, she clucked her tongue and let go, then looked him over with a disapproving expression.

He put a hand to his face reflexively. "That bad?"

"That's all, thank you," Marlena said, and her assistant departed, closing the door behind him. "It looks pretty bad, Chief."

"It's not so bad that I can't take the elevator up to your office."

Marlena glanced at the tray, then back to Greene. "Despite what this may look like, I'm not here to baby you, Chief."

Greene resisted the urge to shrug. Maybe she had elaborate coffees like this all the time. "Won't you sit down?" he said.

Neither of them did.

"You sit down, Chief," Marlena said. "Let me get you something."

She seemed determined to wait on him. Was it pity? It made him uncomfortable. He tried not to be weird about it, not to overanalyze it.

He sat. "Just coffee, please. Black."

She poured a cup and handed it to him. "Anything to eat?"

Greene had a cramp in his stomach. Too many pills and not enough food. But he wasn't feeling so sore now. "Maybe in a bit."

Marlena turned. "Burg?"

Burg was clearly just as uncomfortable at the prospect of being served by the boss. She held up a hesitant hand. "You know, this might be easier if I just—"

She reached past Marlena, picked up a plate, and began loading it up with pastries and protein bars as though she hadn't eaten in a day.

Marlena smiled as she watched Burg stack her plate high and finally sit down. Then she said, "Something to drink?"

Burg was already in the middle of a giant bite of pastry. "Just milk, please," she mumbled around it.

Once Burg was situated, Marlena fixed herself a coffee dressed liberally with cream and sugar, topped by a tall, elegant spiral of whipped cream. The drink was practically a meal in itself.

Greene wondered what Juha, with his bizarre caloric dogma, would say about it. Given his ongoing and total infatuation with Marlena, probably nothing.

Juha ...

Marlena sat in her chair. "Whenever you're ready, Chief."

Greene took a big drink of invigorating too-hot coffee. Then he related in full detail what had happened the previous night from the moment he'd left the tower until he'd returned.

Burg stayed uncharacteristically quiet as he talked, eating and listening.

When he'd finished, Marlena said, "Why do you think Algary would want Juha? Could it be related to the job he did for them?"

"I'm sure that's part of it," Greene replied, "but I think the main reason is obvious. They're working on a stealth suit. What better way to test it than with the man who can see holograms?"

Burg swallowed a massive hunk of pastry. "How do you know he's not working with them voluntarily?"

Greene turned his palms up. "They destroyed his business and he wounded or killed several of them."

Burg shrugged. "Could be a ruse. A cover."

Greene sighed in frustration. "The evidence here isn't in question. You've never liked him. You've always thought the worst of him."

She nodded. "That's true. I don't like him. He's an insufferable jackass. But what does that have to do with anything? You've always given him the benefit of the doubt even when he's explicitly demonstrated that he doesn't deserve it."

Marlena held up a hand, and Greene bit down on the retort he had ready.

"Juha Karjalainen helped us take down Shepherd at no direct benefit to himself," Marlena said. "This company owes him a debt—of gratitude, if nothing else. He's earned the benefit of the doubt in this case."

Burg, sitting where Marlena couldn't see her face without turning, leaned back and rolled her eyes. "So where do we go from here?"

Greene shook his head. "Juha could be in the Algary building, or he could be anywhere."

"I doubt we'll be able to get back in there," Burg said. "Not so easily, in any case, and not the same way."

"I wholeheartedly agree," Greene said. "But as best we could tell, the stealth suit project was offsite. I'm guessing they wouldn't keep unwilling test subjects onsite either. If they do want him to test the suit, it's likely that he and the stealth suit are more or less in the same place."

Burg nodded. "I agree."

"But you have no idea where that is," Marlena said.

"No. But—" Greene leaned forward to brace his elbow on the desk, but he miscalculated the distance. His elbow slid off the desk and he almost fell out of his chair, nearly smashing his face on the edge of the desk.

Marlena was on her feet immediately. "Jesus, Chief, how many meds are you on?"

Greene waved her away and sat back upright, leaving his dignity where it lay. "I don't know. A few. I feel fine."

"Yes, that's exactly what I'm worried about. You look like you could drop at any moment, and you feel *fine*. Medical gave me your file this morning, and that isn't far from the truth. You shouldn't feel fine at all."

"I'm doing my job," Greene said, too sternly. "I'll make it."

Marlena took a deep breath and let it out slowly. "Deputy Chief Burg, would you please go out to the main Security desk and call for an emergency lockdown drill of all entrances? Manual close, manual reopen. Then, once you have everything back open again, come back and let me know how long it took."

"Manual?" Burg looked puzzled, but she set her plate on Greene's desk and stood. "You got it."

"Thank you." Marlena sat back down, waited until Burg had left the office, and then turned back to Greene, a piercing look in her eyes. "This isn't just about Juha. You were running yourself pretty hard before that incident. You stay late, you don't go home. Your work ethic is beyond reproach, no doubt, but there's a deeper issue here, isn't there?"

Greene opened his mouth, then closed it. He hadn't expected a line of inquiry like this.

"You don't like delegating, do you, Chief?" Marlena continued. "Specifically, you don't like delegating to Burg."

Greene said nothing.

"Burg is good, Chief, more than capable of running point on the implementation of new security countermeasures. Hell, she's more than capable of doing *your* job."

"Yes, I know she is," Greene said, much more defensively than he'd intended.

Marlena's eyes widened in sudden understanding. Greene felt as though she was peering into his inmost being, surveying all of his insecurities related to his position—his age, his flaws, his interactions with Shepherd.

Marlena seemed to consider her words as she spoke. "Chief, we've known each other for a few years now, and I haven't been your boss for the majority of it."

"That's true."

"Is this a problem?"

"Not at all," Greene said, and it was the truth. He felt like he knew where he stood with her, at least to a greater extent than he'd felt with any superior he'd had prior.

"All right." Marlena leaned forward. "Then you will believe what I'm about to say to you."

"Yes," Greene said, and resolved that he would.

"I'm not Shepherd, Chief. I'm not out to get you, and I don't have a hidden agenda. I value you. I also value Burg. I'm glad to have you both. Yes, she absolutely could be our chief of security, and I wouldn't have a single qualm about it."

Greene flinched.

If Marlena noticed, she gave no indication. "But the two of you are not the same. She comes at problems like a soldier, and you come at them like an investigator. There's a time and a place for each. My goal is to use each of your skillsets most effectively. I value your abilities, and not just because you solved my husband's murder. You saved this company from disaster when you took down Shepherd. That will not be quickly forgotten. You are our chief of security, and you will remain our chief of security for as long as I have anything to say about it—unless, of course, you get yourself killed."

Greene was taken aback. "That's very kind of you to say, but I'm not—"

She motioned for him to stop talking. "You've got to take care of yourself. You've also got to stop being so goddamned insecure, but I suspect that will take a little longer."

Greene didn't reply—there was nothing to say.

Marlena's expression softened. "You can be a strong leader and an effective delegator simultaneously, Chief. Believe in your people. Empowering them doesn't make you less valuable. As far as I'm concerned, it's the opposite."

"All right," Greene said. He recognized her point intellectually, although he didn't feel it emotionally.

"I'm one hundred percent correct," Marlena said. "You'll learn it for yourself sooner or later."

"Fine. What do you want me to do?"

"The first thing I want you to do is look after yourself. Recuperate. Get yourself healed up. Spend some time at home. You're going to have a baby soon, after all. First one, too, right? That's exciting."

"It is," Greene said. It was true, although he'd been so busy he hadn't had much time to think about it lately. The familiar pang of guilt swept through him.

"Even so, I know you won't be content to sit at home and do nothing. So I want you to coordinate with Garcinia's group about ways to tighten our defenses to keep stealth suits out. That's our number one priority. You ought to be able to contribute on that front without getting yourself shot up, and Burg is more than capable of keeping the ship afloat when you're out of the office."

Greene stifled a sigh. He didn't like this, not at all. But nevertheless, Marlena was right. And without a lead on Juha, what else was there to do?

"I know you're worried about Juha," Marlena said.

Greene looked up sharply. Was he that much of an open book to her?

For the first time, he noticed strain around her eyes. "He's my friend, too, Green," she said.

Greene felt anxiety begin to gnaw at his insides. He'd expected Marlena to come in here and give him some direction—it scarcely mattered which direction as long as he could charge ahead—but instead he was being sidelined. For his own good, he knew, but sidelined nonetheless.

There was a knock on the door, and Burg entered without waiting for a response. "Done and reopened," she said.

Marlena nodded. "Time?"

"Twenty-eight seconds to confirm manual lockdown of all exits. Four minutes, three seconds to get back to normal status."

Greene felt a swell of pride in his people. Twenty-eight seconds was a pretty good time for getting the security gates down.

"Not bad," Marlena said. "But I think we can do better. What was the biggest cause of delay, would you say?"

"The Security staff reacted promptly to the alert," Burg said, and there was pride in her voice, too. "And they've all been well trained on lockdown procedures. The biggest variable is the volume of traffic at the exits. It takes time to get all the people clear of the gates."

"That makes sense. What do you think we could do to speed up that process?"

As they talked, Greene's mind began to wander. This was directly relevant to his responsibilities, but he was about to get sent home, or to Medical, and he'd just received a stern talking-to about giving Burg space to work. For all he knew, this was a test.

Feeling the urge to fidget, he picked up Juha's plush zombie from the desk. It really was quite soothing to squeeze, to feel the pellets inside flow around his grasp.

He glanced absently at the tag. The creature's name, *Tracker*. Doggerel about following and bugs and hugs. He looked at the poorly done stitching down the back as he attempted the impossible task of putting himself into Juha's shoes.

Juha was eccentric, but he wasn't socially awkward. He had method to his madness, even if Greene didn't know what it was half the time. This old thing was a baby gift? Juha had more style than that.

Greene opened his desk, took out a pair of scissors, and meticulously clipped open the stitching.

"What are you doing, Chief?" Burg asked.

He glanced up. They were both looking at him now. "Maybe nothing," he said.

When he had the seam undone, he stuck two fingers inside and poked around. After a moment, he touched something hard, something that was neither stuffing nor pellets. He pulled it out, being careful not to spill the plush's innards.

In his hand lay an electronic device about the size of a fingernail, encased in black plastic, with a cable port.

"Huh," Greene said.

Marlena leaned forward in her chair. "What is that?"

Greene held up the tiny device and looked at Burg. "This is an Evenmorn MM-1991 tracking receiver. Do you concur?"

Burg took it from him and inspected it. "It's an MM-1999, but yes. It was in that doll?"

Greene nodded. "Juha's doll."

"And he gave it to you specifically?" Marlena said.

"Yes. Last night."

Burg handed the tracker back. "What does he want you to find?"

The things Juha had said, that bit about how Greene took care of everyone, even the stupid zombie poem—it all made sense now.

"He wants me to find *him*."

SIXTEEN

Greene studied the tiny device. "Of course he wants me to find him—but he didn't get a chance to tell me."

In fact, Juha had seemed distinctly uncomfortable with the line of conversation, Greene realized—hence all the chit-chat and reminiscing.

"You think he chipped himself and this is the tracker," Burg said.

"Right. He could have set this up easily. All he would have needed was time. And he wasn't really surprised that Algary came for him."

"But from what you said, it doesn't sound like he was particularly prepared for them, either."

Greene shrugged. "I can't pretend I always understand how Juha thinks. Although I'm not really sure what else he could have done with that whole company after him."

Marlena pointed at the tracker. "You can use that, correct?"

"I should be able to."

Greene rummaged in his desk, then picked up his phone and called the Security desk. "I need a cable for an Evenmorn MM tracking receiver. Immediately, please; Mrs. Ranga Rao is waiting. If you don't have one, have someone run over to IT."

"On it, Chief," Krylov said.

"Thanks." After he hung up, Greene said, "It'll be just a minute."

Marlena nodded. "Good. So, Chief, that baby's due any day now, right?"

Greene supposed that polite small talk was an equally productive way to fill the time as allowing his mind to run riot with possibilities, which was the option he would have chosen.

"She is," he said. "My wife has become wildly impatient."

"Just her?" Marlena raised an eyebrow. "You're not excited at all?"

"Of course I am. There's just a lot of other things going on. It's been non-stop around here lately, obviously."

"Can I have your office while you're on paternity leave?" Burg asked. "Your view is better than mine."

"You absolutely cannot," Greene said. "You have rancid protein powder ground into your carpet."

Burg opened her mouth in mock offense. "It is not rancid! Besides, you could clearly use more protein in your diet." She glanced at Marlena. "But nobody around here cares about my opinions about the problems related to having a chief of security who doesn't even lift."

Krylov knocked on the door and opened it at the same time. "Got your cable, Chief."

Greene stood and accepted it from him. "That was fast. Thank you."

"Glad to be of service." Krylov nodded to Marlena and Burg in turn and then departed.

Greene sat back down, connected the tracker to his computer, and opened the Xiong satellite interface.

"Well?" Burg said.

"Give it a second," Greene said. "It's talking to our satellites. All right, now it's triangulating." Finally, a location lit up on the map. "Hm, that's odd."

"What is it, Chief?" Marlena asked.

He turned the screen so that they could see it. "It's the old zoo."

Burg frowned. "Zoo? What zoo?"

"It's on the edge of the city," Greene replied. "It shut down almost two years ago. I used to go there when I was a kid. Xiong and Algary and holography killed demand, among other things.

Every single thing I used to see there you can see in your living room now."

"You still think it's Juha?" Marlena asked. "Why would he be at an abandoned zoo?"

Greene deliberated. "I think it makes sense. It's remote. No one's going there. There have also been several reports of bodies of homeless people being found in that area." He pulled up the most recent news story on his Spec-Trons and scanned it. "Four, within a few kilometers of the zoo, in the last three months."

"Wait." Burg held up a hand, an incredulous smile on her face. "You think Algary is murdering hobos at the old zoo because they're testing their stealth suit?"

"It's a guess," Greene said.

Burg shrugged. "Well, good for them. If you're going to cull the homeless population, an out-of-the-way spot like that is the place to do it. Corporate social responsibility on their part, I say."

Greene didn't hide his scowl. Even if she was only half-kidding, he found the remark in extremely poor taste. But this wasn't the time or place to call her out on it.

"Who owns the property now?" Marlena asked.

Greene turned the screen back toward himself and hunted up the information. "The city."

"Do we have satellite coverage?"

Burg had taken a small tablet out of her thigh pocket, and she tapped away at it while she chewed on a protein bar. "We don't."

Marlena was clearly surprised by this answer. "Not even through our affiliate network?"

"There's no reason to," Burg said. "For what? A couple of dead hobos? Who wants to watch an abandoned zoo? I mean besides Algary, apparently."

Marlena's eyes narrowed. "How many satellites have we got over this city? Get me coverage right now. I don't care what you have to retask."

"Yes, ma'am." Burg went to work. "It's just outside our radius. We'll have it in a few minutes."

Marlena smiled with her mouth but not with her eyes. "Thank you."

"You know, Chief," said Burg, who wasn't looking at Marlena, "I'm fairly impressed that your pal Karjalainen got a signal through without Algary blocking it. That tracking receiver is nothing special, unless he's tinkered with its guts. I wonder what sort of chip he's put in himself."

"If we find him, we can take a look at it," Greene said.

"Juha's always been well-connected," Marlena said. "And he's always had a way with people."

Burg snorted. "He certainly has a way with Algary."

"Maybe you need to spend more time with him," Marlena said.

Burg turned so that Greene could see her roll her eyes but Marlena could not. "Yes, I'm sure that's the solution. That's just what my life was missing."

"I'd like to hear exactly what it is about him you don't like," Marlena said.

"I'd love to tell you," Burg said, "but I've got a satellite in position now."

Marlena rose from her chair. "Let's see it."

Greene reached to turn the screen again, but Marlena came around the desk, and Burg followed.

"Is this live?" Marlena asked.

Greene nodded.

They had a clear top-down view, and even from a great distance, Greene could tell the zoo had gone to seed. The paths were overgrown, the enclosures were empty, and the grass was so tall in places that he could see it rippling in the breeze—the place was utterly desolate.

"If Algary's there, they're keeping a low profile," Burg said, chewing too close to his ear.

Marlena pointed. "What's that big building there?"

Greene zoomed in where she indicated, on a wide, sloped edifice with multiple skylights, one of which was broken. "That's the event lodge."

"Zoom back out." Burg waved her tablet. "I've found a map from back when the place was operational. Look: penguin house, reptile house, zombie habitat, panda habitat, mammoth enclosure. It all there, just storm-damaged. There's nothing here that looks like a newer facility."

"They could be inside one of the existing structures," Greene pointed out. "You wouldn't dress up the outside; it would draw attention. Besides, they don't have to be researching and testing in the same place."

Marlena drummed her fingers on the desk. "No, but it would be convenient. And the zoo is a good spot for it. Where is Juha now, according to the chip?"

"One second. Here." Greene pointed to a wide-open area with a playground and several picnic tables.

Burg bent down to put her protein bar wrapper into Greene's wastebasket. "I hate to be that guy, but there's nobody there."

"How accurate is this chip?" Marlena asked.

"Hard to say exactly," Burg replied. "Ordinarily, it's to within ten meters. But if Algary *is* there, they'll have countermeasures in place, because they would be stupid not to. They could be affecting the accuracy even though the signal's coming through. Clearly, Karjalainen is not in that radius unless he's hiding. Hell, maybe he's just dicking with us."

"Or he could be underground," Greene said.

"What?"

"Think about it. It would make all the sense in the world for Algary to have an underground facility there. It's abandoned, and it's been an extremely low-traffic area for two years. They could have built it without drawing much if any attention. Nobody would think to look for them there. And it's the perfect environment for running hide-and-seek tests with stealth technology."

Burg sighed. "This is a fascinating jumble of speculation, circumstantial evidence, and wishful thinking, I'll give you that."

Greene jabbed a finger at the screen. "He is *there*, Burg!"

"*Something* is there. It doesn't have to be him. Maybe it's something he wanted you to find."

Greene recognized that he had already made up his mind, but he was certain that he was right. "Why would he hide something at the old zoo?"

Burg shrugged. "I don't know. Why would he do half the dumbass things he's done since he's appeared in our lives?"

"No. He knew they were going to take him. It's him. He's there."

"Send a drone," Marlena said. "Let's get a closer look."

"Hang on," Greene said. "If Algary *is* there doing all the things I think they are, they're probably on the alert for drones. It could give us away."

Marlena straightened and took a deep breath. "Chief, I am trying to bear with you on this. But how, if they have an underground facility, are you going to find the entrance?"

Greene motioned to the screen. "Satellite surveillance. Look, the zoo is a big open space. It has a lot of cover. A lot of hiding places. But it's also completely enclosed, assuming the exterior fences are intact. If you wanted to test a stealth suit in tactical situations, it checks all the boxes."

Burg grunted. "You think they're playing hide-and-seek with Karjalainen over there."

Greene thought of the bodies that had been found in the area. "Hopefully that rather than the most dangerous game, but yes."

Burg considered this. "*If* you're right about all of it—*if*—then we can use the tracker and the satellite footage to find the entrance, or at least close enough to work with, the next time they run Karjalainen out there."

"Exactly."

Burg shrugged. "Could work."

"And then?" Marlena asked.

Greene blinked. "I'm sorry?"

"Say you find the entrance. And then what?"

Greene was confused by the question. The answer was obvious. "Then we take a squad and go in and get him, of course."

Marlena crossed her arms. "A raid. God damn it, Chief, what did we *just* talk about?"

"This isn't about me! Yes, a raid. They don't know we know about them, and they won't see us coming until we're on their doorstep. We can hit them hard and fast."

Marlena's face was stony. "No."

Greene threw up his hands. "What do you mean, *no?*"

"It's out of the question."

Greene's agitation increased, and he fought off a wave of dizziness. "If I'm right, everything is there. *Everything.* Not just Juha, but our stolen device and Crestridge's stolen device."

"I understand that, Chief. I'm not an idiot."

Greene winced. "I didn't mean—"

Marlena held up a hand. "What you're proposing only ends one way, whether you succeed or fail: in all-out war with Algary."

"For God's sake! The stupid Corporate Code again? Why should it mean war? They're the ones stealing, kidnapping, and murdering people."

"Can you prove it, Green?" There was fire in her eyes now. "Can you prove it beyond a reasonable spin? Do you have some good optics for me?"

Greene scoffed. "Optics?"

"How it looks to the public. To the press. To the shareholders."

"I'm worried about what's *true*. What's right and wrong. Not how it looks. Never mind that this is an *opportunity.*"

"And I'm worried about this company. And *that* company. And what they can justify doing."

"Seriously?"

Greene had more to say, but he closed his mouth when he registered the anger on her face. He realized he'd never seen her mad at him before, but she certainly was now.

Marlena's voice was even, measured. "Chief, take your sanctimony and cram it up your ass."

Behind him, Burg stifled what was probably a laugh.

Marlena shook her head. "What do you think, that the Corporate Code is just an arbitrary set of rules? Written in stone and handed down from ancient times for us to blindly follow? We are not a state. We are not a government organization. We aren't the police. We are a *business*. Our *raison d'être* is to generate profit. If we don't do that, we will cease to exist."

"Yes, but—"

"What you're proposing means a shooting war. War with Algary would be drawn-out and devastating for both sides. *Expensive*. Bad for business. Bad for the stockholders. Bad for our long-term prospects even if we win. Because let me tell you what the optics are going to be: Xiong personnel in an Algary facility, possibly shooting Algary people, causing destruction. And why? For what? Without proof, Algary controls the public narrative. We'll be the bad guy regardless, and it is therefore not in the company's interests."

"But if we go in, we could get proof," Greene said.

"That's not how it works. That's backwards."

Greene slammed a fist down on the desk. "Juha is my friend. And he's your friend, too. You *just* said that."

Marlena's face was hard. "I know that."

Greene motioned at the plush on the desk. It had tipped over, and plastic pellets trickled out. "He's counting on us. On me."

Burg went to the cart to refill her milk. "That's awfully damned presumptuous of him."

Greene swallowed a retort. "What do you want to do? Just leave him in there?"

"Give me an alternative," Marlena said.

Green frowned. "What?"

Marlena returned to her seat. "Everything isn't A or B, Chief. Is there a way to go in and get him that's in the company's interests? Persuade me."

Greene made himself take a breath. Maybe she was willing to work with him after all. God knew he hated all the politics and games, but if that was the only way to get things done, then that's what he would have to do.

"If we could discover the source of the homeless murders, we could score some CSR points," he said. "And maybe make Algary accountable."

"*If* they're behind it," Marlena said. "Still, that isn't nothing. Keep going."

"Juha has been an asset to this company in the past. He may well be again. It could be advantageous to have him in our debt."

"Indeed." Her expression had softened slightly. "What else?"

"Just a minute. An altercation is what's bad for business, but maybe we don't need to have one."

Marlena's eyebrows went up. "How do you mean?"

"If they want Juha for testing, they won't bring him out just one time; they'll run him out there again and again until they get it just the way they want it."

Burg nodded. "Seems reasonable."

"So we could set up a perimeter, wait until the next time they bring him out, and then grab him."

"That doesn't get our device back, though," Burg observed.

"It's too late to get it back," Marlena said. "They'll have dissected it and copied it by now."

"It's our best chance to get Juha, though," Greene said.

Marlena considered this. "That's better, but it's still the problem of a Xiong assault on Algary."

"Is it?" Greene asked. "They're not even supposed to be there—how can they publicly acknowledge an attack?"

"Maybe they wouldn't. But it's an attack nonetheless, and it's sure to provoke them."

Greene sighed. "Maybe—I *hope*—'attack' is the wrong word. If we're just snatching him, it doesn't have to be a big squad. We might be able to do it with just three or four people."

Marlena gave him a pointed look. "That sounds a lot better. However, it's still Xiong on Algary."

Greene felt a new wave of confusion. Why was she looking at him like that? Unless—

"I would have to do it myself," he said suddenly. "Off the books. Here, you were practically ready to send me home and put me on bed rest. Put me on medical leave, and then once I walk out of here, you're not responsible for what I do."

"Hm." Marlena had surprise on her face, and Greene was sure it was feigned. "What a remarkable idea. Since you seem bound and determined not to take care of yourself no matter what anyone says to you, that might in fact solve all our problems."

Greene let out a breath of relief. Maybe he could learn this game after all.

"Just a minute," Burg said. "If he goes over there, that's still Xiong running around on Algary land. If they ID him, they'll know it's us."

"What the Chief does in his free time is his own business," Marlena said. "It doesn't matter what they know. It matters what we can sell and what we can deny. The Chief being on leave helps a great deal, as does the fact that Algary doesn't own that land."

"It's still pretty thin," Greene admitted.

"Yes, well." Marlena brushed a speck from her sleeve. "I assume you know that means that you go under the bus for it if you fail."

Greene felt his stomach knot at the thought. At least she was upfront about it. Then again, if he failed, he'd be in Algary's hands again, and he'd have a lot worse things to worry about than losing his job.

"I know," he said.

Marlena nodded and stood. "Excellent. Is there anything else we need to discuss right now? Because I'm very busy and you are now officially on leave, and therefore whatever it is you're doing right now doesn't concern me at all."

A smile tugged at one corner of Greene's mouth. "No, ma'am."

Marlena paused at the door. "But just so we're clear on one thing. When this is over, you're taking a break to recover."

"Yes, ma'am."

"Send the food cart back up when you're done with it. Oh, and it wouldn't hurt my feelings if you brought me back a stealth suit."

When Marlena was gone, Greene leaned back in his chair and let out a sigh. "That was a song and dance."

Burg lounged in her chair, her glass in one hand and the pitcher of milk in the other. "You're lucky she's letting you go at all."

"I guess I am."

"You're really going to throw it all away for Karjalainen, huh?"

This stung Greene for reasons he couldn't immediately identify. "I—"

Burg shook her head. "You don't have to explain it to me. I don't suppose it's much fun, being a better person than the rest of us."

Greene scowled. "You're making fun of me."

"Yes, I am. Now: how can I help?"

"You? Help? You hate Juha."

Burg sat up straight and set the pitcher on the cart. "Who said anything about him? I think you'll agree that it's in the best interests of all parties concerned for you not to fuck up this mission, and you sure aren't going to be able to do it by yourself. So how can I help?"

Greene fought to keep a smile off his face. To whatever extent Burg actually cared about him, she wasn't going to show it. He respected that.

"Thank you," he said. "But I'm on leave and you're not, plus whatever deniability the company has goes right down the toilet if you and I are seen together."

Burg finished her milk and wiped her mouth on her sleeve. "I agree."

Greene considered. He was hesitant to ask her for anything, but she *had* offered. "I'd like to have you on comms. On site, in the car. Monitoring the satellite feed, maybe running a drone."

She nodded. "I can do that. Who else are you thinking for on the ground?"

"I haven't gotten that far yet."

"Half the Security team would go for you."

Greene sighed. "Maybe they would, but I wouldn't presume to ask any of them to risk their lives or their careers on an operation like this."

"No shit. You're kind of a pussy like that. *Sir.*"

Greene chuckled. "Why don't you tell me what you really think?"

"How many more people are you thinking? Two? Three?"

"Yes. I'd like it to be as small a team as possible for all the reasons we discussed, but I also need to see some video of whatever it is they're putting Juha through first."

"Fair enough."

"But it can't be all Xiong people. That's a bad look."

"Do you have anybody outside the company you'd trust for something like this?"

Greene thought about the connections he had left over from his police days. "Who can also drop everything in the next forty-eight hours for a clandestine operation that will take who knows how long? Maybe a couple. I'd have to make some calls." He snapped his fingers. "No, wait. I do have one person in mind from outside."

Burg refilled her glass. "What about Sonnenschein? She's one of the best we've got, and she absolutely adores you. In a purely professional capacity, I mean. I'm sure she'd agree. And if things go bad, the company can say she'd fallen under your bad influence. It would be no problem to put her on special detail for the next couple days."

Greene opened his mouth, then closed it again. Sonnenschein would be a great addition: she was smart, she took initiative, and she followed orders without hesitation. And there was no doubt she would agree if he asked.

But he couldn't bring himself to say her name out loud—the instant he did, he became responsible for anything that might happen to her.

"Plus the less we have to spread this secrecy around, the better," Burg added.

"That's true."

"I assume from that frown and the fact that you haven't immediately embraced my good idea means that you agree it's the right choice but you're feeling bad about getting her involved. *Sir*."

Greene stared at her. "Am I that much of an open book?"

"An open large-print read-along book? Only sometimes. All right, don't worry, I'll go talk to her."

This was perfect. It was everything he wanted. And yet he was hung up on what? His feelings?

Burg rolled her eyes again. "For God's sake, I'm not talking about coercing anybody. I know you would rather die than ask for help, but for just five minutes, take your head out of your ass and stop being so difficult."

Greene sighed, then gave in and accepted the path of expediency. "Thanks, Burg. But I'll talk to Sunny myself."

"Fine. You're welcome. Just let me know when you're ready to go." Burg put down her glass, gathered up an armload of snacks from the serving cart, and left.

Greene turned and stared at the feed of the desolate zoo and the motionless signal from the tracker. "What are they doing to you, man?" he muttered.

Now that he was alone, doubt began to creep in. Burg had been right—the evidence was all circumstantial. What if he was wrong?

Greene tried to settle his mind. He was mentally and physically exhausted, and worried—about Juha, about how Xiong was going to counter Algary's stealth suits, about the pregnant wife he'd been neglecting.

He leaned forward and rested his chin on his hands, still staring at the screen. He didn't have the energy to ask other people to risk life and limb for him.

Eventually, he fell asleep at the desk, his head pillowed on his arms like he was in grade school.

A persistent pinging by his computer awakened him from a dream that he couldn't remember beyond the lingering sense that he'd failed in some task.

Greene oriented himself and deactivated the computer alarm. He saw movement on the satellite feed: a lone figure, making its way across an open section of the zoo. The tracking signal moved along with it.

Greene rubbed his eyes, squinted at the screen, and zoomed in on the figure, who was moving quickly away from what the map indicated had been the reptile house.

The figure wore what looked like khaki coveralls, and Greene felt a jolt as he recognized a dark brown topknot ponytail. It was Juha, it had to be.

"Perfect," Greene murmured.

Juha was moving quickly from cover to cover, clearly making his way toward the zoo's main entrance. Greene lost him in the trees in places, but the tracking signal indicated that he was making steady progress.

Juha was doing well—except that Algary had to have chipped him as well. Of course, Juha would know that—but what alternative did he have but to try?

Greene zoomed out, searching for any other movement, but didn't see any.

In a matter of minutes, Juha reached the front entrance, where he stopped. It would be locked and gated, of course. But instead of attempting to climb over, he turned around, clearly looking for something.

Juha squared up as though ready for close combat. He feinted to his right, then shuddered and collapsed.

As Greene winced at the sight, a second, larger, figure appeared next to Juha as if out of thin air, wielding a shock baton.

"It's true," Greene muttered. "It's all true."

This bulky assailant, dressed in a drab grayish bodysuit, stood over Juha's motionless body, apparently waiting.

A minute later, two other men arrived, jogging along the path Juha had followed. They picked Juha up—one holding his arms and the other holding his legs—and carried him back the way they'd come, the man with the shock baton following.

Finally, they all disappeared into what the old zoo map indicated had been a concession stand.

Greene sat back and let out a breath. What had he just seen? Juha subdued by a man in a stealth suit. He rewound the feed and replayed that part. Yes, that was what it was. It had to be.

However, Greene felt his satisfaction with this discovery quickly swallowed up by his apprehension at what Algary might do with their very real stealth technology—specifically what they might do against Xiong.

Now that the action was over, Greene realized that he had a foul taste in his mouth, a combination of coffee and too much medication. How long had he been asleep?

He glanced at the clock and couldn't believe it. A quarter to one. Three hours? Maybe Marlena was right. Maybe he was falling apart.

Greene rewound the feed to when Juha had first appeared. Juha moved directly toward the main entrance, with purpose, and he showed a basic familiarity with the area. That meant they'd run him out there at least once already, probably several times. He managed to stay on the move for just over seven minutes before Algary caught up to him.

Greene watched the altercation between Juha and the man with the stun baton several more times. Without question, the man had appeared out of nowhere, and Juha had braced for an attack from the precisely correct direction *before* he did.

The stealth suit worked. And Juha could see it.

Greene grabbed his phone and sent Burg a message: *Have confirmation. We're good to go.*

He took a deep breath, braced himself, and phoned Perseverance Ojukwu.

"Greene," she said by way of greeting.

"I have a proposition for you," he said. "Algary has abducted Juha Karjalainen, and I need your help to get him back."

"How sad for him," Ojukwu said. "My help? How desperate are you? And get him back how? From where?"

Greene briefly sketched out the situation.

"What has all this got to do with me?" Ojukwu asked, and Greene could hear the suspicion in her voice. "If your company is starting a war with Algary, we want nothing to do with it. Get your own people killed."

"This is not a Xiong request. And I'm not asking for Crestridge's help. It's just me, asking for yours. Off the books."

"You're going up against Algary by yourself? I don't owe you any favors, Greene, and certainly not one that big. But you have my curiosity. What would be in it for me?"

"The location of an Algary blacksite. A blacksite where they've got the tech they stole from you."

"Not bad," she said. "But I think you mean a *compromised* blacksite that they'll be closing up and relocating once you go through with this operation of yours."

"Give me a little more credit than that." Greene gave her a brief outline of his plan. "We'll be in and out, and they'll never know who we were."

"I appreciate your optimism, Greene, but I don't share it. You have a nose for trouble. Bullets go looking for you."

He sighed. "I can't argue with that."

"You know, you must really be in a bind to call me for help. What else do you have to offer?"

"I can give you our satellite footage of the stealth suit tests."

Ojukwu laughed. "Either the stealth suit doesn't work, in which case we don't need the footage, or else it does work, in which case you're going to give me footage of nothing. Come on, Greene, this is all very interesting, but I'm a busy woman."

"What about money?"

"Money? Whose money? You said it was off the books."

"I can pay you after," Greene said, wondering as he did exactly how he might arrange that.

"Money is always nice, but I think you can do better. Stop wasting my time and give me your best offer."

Greene took a deep breath. He felt like he was about to make a mistake. "I will have the man responsible for stealing your tech walk through in precise detail how he breached your security and took your device."

Ojukwu clucked her tongue. "Greene, you son of a bitch! You goddamned cheeky bastard! It was Karjalainen all along! You lied to me!"

"I just found out. Really."

"Maybe you did and maybe you didn't, but you weren't going to tell me! Karjalainen indeed."

"I—"

"Oh, I *should* come on your mission." She had vitriol in her voice now. "I should come just so I can shoot him myself."

Greene put a hand on his forehead. Why had he thought this was a good idea?

After a long silence, Ojukwu said, "Greene."

"Yes?"

"If I do this for you, you owe me a debt, beyond everything else you've promised. A considerable one."

"Agreed."

She sighed. "All right. When?"

"I'm going to monitor the feed and try to pick up a pattern. I'm guessing they'll run Juha out again after he's recovered from the stun baton. Can you be ready this evening?"

"I'm already regretting this," she said. "But fine."

"Excellent. Thank you."

Greene hung up the phone, dragged himself out of his chair, and went to find Sonnenschein.

SEVENTEEN

The sun was beginning to set when they picked up Ojukwu on the seemingly random street corner she had designated. She was dressed similarly to the rest of them, in jeans and a canvas jacket, presumably with body armor underneath.

Ojukwu dumped the duffel bag she carried into the trunk, closed it, and then slid into the backseat. "Greene. You look terrible."

Greene tugged on his knit cap. "I know."

She nodded at Burg and Sonnenschein in the front seat. "Ladies. I see we all got the memo to dress like down-on-our-luck scavengers."

From the driver's seat, Burg nodded in return, then ordered the car into motion.

"Hello!" Sonnenschein said. She was smiling like she was on her way to a festival, and in the dim light, the colorful gaiter bunched around her neck looked almost like a lei.

Ojukwu looked at Sonnenschein. "Burg I know about. Are you Xiong as well?"

Sonnenschein winked. "I'm on vacation."

Ojukwu didn't try to stifle an exasperated grunt. "Greene, this is looking an awful lot like a Xiong–Crestridge collaboration. That is not what you promised me."

"Xiong is going to disavow all of us," Greene said. "Probably we're a trio of ex-employees out for ourselves as mercenaries, or else I'm the bad apple and dishonestly co-opted company resources to pursue my own personal agenda."

Ojukwu snorted. "You? Who's going to buy that? I wouldn't believe a report that you had littered on the street."

In the front seat, Burg laughed. "I like this one."

Greene scowled. "The PR people will come up with something. Maybe I've become unhinged because I can't manage my job-related stress. Maybe I'm forming a problematic addiction to pain medication that's making my behavior erratic. Maybe both of those."

Burg glanced back, her eyes narrowed, but only for an instant.

Greene rubbed the stubble on his face. "Sunny, have you got the demo charges?"

"Right here, Chief." She handed back a small brown satchel.

Burg raised a hand. "What demo charges?"

"I'm assuming they're going to run Juha out another time today because they'll be eager to see how he does in the dark," Greene said. "I think it's a safe bet, but we can't be sure. I'm willing to hide in the bushes and wait, but not forever. I'm not going home emptyhanded. Too much back-and-forth is likely to draw attention. Plus the longer they have him, the closer we get to the end of his usefulness to them."

Burg frowned. "You pitched me a grab-and-go. You didn't say anything about storming the castle."

"Same," Ojukwu said.

"My views on the situation have evolved," Greene said. Indeed, he'd spent most of the afternoon stewing over it. "I'm sorry. But we're only going to get one shot at this. Are you opposed?"

"Not necessarily," Burg said. "But Mrs. Ranga Rao isn't going to like it."

"Mrs. Ranga Rao doesn't know about it," Greene said. "Mrs. Ranga Rao didn't *want* to know about it."

"*I'm* opposed," Ojukwu interjected. "That isn't what you sold me, and we're a little understaffed for a frontal assault, aren't we? You don't know how many people they've got in there, but I'm guessing it's more than four."

Greene fought the urge to throw up his hands. "I am not telling you that this is what I'm planning to do. I hope to God it doesn't come to that. I fully intend to get in, grab him, and get out. But nevertheless, this is what I'm *prepared* to do."

All three women were just looking at him now.

"Look, it's a secret base, so they'll want to keep a low profile. That means as few personnel as possible, and I'm guessing that most of the people there are on the technical side anyway." He realized that he was trying to convince himself as much as the others. "So that's what I'm prepared to do. Do you want to get out?"

Ojukwu sighed. "If we're going to do it, I suppose there's no sense half-assing it. But I insist on being compensated commensurately with services rendered."

"Absolutely," Greene said, having no idea what sort of promise he was actually making to her.

She was still frowning. "Have you got anything new on the security?"

Greene took out his phone and put the zoo map up on the car's windshield display. "Nothing concrete since the last time we talked. It's safe to assume that they're monitoring everything on the zoo premises, but I've seen nothing to indicate that they're keeping as close an eye on what's going on outside their fences. So we'll wait outside the perimeter until Burg tells us Juha is out. Then, when he gets close to us, we'll go in and grab him before the Algary people catch up, just like we planned it. Quick and quiet."

Ojukwu studied the map. "Even without climbing a fence, that's a lot of ground to cover. It's half a kilometer from the perimeter to where you saw Karjalainen come out."

Greene highlighted several spots on the map. "I've identified some easy entry points. We'll fan out and go in here, here, and here."

"That only covers about a third of the property," Ojukwu said. "What if he goes the other way?"

"He won't. He chipped himself and gave us his tracker. He'll be expecting us. He's going to be as predictable as possible."

Ojukwu snorted. "That's utter presumption."

"I worked with him for five years. I know how he thinks. As much as anybody does. And if I'm wrong, well ... Sonnenschein here is the fastest sprinter in Portsmith. Right, Sunny?"

Sonnenschein nodded enthusiastically. "Right, Chief!"

"Right. What else do we need to cover?"

"Call signs," Burg said. "Keep our names off the comms." She pointed at Ojukwu, Sonnenschein, and Greene in turn. "'Raptor.' 'Speed.' 'Browne.'"

Greene blinked. "My codename is 'Browne'?"

"It has an 'e' on the end," Sonnenschein said. "That was my idea."

"Thanks."

Burg looked quite pleased with herself. "You were busy when we put them together. Anyway. I'm 'Castle.' Karjalainen is 'Jester.'"

"I have to admit, 'Jester' is kinder than I was expecting," Greene said.

The car came to a stop. There was just enough daylight left to show that the zoo was nowhere in sight.

"Where are we?" Greene asked.

Burg glanced back at him. "Sorry, boss, did you want me to park in the parking lot?" She tapped at the dashboard panel and zoomed the map out, then pointed. "We're here, on the main street outside the park. The road through is winding but clear. There's a good chance of being noticed."

Greene nodded. "The city doesn't keep the area up anymore, and there aren't any other reasons for people to come up here." He leaned forward and pointed at the map. "From here, it's a short distance through a thick wooded area to the outside of the zoo. A straight shot, good cover."

Burg glanced out her window. "Dark enough for you yet?"

"It's good enough." Greene felt a sudden pang of fear that Juha would be set loose before they were in position. It was an irrational fear, he knew—mathematically, the odds of it happening were low—but he couldn't shake it.

Burg nodded. "Have you got everything you need?"

"Gear check," Greene said.

"I'm set," Sonnenschein said immediately. She carried only a pair of pistols: speed was her best asset, and Greene hadn't wanted to compromise it.

Greene unzipped his jacket and patted himself down. To the harness he wore over his body armor he'd clipped two flashbangs, a smoke grenade, a plasma grenade, and an experimental one-shot field-disrupting device that Garcinia wasn't confident would work against Algary's stealth technology. His pistol and his heat ray were secure in their holsters. He was ready.

Ojukwu eyed the armaments hanging from his torso. "Quick and quiet, eh?"

Greene zipped up his jacket. "I like to be prepared."

"You look prepared for a *war*. Can you run with all that?"

"Well enough," Greene replied. He'd taken fresh doses of all his meds right before they'd left.

Ojukwu shrugged and opened her door. "I need you to pop the trunk," she said, and Burg complied. Ojukwu got out of the car, and Sonnenschein followed.

Greene turned to Burg. "You're going to be right here?"

She nodded. "I'll pull off the road and be as inconspicuous as I can, and I'll be ready to go when you get him back here."

Greene felt a sudden surge of emotion, which he tried not to show. "Thank you."

Burg jerked her head toward the zoo. "Run along, Chief."

Greene emerged from the car, then grabbed the satchel of demolition charges and his little bag of water and snacks. He shut the door, and the lights went out inside.

In the gathering darkness, he found Ojukwu standing in front of the trunk, a heavy long-barreled automatic rifle slung across her front.

"Can you run with that?" Greene asked.

"Still faster than you," she said. "But I'm the support: if you do your job, I shouldn't have to run anywhere except back to the car."

"Fair enough," Greene said. "All right, time to take a walk. Spec-Trons on. Check your night vision."

Greene activated his, and the world lit up in shades of green.

Ojukwu nodded. "Ready."

Sonnenschein pulled her gaiter up over her nose and mouth. "All set, boss."

Greene pulled his own gaiter out of his pocket and put it on. It was possible that his face was so bruised and swollen that he wasn't recognizable, but it was better to be safe than sorry.

"Let's go," he said.

They entered the trees together but split up after a few minutes: Ojukwu off to the north, to Greene's left, and Sonnenschein to the east on his right. He soon lost sight of them.

It was all Greene could do from tripping over the brush and branches that littered the ground. The night vision helped quite a bit, but seeing the world in this spectrum was disorienting. The amount of noise he was producing made him cringe.

The comm wired into his hearing aids crackled to life, and he jumped.

"Comm check, Browne," Burg said.

"Receiving you clearly," Greene muttered.

Some thirty meters ahead, through the trees, Greene spotted a wall, brick overgrown with ivy.

"I've reached the perimeter," he said softly.

"One sec," Burg said.

A green-scale satellite map of the zoo appeared on his Spec-Trons' heads-up display. A moment later, a marker appeared near his position.

"Head to your right about twenty meters," Burg said. "There might be an easy way in for you there."

"I see it."

Greene worked his way around, keeping his distance from the wall—there would be no crossing the perimeter until they were ready for Algary to know they were there.

The rustle of branches nearby, unacceptably close, made him start, and as he reached for his pistol, some small animal—a squirrel, probably—dashed away into the night.

"Perfect," Greene murmured as he willed his thudding heart to slow.

He reached his marker without further incident. A sizeable dead tree had knocked down a section of the wall when it fell. The rubble was knee-high—he would have no trouble getting over it, assuming he didn't trip and fall on his face.

He found a concealed spot a short distance away that gave him a relatively clear path to the wall. There, he sat down and leaned against a tree.

"I'm in position," he said.

"Copy," Burg said. "Speed is already set. I'm still waiting to hear from Raptor."

Sonnenschein was the fastest, but she also had the farthest mark. What was taking Ojukwu so long? Had she gone rogue, chosen to go off and do her own thing, to make her own move against Algary or against Juha?

Greene realized that his mind was wandering toward paranoia, considering all of the things that could go wrong, including and especially the unlikeliest and stupidest possibilities.

"Connect the lines," he said.

"Done," Burg said. "All channels open."

What was Ojukwu's call sign again? "Raptor, where are you?" Greene said. "Are you in position?"

Ojukwu's voice was a harsh whisper. "I'm working on it! You didn't tell me I'd be crawling through bushes and brambles!"

Greene let out a slow breath. "Carry on."

Perhaps a minute later, she said, "All right. I can see the service entrance. It doesn't look like anyone's been through here in some time. It's quite overgrown."

"Can you get over the fence there?" Greene asked.

"Over, yes, or through."

"All right, good. Both of you check my mark. This is where we're all coming out.

"Acknowledged," Ojukwu said.

"Got it, Chie— Browne," Sonnenschein said.

Greene settled in to wait. The night air was cool, but he soon became uncomfortably warm under all his layers. He took his jacket off, rolled it up, and put it between his lower back and the tree.

No further conversation took place, no chit-chat. There was no need for it. He forced himself not to overthink. They were all professionals; they all knew their jobs. If there was something to report, they would report it.

There wasn't much to see out here in any case. Greene turned off his night vision and let his eyes adjust to the natural darkness. With the tree cover, the blackness was shockingly deep away from the glow of the city. Greene found the total lack of light in the zoo unfamiliar and uncomfortable.

Greene's mind went to the last time he'd been in darkness like this. He and Juha had gone to the Hollow Hills Recreational Forest, investigating the Ranga Raos' car crash and looking for Marlena. He didn't care for the association.

The sounds out here were equally strange—the chirping of insects, the calls of night birds, and the wind rustling the leaves and the tall, unmown grass were all completely alien to his city life.

He pushed up his sleeve and glanced at the barely luminous hands on his watch. He'd been out here for thirty minutes. He reached into his supply bag, found his water flask, and sipped from it.

Greene's thoughts drifted to Nisha. This would be yet another night he didn't make it home. When had he last been there? It had been at least two days.

Accept the reality, he told himself: you live at Xiong Tower and visit your apartment.

He hoped Nisha wouldn't be too angry. He hoped he wouldn't miss the birth of the baby. He hoped Nisha wouldn't call or text him in the middle of this operation.

He hadn't told her what he was doing, hadn't even mentioned what had happened to Juha. He wondered if he should have.

Greene shifted his position, trying to work out some soreness. The meds weren't working at full effect anymore—he was building up a tolerance.

How long could he maintain this pace? How long would Nisha put up with it?

It was bad enough he was so inconsistently around for her, neglecting her. Now he was about to have a kid on top of everything—and when she was born, what would change?

Nothing. Nothing at all. What *could* he change?

He liked his job. He liked the money and the prestige that came with it, and he could live with the long hours and the danger.

No, he'd end up neglecting his daughter sooner or later just like he neglected his wife.

Greene pushed back against the blanketing resignation that hovered over him. That future wasn't good enough. He felt a compulsion to do something—but he didn't know what.

He probably never should have gotten married in the first place. It would have saved a number of people a great deal of grief and trouble. Why hadn't he—

"Browne!" It was Burg's voice.

"Huh?" Greene came back to the present. He'd dozed; his mouth was dry. Sloppy.

"He's out!"

"What?" Greene reactivated his night vision, willing his brain to engage.

"Jester is out. He's on the move."

"Wake up, Mister Browne!" Ojukwu said, sounding almost gleeful. "Are you going to sleep through your own operation? Jesus Christ."

This remark snapped Greene back to full alertness. "I'm standing by. Which way is he going?"

"About like you figured," Burg said. "Somewhere between you and Raptor, roughly. You want him on your heads-up display?"

"Yes, for everyone." Greene stood up carefully and tried to work out the kinks. He glanced at his watch. They'd been out here for nearly two hours. He'd really slept.

"Roger, pinging him."

The satellite map of the zoo reappeared in the upper right corner of Greene's field of vision. He, Sonnenschein, and Ojukwu appeared as tiny blue dots; the little yellow dot that was Juha moved toward them now, little by little, with distance as the crow flies displayed. Currently 457 meters and closing.

Greene picked up his supplies and took a drink of water. "Get ready."

"Ready," Ojukwu said immediately.

"Good to go," Sonnenschein said.

"Make the call, Browne," Burg said.

Greene unzipped his pants and urinated into the nearest bush. Who knew when he'd get another chance? "Wait for it."

He put his jacket back on as he watched the map. Juha had made his way through a picnic area and was now moving more slowly past what had been the children's zoo. Now 358 meters away.

"I've got a satellite visual on two people," Burg said. "Stationed near the building where he came out. Pinging them now."

Two red dots appeared on the map, farther away than Juha was, and stationary.

"Copy." Greene bent down and tightened his ankle brace. "So far, so good."

On the map, Juha's dot was heading through the Penguin Palaver Sponsored by SinusBlaster Mentholated Gum. Now 233 meters.

"What are you waiting for?" There was urgency in Ojukwu's voice now.

"On my mark," Greene said.

Juha was now closer to them than to where he'd appeared, and those red dots still hadn't moved. It was time to move, before whoever was wearing the stealth suit intervened.

Greene took a deep breath. "Go!"

EIGHTEEN

"Copy," Ojukwu said.

"Going!" Sonnenschein exclaimed.

Greene charged forward. He still felt stiff, but not to a degree he wasn't used to. He vaulted over the broken zoo wall, and his sprained ankle almost gave out when he landed. But the brace held and the pain meds kept him upright.

Out from under the tree cover, the moon and stars glowed shockingly bright. Momentarily blinded, Greene had to slow down for the several seconds it took his Spec-Trons to adjust. He pushed on through the tall grass, arms out in front of him, and when he could see clearly again, he found himself outside the zoo's ReHistory Genomics Foundation Discovery Center, whatever that was.

Ahead he saw the gift shop and the solid pavement of the welcome plaza, at the center of which stood the ruins of an enormous statue. A life-sized mammoth loomed, tusks and trunk raised, with an African elephant standing on its back in a similar pose, facing the opposite direction. The colossal wreck of an Indian elephant, which had clearly once been mounted atop the other two, now lay in several pieces beside them.

Greene could still see Juha's location on his display, but he couldn't find the path amidst the overgrown hedges and overgrown lawns, and he nearly ran into a row of recycling bins that were barely taller than the rippling grass.

"Castle, I need a direction!"

"There's a path to your left," Burg said.

"Same!" Ojukwu said a moment later.

"Raptor, bear about fifteen degrees to your left," Burg replied. "Speed, you should be clear straight ahead."

Greene found the paved path where Burg had said, flanked by a totem pole of carved directional signs. The paint had faded, but he could still read them: Hippo Haven, Rhino Retreat, Woolly Mammoth Walk—all emptied long ago.

Greene wondered idly what had happened to the animals. Sold to the rich and eccentric, most likely, to be kept as exotic pets, or else to be eaten; he couldn't imagine anyone else who might want a real pachyderm, or why.

He soon came to a copse of bamboo that, unattended, had erupted from its boundaries, pushed through the cracks in the pavement, and formed a thick and impenetrable wall.

Greene stopped, frustrated but glad to catch his breath, if only for an instant. Juha was only 72 meters away now.

"The path is blocked," he said. "What's my best route?"

"There's an open-air exhibit to your right," Burg said. "You should be able to cut through it, or around it."

"I see it."

Los Estados Presents the Florida Wetlands Featuring Real Florida Men, the sign read. The exhibit's paths too were overgrown, but the way through looked fairly clear—the water had dried up long ago. He saw a short fence, easily climbable, and after that a dry moat close to five meters straight down.

Greene hopped the fence, then turned around, grabbed the edge of the moat, and let himself down. Dead leaves, loose soil, and weeds lined the bottom—a nice soft landing for his ankle.

He had to clutch the tall grass with both hands as he climbed up the bank to the exhibit. Before he'd reached the top, he was breathing hard again. That wasn't right. It was too soon.

"I'm almost there," Sonnenschein reported. "I've got eyes on the Forbidden Kingdom exhibit; he seems to be in there. I'm going to go in and get him."

"I'll be there in time to give you support on the way out," Ojukwu said.

"Confirmed, Jester is in the Forbidden Kingdom," Burg said. "Browne, it's just on the other side of the exhibit you're in."

"Understood." Greene reached the top of the hill and grabbed the slender trunk of a palm tree growing at the edge to pull himself up, wondering if the moat went all the way around, and if so, how he was going to get up a sheer five-meter wall.

As Greene straightened, movement close by made him start, and a hand closed over his arm.

The stealth suit. Algary had found him.

Greene's adrenaline surged, yet the ease with which he wrenched free from the grip surprised him. He dodged away, trying to create some distance as he went for his gun.

But no, this wasn't the stealth suit—he could *see* this figure. Some other Algary security, then.

Greene brought up his pistol, wondering why they hadn't just shot or stunned him, since they'd clearly seen him first, when the smell hit him.

Reeking of soil and sulfurous decay, the gaunt figure lunged toward him, barely more than a skeleton covered in skin. Clothed in tattered rags, baring broken teeth, it swiped at him with long, ragged fingernails.

"Jesus Christ!" Greene stumbled back, gasping for breath, fighting down visceral horror that twisted his stomach. He'd never seen one in person before.

"What's happening?" Burg demanded.

"There's a zombie in the Florida zombie exhibit!"

He heard a chuckle that surely came from Ojukwu.

"Shit!" Burg exclaimed. "I thought this place had been cleared out. Sorry. Get the hell out of there! And don't let them bite you."

"No kidding," Greene muttered. *Them?* One wasn't much of a threat if he could keep his distance, but several ... Never mind how much time he was wasting in here.

The thing came toward him again, surprisingly fast. How was it still alive, trapped in here by itself? What was it eating? Insects? Birds? Squirrels?

Greene raised his pistol, then hesitated. Firing would give away the team's presence with certainty.

It was upon him now. He kicked it in the shin as hard as he could. Its brittle leg bones snapped, and it crumpled in a heap in front of him.

Undeterred, the creature dragged itself forward, clutching at Greene's ankles. He kicked it again, sending it tumbling down the embankment into the dry moat.

Not waiting to see the creature inevitably attempt to crawl back up to him, Greene turned and ran toward the other side of the exhibit, between stands of tall grass that sprouted here and there from the cracked earth. He didn't see any more of them— but he hadn't seen this one, either.

He'd almost reached the other side when he heard a pistol shot.

"Shit!" Sonnenschein cried.

"The two guards are now moving toward Jester," Burg reported.

More shots followed, from multiple guns.

"What's happening?" Greene demanded. He'd arrived at another embankment, another dry moat.

"It's Algary!" Sonnenschein exclaimed. "They— Ah!"

"Sunny!" Greene said, before he could help himself.

A burst of automatic fire resounded ahead and above him.

"I'm here," Ojukwu said. "And it seems like the stealth suit works pretty damned well if you ask me."

Greene ground his teeth in frustration. "Castle, get me the *hell* out of this zombie hole!"

"The moat doesn't go all the way around," Burg said. "Over to your right is the maintenance side. There's just a fence."

Greene didn't see it, but he moved that way, searching frantically, taking her on desperate faith.

Then he saw it: a tall chain-link fence, completely overgrown with vines, half-hidden by all the other foliage.

Ojukwu's automatic rifle thundered again.

Greene holstered his pistol and sprinted for the fence. He sprang at it, dragging himself up, heedless of the barbs at the top that tore his hands and ripped his clothes, and flung himself over.

He landed hard on uneven ground and his ankle gave way, sending him sprawling into a prickly shrub.

More gunfire sounded as he hauled himself upright and lurched in the direction of all the dots on his heads-up display.

"God, I hate nature," he muttered.

"Straight ahead of you, Browne, you're right there," Burg said.

Greene pushed forward, through bushes and branches that snagged his clothes in a hundred places and threatened to trip him a dozen times. Then, suddenly, he was in the open.

"I see it," he said.

The façade of the Forbidden Kingdom was so immense that Greene couldn't tell if the exhibit itself was indoors or outdoors. Done in a generic pan-Asian style clearly intended to create in the unimaginative viewer a sense of the exotic, it featured columns, stones, tree trunks and roots, and carvings of tigers, all cast in molded concrete. A set of metal doors, their glass broken out long ago, stood open.

According to Greene's heads-up display, Juha and Sonnenschein were inside, with Ojukwu just beyond. The two guards were also farther away, but Greene couldn't tell if they were inside or out.

"Browne, I'm not getting a response from Speed," Burg said. "I don't know what's happened."

A wave of terror ripped through Greene like an icy wind, leaving his hands tingling and his testicles retracted.

"Acknowledged." He drew his pistol and dashed for the entrance.

The Forbidden Kingdom turned out to be a fully enclosed structure. Greene stepped into a wide corridor meant for heavy foot traffic, with exhibits on either side behind walls of now-dirty glass and a ceiling lined with skylights blacked out by carpets of half-rotted leaves, all of it done in the same style as the outside. Paper cups, torn zoo maps, and snack wrappers littered the floor.

The gunfire in here was much louder, echoing upon itself, and Greene was grateful when his hearing aids adjusted to compensate.

Greene ran down the corridor, which hooked to the right at the far end. He found Sonnenschein slumped on the floor, propped up against the nearest column, her chin on her chest. Her gaiter was pulled down; blood trickled from her mouth. When she saw him, she looked up and said something he couldn't make out.

Greene crouched beside her. "Sunny!"

Her breathing was shallow and her voice thin. "Chief. I'm sorry. Just give me a minute to catch my breath."

Greene looked her over, but in the darkness, he couldn't determine the damage. "Where are you hit?"

Sonnenschein took a deep breath, then coughed, clearly fighting to keep the pain off her face. "One in the gut. One in the shoulder. Maybe two. They got through. I can't tell how badly it's bleeding. I know you wanted us to wear the heavy armor, but it really slows me down, so I just wore the light vest, and I guess they're using a larger caliber than I was expecting, and—"

Greene took her hand in his. "It's all right."

"I didn't want to let you down. I'm sorry."

"You haven't," Greene said. The reality was entirely the opposite. "Can you get up?"

"I'm working on it. Don't worry about me. Finish the mission."

"Sunny—"

She jerked a thumb behind her, down the far hall. "I did find your friend, though. I gave him one of my pistols after I got hit. You'd better get down there."

Greene squeezed her hand, fighting down a sudden swell of emotion. "I'll come back for you."

She gave him a tiny smile. "I know."

Greene stood, hesitated, and then jogged down the corridor.

"Castle, you heard all that?" he said.

"Copy that," Burg replied. "What do you want to do?"

"She's put on a brave face, but I don't trust that she can get back to the car on her own. She might need a medkit before we're able to get her out of here."

"I've got one. Do you want me to bring it?"

That meant giving up Burg running point and having dedicated eyes on the big picture. But if it meant saving Sonnenschein ...

"Yes, please, get here as fast as you can," Greene said.

"On my way."

The corridor opened onto the Forbidden Kingdom's central area. The moon shone brightly through the shattered glass ceiling on a broad square with an inscribed circular path ringing a central exhibit, which had been encased by glass when it had housed tigers. Now it was completely open, and home to nothing but dead jungle trees and overgrown weeds. On the far side, another corridor led to the other half of the building.

In the center, his back against a withered tree, stood Juha, clad in khaki coveralls, Sonnenschein's pistol in his hand. He seemed focused on the far corridor. A noise like a trashcan being tipped over echoed toward them, and Juha fired at it.

Greene identified another tree wide enough to give cover near Juha's position. He sprinted for it, staying low, and slammed his back against it, both hands on his pistol.

Gunfire sounded from down the corridor, and he and Juha both crouched reflexively.

Juha looked at him, eyes wide, and then recognition dawned, even with Greene's face fully obscured by his hat, Spec-Trons, and gaiter.

"Welcome to the party," Juha said. "I'm glad you made it. What took you so long?"

Greene sighed. "It's nice to see you, too."

"You'll have to speak up," Juha said, motioning to his ear. "Stun grenade, you know."

"Oh, I know."

Greene was now close enough to see that Juha was in about as bad a state as he was. One eye was black, and the side of his face was caked with dried blood from a gash on his temple.

"I'm at Jester," Greene said. "Raptor, where are you?"

"I'm outside the building you're in, on the far side," Ojukwu said immediately. "I've got two of them here. I'm keeping them pinned down so they can't get in, but they seem content to wait. I'm guessing they have reinforcements on the way."

"Agreed," Greene said. "Are you clear to withdraw?"

"I am now. A few minutes from now, who knows?"

"Point taken. As soon as we can get Speed out, we're ready for evac."

"Acknowledged," Ojukwu said. "I'll hold them out here until you're clear of the building and then catch up."

"Copy that. And thank you." Greene turned to Juha. "Why are you still here?"

Juha peered into the darkness. "I need directions to the evac point, for one. And I didn't want to abandon your squadmate, for another."

"Well, let's fall back to her position and see if we can't get out of here before reinforcements show up."

"They don't need reinforcements," Juha said. "They have the invisible man."

"The stealth suit! Do you know where it is?"

"Oh, it's much more than a stealth suit. But yes, I'm fairly certain he's in here with us."

Greene glanced around sharply, then felt like an idiot for doing so.

He thought of Sonnenschein, hurt and slowed, and of Burg, rushing toward their position. "My team—"

Juha shook his head. "Nah, they don't care about you guys. I mean, comparatively. They'll all be focused on not losing me. Because I can see him. Well, kind of."

"Kind of?"

"Yeah. Sometimes. Basically, when he— Shit."

Juha turned and fired past Greene's ear, too close. Before Greene could react, Juha fired a second shot, and then his gun clicked empty.

His ears ringing again, Greene turned, raising his pistol, and was immediately knocked to the ground by a blow to his chest that came out of nowhere.

As he rolled over onto his stomach, Greene sensed but did not see something go past him with heavy footsteps and a rush of air.

Juha reversed his pistol, holding it by the barrel. As he lifted it to strike, he went rigid, as if shocked, and then collapsed.

Greene got to his feet, mind racing. The stealth suit, what else—and he hadn't seen it even when it had been right on top of him.

Greene brought his pistol up in Juha's direction, but he had no target.

A blow like a hammer impacted him center mass, and electricity coursed through his body. His pistol slipped from his limp fingers, and he fell to the ground, convulsing.

For a moment, Greene could only lie on his side and wait for the white-hot pain to dissipate. When he could focus his eyes again, he saw Juha in front of him, in a similar state, twitching.

Greene thought he heard a pneumatic hiss. One of Juha's legs rose into the air, and then his entire body began to move, as though an invisible force pulled him by the foot.

The stealth suit. Greene squinted, but he wasn't sure whether he could detect any movement.

Juha's body moved at a brisk pace, close to jogging speed. He wasn't obese anymore, but he was still a large man. The strength needed to drag him that fast was inhuman.

Greene commanded his body to respond. "You have to go after him," he told himself.

He managed to get up onto his tingling hands and knees. His heart raced, and he couldn't seem to catch his breath.

A service door Greene hadn't noticed before banged open, and their invisible assailant pulled Juha through.

"They're falling back," Ojukwu said, as if from a world away. "I don't know why. I'm not picking up any reinforcements on the infrared."

"They got him back," Greene managed to say. "They're trying to take him back inside."

"I see." Ojukwu's voice was icy.

"I'm sorry," Greene said. "It was the stealth suit."

After a brief pause, she said, "I'll try to cut them off."

Greene fumbled on the dirty floor for his pistol and jammed it into its holster. "I'm on my way."

He tried to get up, but his twitching thighs wouldn't bear his weight. He couldn't seem to get the muscles to fire.

"Come on, legs," he said.

So exhorting himself, he grabbed the trunk of the nearest tree and pulled himself upright, afraid that if he fell again, he wouldn't be able to get up a second time. He staggered after them, his skin prickling all over.

Wobbly as he was, he supposed he'd been fortunate that his armor had taken the brunt of the attack. Juha had been completely incapacitated.

Greene didn't attempt to follow the stealth suit through the service door; all things considered, blundering around in dark hallways seemed like a great way to get himself lost. Besides, he had no chance of making up the distance on them at this point.

The place where Juha had emerged each time was presumably the entrance to their facility. That's where they'd take him. He could see it on his display, and he could see Juha's glowing yellow dot headed roughly that direction. The red Algary pings had disappeared, though.

Greene made it through the remaining corridors of the Forbidden Kingdom without encountering any more Algary forces. He drew his pistol as he stepped out into the warm moonlight, and the fresh night air revived him slightly.

"Raptor, where are you?" he said.

"I'm moving," Ojukwu said. "They're withdrawing, and I'm trying to keep them flanked, at least slow them down. Jester is moving. Are we going after him?"

Greene couldn't see or hear his quarry. No doubt it was well ahead of him, and his hearing wasn't good in any case.

"No," he said. "Don't try to get to him. We've got to reach the entrance to their facility before they do. Can you make it?"

"I'll do my best," Ojukwu said, her tone resolute.

Greene tried to pick up his pace, but his movement remained frustratingly slow.

He opened his mouth to tell Ojukwu that he wasn't going to get there in time, then chose not to say the words. Instead, he urged himself to go faster, to do better, to *be* better.

"Run," he muttered to himself. "*Run*, damn you."

Greene gritted his teeth and commanded his limbs to obey. His hobble became a trot, and then a lope, and finally a stiff-legged dash down the path. He felt as though he might lose his balance at any moment, but at least he had a chance.

"I've reached Speed," Burg announced in his ear. "What are you doing?"

"Trying to finish the mission," Greene replied, his breath short. "Get her stable. Get her back to the car."

"But what about you? You're going to—"

He didn't have the energy for more words. "Don't worry about me. Just do it!"

From ahead came the sound of gunfire: the booming reports of Ojukwu's rifle, answered by Algary's smaller weapons.

Greene got off the path, almost falling, and into the tall grass for cover, realizing as he did so that it was for naught if their adversaries were using infrared. But as he pushed onward, he realized that no one was firing at him.

Ahead stood a small building backed up against a stone retaining wall about two stories high and otherwise surrounded by a paved area filled with picnic tables. His heads-up display indicated that this was the building that Juha had come out of. A faded sign reading *Alluring Appetizers Presented by Algary Applications* confirmed it.

Greene took cover behind a large tree about twenty meters from the snack stand, switching his Spec-Trons to infrared to see what he could pick up.

Ojukwu was coming up hard on his left. On top of the retaining wall in front of him stood three figures, maybe more, all seemingly oriented on Ojukwu. There was no telling whether Juha had already been taken inside.

He cast his infrared gaze around almost wildly, hoping by some miracle to see Juha—and did. There, to his right, at a distance, a prone, still figure moved swiftly through an open patch of tall grass toward the Algary concession stand.

How had Greene arrived first? Whoever wore the stealth suit must have taken a circuitous route, likely to try to shake any pursuers. This reinforced Greene's belief that Algary didn't have the slightest suspicion that Juha had chipped himself.

No one seemed to be looking in Greene's direction—at the very least, no one had shot at him. He had just made up his mind to advance when he saw several small objects sail through the air from the top of the retaining wall. They bounced in front of the concession stand, spewing prolific volumes of thick white smoke.

Greene heard more fire from Ojukwu's rifle, and one of the figures on the top of the retaining wall fell. An instant later, the others vanished from his view.

"They're trying to fall back!" Ojukwu called.

Greene glanced to his right again. Somehow, Juha—and their stealth-suited assailant—had already reached the concession stand, might already be inside.

"Oh no," he muttered. "All right, I'm going."

Greene charged toward the building and reached it without being shot. The smoke had begun to dissipate on the night breeze, but it remained sufficient to sting his eyes and impair his vision.

Moving as fast as he could, Greene used his free hand to feel along the small building until he reached the side door, which he found ajar. He dropped his shoulder and slammed it open, then leapt inside with his pistol raised close to his body.

He saw no one inside. At a glance, the place appeared ready for business: the cash register, popcorn machine, and soda fountain remained, and towers of Paleocola-branded disposable drinking cups lined the back counter.

They'd come in here, he was certain of it. They couldn't have gone anywhere else. But the only other way out of this tiny area was the stainless steel door to the walk-in freezer. Surely they wouldn't have …

Greene yanked on the handle, but the door didn't budge. "Locked from the inside?" he said. "That means …"

To his right, a figure loomed in the doorway, obscuring the little moonlight that was getting through.

"It's me," Ojukwu said as Greene pivoted toward her, weapon raised. "I'm here."

Greene felt the energy drain from his body, and he slumped against the nearest counter to keep his balance.

"We're too late," he said. "They're gone."

NINETEEN

They had vanished in the smoke, Juha and all of the Algary people, including the one Ojukwu had shot.

"Damn it!" Greene kicked an open cardboard box on the floor, sending individually wrapped packets of disposable tableware flying everywhere. He cast about for something to hit with his fist, then clenched it hard and pressed it to his forehead, struggling to rein in his raging frustration.

Ojukwu ejected the magazine from her rifle, stuck it into a jacket pocket, and pulled out a fresh one. "What do you mean, 'they're gone'?"

Greene made himself take a deep, slow breath. "They must have gone through there," he said, nodding at the door to the walk-in freezer. "There's no other option."

Ojukwu reloaded her rifle, then checked it over. "A freezer."

"Where else? We know this building is where they came out, and we both saw them come back here. Look—this side of the building backs right up against the hill. It's a perfect configuration for them to have constructed a tunnel into the hill, and then underground, most likely. And besides, why else would a walk-in freezer be locked from the inside?"

"Oh, I agree with you completely," Ojukwu said. "It's exactly the sort of secretive nonsense Algary would do. So now what? You think you can break it open?"

Greene unslung the satchel from his shoulder and began to remove the demolition charges. "I'm certainly going to try."

"If they're smart, which they are, they've got the door reinforced."

Greene began planting the charges around the doorframe. "I'm sure it is."

"Possibly even with a force field."

"I thought about that, too. I've got to try, though, right?"

Ojukwu looked at him, then at the devices mounted on the door, then back at him. "Greene, are you demo-rated?"

Greene opened his mouth, then paused. "Why do you ask?"

Ojukwu cocked her head. "You're putting an awful lot of explosives on there."

Greene realized he had emptied the bag except for the detonator, then decided to leave the charges where he'd put them. "I want to make sure we get through the first time."

"It just seems like a lot. If this door leads underground, there'll be a tunnel. What if you collapse it?"

Greene peered at her. "Are *you* demo-rated?"

"No," she said, her tone defiant.

Greene began to arm the charges. "A second ago, you were worried I didn't have enough explosives, and now you're afraid I'm going to—what? Somehow blow up their entire operation from here? If you don't want to keep going, if you'd rather just pack it in, just say so."

"You bastard." Ojukwu jabbed a finger under his nose. "I'm not a coward. But I'm not here to get killed for you or for Karjalainen, either. This reeks of desperation and half-assery, and you aren't exactly at your most reliable right now."

"Every second we stand here talking is a second they have to get ready for us."

"So eager to run inside and get killed!"

Greene crossed his arms. "Just say what you have to say."

"Nothing!" She snapped her fingers in front of his eyes. "I have nothing to say. If I leave now, you'll get yourself killed for sure, and then I'll never get what you owe me. Blow this thing and let's get on with the evening."

Greene felt a wave of relief wash over him. He hadn't really thought about going in alone—then again, he hadn't expected anything that had happened in the last few minutes. But he would have pressed on by himself rather than turn back.

Greene motioned to the concession stand's entrance. Ojukwu stepped outside, and he followed.

They crossed the picnic area and reached the thick tree Greene had sheltered behind a few minutes prior. Ojukwu stood squarely behind it, and Greene squatted next to her.

"Ready?" he asked.

"Do it!"

Greene pressed the detonator, hoping, praying that the explosives would be sufficient to enable them to continue.

A lime-green light, painfully bright, illuminated the interior of the building. Then, with a roar that shook the earth, the concession stand disintegrated, transformed into a million tiny particles accelerating upward and outward almost too fast to see.

The emerald blast wave and the fragmentation hit Greene at the same time, the countless tiny bits of wood and aluminum like a sandstorm that plinked off his Spec-Trons, stung his hands, and tore his clothes as the force knocked him over.

Greene lay on his back, pieces of the building falling around him, and reflexively raised his arms to shield his face. Several objects struck him with enough force to make him grunt in pain but not to do any serious damage. When he opened his eyes a moment later, he saw a cloud of debris settling on and around him.

Safe behind the tree, Ojukwu began to laugh, a chuckle that bloomed into an almost maniacal cackle.

Greene sat up, feeling a soreness that no meds could remove without separating him from his senses. "That was funny to you?"

"Think you used enough dynamite there, Greene?" she said, still giggling.

"Plasma," Greene said. "Sunny didn't tell me they were plasma."

"On the bright side, I bet Algary wasn't expecting it either." Ojukwu reached down, took his hand, and pulled him to his feet. "Let's go."

Greene's comm activated. "What the hell was that?" Burg demanded. "We heard that from here. Are you guys okay?"

"We're fine," Greene said, picking the splinters out of his hands.

"All part of the plan, or so I am told," Ojukwu added cheerfully.

"Carry on, then, I guess," Burg said. "I'm on my way back to the rendezvous point with Speed."

Greene attempted to brush the dirt from his Spec-Trons but only succeeded in smearing the mess around. They were too scratched now to see through properly anyway, and he stuck them in his jacket pocket.

He dusted himself off, drew his pistol, and advanced toward the smoldering remains of the Algary concession stand and the collapsed retaining wall, Ojukwu following.

Perhaps "remains" was too kind a word, Greene reflected as they approached. What had been the roof and walls was now scattered across a hundred-meter area. The contents of the building had been atomized. The shattered foundation radiated heat through his shoes when he stepped onto it.

"Huh," Ojukwu said.

The freezer door still stood in its frame. Ojukwu had been right—it was reinforced with force fields. But the walls on either side had collapsed, and light glimmered from within and below.

"I think you found a hole in their security," Ojukwu said, still clearly amused.

"I think we *made* one." Greene motioned. "We can fit through here on the left."

She pointed her rifle into the opening and peered down. "It looks like a bit of a drop. I can't see what's down there."

Greene reached into his jacket for a flashbang, pulled the pin, and dropped it into the hole. As soon as it detonated, he climbed in.

The drop was farther than he'd guessed, perhaps five meters, and his bad ankle gave out as he landed with a loud *clang* on the metal floor. He rolled with the impact and came up on his knees, weapon up, fighting for mastery over the shooting pain.

Ojukwu dropped down beside him quite a bit more gracefully, rifle and all, landing in a poised crouch. "It's clear," she said.

Greene glanced around. The small two-story room appeared to be some sort of security foyer. The metal walls, ceiling, and floor reflected the cold fluorescent lights. Behind him, a ramp led up to the walk-in freezer door, and ahead stood a more conventional metal door. Backless aluminum benches lined the side walls; the room was otherwise empty.

"Castle, we've entered the facility," Greene said. "We—" he broke off as static hissed in his ear.

"I think we've lost comms," Ojukwu said. "This place is shielded at best and they're jamming us at worst."

Greene tightened the brace around his ankle until it hurt, then stood. A limp was unavoidable at this point, but it would have to do.

He went to the door ahead and peeked through the small window in its center. On the other side, a straight hallway, lined on both sides with lockers, ran down to an identical door at the far end. No Algary people were visible.

Ojukwu joined him at the door. "I don't like it," she said, evidently thinking the same thing Greene was.

"Would you like it better if we could see them?" he said.

"Probably not. I don't like anything about any of this. Shall we?"

Greene pulled on the door handle and was slightly surprised when it opened. When he stepped into the hallway, no invisible force assaulted him, and he concluded that they were indeed alone there.

Ojukwu advanced with her rifle raised. "You don't have any idea how big this facility is?"

"None whatsoever." Greene took out his battered Spec-Trons and put them on to check the display, which was still mostly visible. "We're close, though. Juha's signal is thirty meters ahead and ten meters down."

Klaxons sounded ahead and behind them, the harsh noise reverberating off the metal walls.

"*Now* they sound the alarm?" Ojukwu said, raising her voice. "I guess we've managed to exceed their expectations."

Greene limped gamely onward, determined to match Ojukwu's pace, unwilling to show any more weakness than necessary.

Ojukwu paused, then scowled at him. "You're hurt."

Greene was hurt in more ways than he could articulate. "I can keep going."

Ojukwu shrugged, then continued.

Greene wished he'd brought some meds, then remembered that he had already taken every med he had access to and that they just weren't getting the job done anymore. One way or another, he figured, he'd put himself on the fast track to death.

The thought didn't bother him the way it normally would.

"God, Jesus, just help me make it through this," he muttered through gritted teeth.

They reached the far end of the hallway. Greene realized his grip on his pistol was too tight and forced himself to take a deep breath. Then he pulled on the door handle. It didn't budge.

"Got any more of those demo charges?" Ojukwu asked.

Greene patted himself down and took inventory. "No, but I've got a plasma grenade. That would do it."

"Just one?"

"Just one."

"Then here's hoping this is the last locked door we come across, although I don't like the odds of that."

Greene didn't either.

"You understand," Ojukwu said, "that we've gotten farther than they thought we could, which means that however many troops they've got, they're *all* right through there."

Greene leaned against the wall. "I know."

"It could be twenty for all you know. Or more."

"Yes. I've got one more stun grenade. Between that and the plasma charge, we might get through most of them."

Ojukwu looked back. "Before we do this, how are we getting out of here?"

Greene followed her gaze. The freezer door was still sealed, of course, and the hole they'd entered through would be difficult if not impossible to reach with a bad leg.

"We'll find the door controls," Greene said.

Ojukwu shook her head. "Just like that, eh?"

"Or you could climb out with Juha and leave me behind."

She tilted her head sideways, but Greene couldn't read her eyes behind the Spec-Trons. "You'd be all right with that, wouldn't you? Well, let's not get ahead of ourselves. Okay, how do you want to handle it?"

"I don't want to throw the grenade from down the hall. It could bounce back. I'm going to plant it at the base of the door, pull the pin, and run back down the hall."

"You're going to run?"

"Well ..."

She held out a hand, palm up. "Give it here. I'll do it."

Greene hesitated. "Are you sure?"

"Just give me the damned grenade."

He handed it over. "Thank you."

Greene limped back to the foyer doorway, took cover, and checked his pistol. "Ready!" he called.

Ojukwu planted the grenade at the base of the door and pulled the pin, then sprinted back to Greene's position. Half a second after she reached shelter, the grenade detonated.

The explosion blasted the door from its hinges, destroying the wall and a section of the floor beneath it. Most of the lights in the hallway went out.

Greene peered ahead, trying to see through the viridescent haze, then jerked back as gunfire echoed from the far end of the hallway.

Ojukwu blind-fired several rounds in return, just to keep them honest.

Greene couldn't tell how many there were—at least six, probably more. He chewed his lip. He and Ojukwu weren't going to win a shootout against so many, and they definitely couldn't charge them, not down a straight hallway.

They were stuck. The longer they remained here, the more likely it was that Juha would be moved out of their reach, never mind that eventually, Algary reinforcements would surely arrive.

A prolonged firefight was death one way or another. They had to press forward or they had to abort the mission.

Greene holstered his pistol, drew his heat ray, and set it to maximum power and wide spread. He pointed it down the hall and fired, holding down the trigger. For an instant, all enemy fire stopped, and Greene heard several cries of pain.

He took the opportunity to peek out for a better look. The plasma grenade had blasted a bigger hole in the floor than he'd realized, close to three meters across.

Greene had an idea.

He fell back as the firing resumed. Ojukwu said something that he couldn't hear over the gunfire.

Greene put away the heat ray, then reached into his jacket and pulled out his smoke grenade and his remaining stun grenade. With one hand, he held them up so that Ojukwu noticed.

"No matter what, keep them pinned down!" he bellowed over the din.

She nodded in agreement, if not understanding.

He pulled the pins from both grenades, then, before he could overthink what he was doing, winged them sidearm through the doorway, one after another. The flashbang sailed true, landing amidst the Algary forces, spinning across the metal floor. His aim with the smoke grenade wasn't as good. It bounced off the wall three quarters of the way down the hall and clattered to a stop on Greene's side of the gaping hole in the floor.

The stun grenade's explosion resounded down the hall, and an instant later, the hallway began to fill with thick pink smoke, which quickly obscured both the Algary security team and the hole in the floor.

"Good enough," Greene muttered.

"Pink?" Ojukwu said.

Greene shrugged, then put his head down and charged.

Staying low, Greene ran down the hall as fast as his bad ankle would carry him. He half-expected to catch a bullet fired in his general direction, but the guards still weren't shooting.

Good, Greene thought—let Algary shell out for a few hearing aids and bioprinted eardrums.

He approached the billowing cloud of smoke, realizing that he couldn't see the hole. Focused on holding his breath, he dropped into a slide and closed his eyes as he entered the smoke.

Greene pitched into the void an instant before he'd expected to, and he experienced a momentary surge of terror. Then his jacket caught on the jagged lip of the hole. The fabric held just long enough that he was thrown off balance before it tore.

Having lost his sense of direction, Greene tried to tuck and turn his face sideways. His hip and elbow impacted a hard surface, and as all of the air went out of his body, he fell again, perhaps a meter, onto cold metal.

Gasping for breath, coughing from the smoke in his lungs, he forced himself to open his eyes.

He lay on the floor, seemingly alone, in the middle of what looked like a break room. Several metal tables—he'd landed on one—stood in the middle of the room, each surrounded by chairs. Along the bare concrete walls, he saw couches, a large television screen, a fridge, a microwave, a sink, and several vending machines. The room had one exit, straight ahead, the direction they'd been heading on the floor above—toward Juha.

Upstairs, through the cloud of pink smoke drifting down, Ojukwu's rifle sounded again.

Greene hauled himself to his feet and took stock of his injuries. He'd added an aching elbow to his sizeable collection.

The archway leading out of the room had no door. Greene drew his weapons and headed for it.

On the other side he found a squarish room, clearly the junction of this place. All three of its other sides had doorways, and a metal staircase ran both up and down.

Up would take him right into the thick of the Algary forces. As for the rest—

Boots rang on metal as two men in Algary uniforms came down the stairs, carrying pistols. Covering against the very move Greene had made, no doubt.

Greene quickly faded back into the break room, contemplating whether he could overcome them without giving himself away to the rest. The pistol was too loud; he'd have to use the heat ray. He hoped this new and improved model was up to the task. He hadn't had a chance to use it in the field before tonight.

As soon as the Algary men entered the room, Greene gave them a sustained blast. The results were immensely satisfying: the nearer one doubled over and the other dropped his gun, writhing where he stood.

Greene went for the closer man first, striking him on the back of the head with the butt of his weapon and sweeping his legs out from under him. The man hit the floor face-first and didn't immediately attempt to get up.

The second guard was already beginning to recover. Greene shot him again with the heat ray, then dropped his shoulder and knocked the man onto his back.

Now what? Greene didn't intend to shoot them in cold blood, but they wouldn't stay down for long, and they'd be right back after him again once they got up.

The nearer of the two men stirred, and Greene pounced on him, digging a knee into his sternum. Greene holstered his heat ray and rifled through the man's pockets, hoping, perhaps, for an access card of some kind. He didn't find one, but he did discover a set of handcuffs and their key.

"That'll work," Greene muttered.

He checked the second man's pockets, found nothing useful, then looked around the room for something to cuff them *to*. At a glance, nothing seemed viable, and he settled for binding one man's wrist to the other's ankle.

Greene rose, collected their pistols, and, seeing that neither of the men was in a state to observe him, put them in the fridge behind a takeout bag from SynthBurger.

As the gunfire continued upstairs, he ventured again into the junction room. According to his battered Spec-Trons, Juha was to his left on this level, not far at all.

Pretty impressive that he was still getting a signal from Juha's chip down here when they didn't even have local comms, Greene thought. Quite a piece of work. It couldn't have been cheap. Greene wondered how that squared with Juha's purported financial difficulties. He wasn't sure what the truth was, but he knew he didn't have all of it.

And here Greene was, down in the bowels of God knew where, risking his life and the lives of others to save a man—a *friend*—he couldn't rely on to tell him the truth.

"I'm never doing this again," Greene informed himself, not believing it, fighting off the urge to ponder what was wrong with him.

An odd quiet fell as the facility's alarm stopped blaring. Greene didn't know what this portended, but he felt motivated to pick up his pace.

Before him stood a conventional metal door with no apparent security features. He tried the handle, and it opened.

Weapon raised, Greene advanced into a short hallway with three doors on each side and one at the far end. Each door had a rectangular window at head height, and lights were on in all of them.

Greene glanced into the nearest and saw an office chair and a metal desk with a computer screen atop it. The room across from it had an identical setup. Both were unoccupied.

He moved up as movement caught his eye.

In the second room on his right, a towering, muscular man with his back to the door held a second person down on a medical examination table. Greene processed what he saw in an instant: a medical scanner, a scalpel, a splash of blood.

According to his Spec-Trons, the second person in the room was Juha.

TWENTY

Greene turned the handle and slammed the door open with his shoulder.

His first thought was that Algary had decided to kill Juha. His second, right on its heels, was that Algary had figured out that Juha had a chip in him after all and intended to cut it out.

Yes, Greene realized as he turned his heat ray on the man with the scalpel and watched him straighten and squirm, that was exactly what was happening, in a decidedly non-surgical manner.

The room was too small, the big man too close. He fell into Greene, turning, lashing out. Greene's hand struck the doorframe, and the heat ray fell from his grip.

As Greene fell backward, fumbling for his pistol, he saw Juha slump to the floor, his coveralls torn and bloody. He didn't try to get up.

The big man found his footing and drove his shoulder into Greene's chest, carrying them both out into the hall. Greene tried to bring his pistol up to shoot or to strike, but he had no room to maneuver.

The Algary man outweighed him by at least twenty kilos, and it was all Greene could do to grab a fistful of his uniform and spin out of the way as the man tried to slam him into the wall.

Greene backed up, trying to create space to bring his gun to bear, but his shoulder blades hit the door at the end of the hall.

With his free hand, Greene grasped at the door handle. He turned it as the man lunged into him, and they both fell into the room.

Greene kicked wildly with his good leg, got free, and used a nearby desk to pull himself back upright. As he took in his surroundings, a wave of vertigo hit him, and he almost fell down again.

He stood in mid-air, with no visible support, at least a kilometer above Portsmith. Beside him, a desk and chair occupied the same plane. Puffy white clouds drifted close by overhead, and the sun shone bright far above him. Below and directly in front of him, he could see the Algary building and the serpentine dragon that kept watch above it, and across town, he could just make out the giant golden bear that prowled atop Xiong Tower.

The hologram was so vivid that Greene had to fight down nausea.

Greene made himself lock his eyes on his adversary, which was easy to do, because the big man was on his feet again.

He reached Greene in an instant, shoving, pressing, seizing Greene's wrists in an iron grip. As he tried to bend Greene back over the desk, Greene twisted sideways, and they went down in a heap together, Greene's pistol clattering across the invisible floor.

Before Greene could react, the man was on top of him, his hands around Greene's neck. Greene tried to strike at the man's face, but he was already desperate for oxygen, and his blows were feeble. His vision blurred, then began to darken as he descended toward the edge of consciousness.

In an instant, the pressure on his throat was gone and the crushing weight on his chest lifted.

Greene lay on the floor, gasping for air like a blind fish. When his vision cleared, he saw Ojukwu standing over him, holding her rifle like a club, and his opponent unconscious on the floor beside him.

Ojukwu held the butt of her rifle out to Greene. He grabbed it, and she pulled him to his feet.

"Thank you," Greene said after he'd caught his breath.

Ojukwu straightened her gaiter. "Looks like I got here just in time. What in the world is this room? I'm dizzy just standing here."

"Just an office, as far as I can see."

She clucked her tongue. "An office for someone with a very inflated view of themselves. You can literally look down on everyone while you work."

"It could appeal to a certain ego," Greene admitted as he retrieved his pistol.

Ojukwu inspected her rifle. "Speaking of looking down on people, did you find Karjalainen?"

"Juha!" Greene lurched past Ojukwu into the hall and found the room Juha was in. The blood spatters made it hard to miss.

Juha had managed to stand and was leaning shakily against the exam table. The top of his coveralls had been ripped open, and blood ran down his muscled chest, over and between his upper abdominals and onto the wrinkled pouch of loose skin around his navel.

Juha nodded at Greene as he entered the room, and then his eyes widened. "Ojukwu?"

"I suppose Greene hasn't had a chance to tell you yet," she said from the doorway. "You're coming home with me."

Juha's eyes narrowed. "I don't know what that means, but I don't like the sound of it. Then again, it's got to be better than hanging around this place, so sure, lead on and let's get the fuck out of here."

"You look awful," Greene said. "Are you all right to move? Do we need to patch you up first?"

"Well, I *feel* awful. But if the alternative is staying here, then how I feel doesn't matter."

"Did they get the chip out of you?" Ojukwu asked.

Juha glanced at a puddle of blood on the floor that contained what might have been bits of flesh. "I'm not sure. It's likely. You know, if this happens again, I'm going to put the chip directly in my ass cheek, I tell you what."

Greene glanced back at Ojukwu. "What's the situation?"

"It's clear up top as far as I can tell," she said. "Or at least, it was when I came down here."

Greene was both surprised and impressed. "You got them all?"

"All the ones I saw. There weren't actually that many."

"Come on," Greene said. "We can't take the chance of losing him again."

"You won't," Juha said. "Just follow the blood trail."

Greene picked up his heat ray and holstered it, then put his arm around Juha's shoulders and helped him to the doorway.

"My God, both of you can hardly walk," Ojukwu said. "Let me take point."

"By all means," Greene said as she moved in front.

Ojukwu headed toward the stairwell at a pace Greene had trouble matching. "Karjalainen, how many security staff are there here?" she asked.

"Uh ... I don't know, honestly. But I can tell you that I've never seen more than four at a time."

"And the labs? Where are they?"

"Labs? They never took me to any labs. But the rest of the facility, whatever it is, is down."

Ojukwu shook her head. "With the understanding that this entire operation is off the books, I've got to say, it seems like we've got this place about clear. If we had a proper team, we could sweep the whole place clean before the Algary reinforcements showed up. Take it all." She glanced back. "What do you think, Mister Browne?"

"*If*," Greene said.

But Juha laughed. "Clear? Hardly."

At the end of the hall, Ojukwu opened the door with one hand, keeping the rifle raised with the other. "What are you worried about, the stealth suit? One guy? He's probably long gone from here, saving their precious tech."

"Or else locking down whatever facilities are below us," Greene said as they moved out into the junction. "Looting this place isn't the mission. It was never the mission. The objective is to get out of here."

Juha slipped out of Greene's supportive grasp and leaned on the staircase railing. "Both of you are astoundingly wrong."

Greene looked at him sharply. "What?"

"The suit. It's not what you think."

Ojukwu paused at the bottom of the staircase. "And what does *that* mean?"

"You're thinking, what, stealth? Infiltration? Espionage? That's what you're worried about?"

Greene felt his brow furrow. "Isn't it?"

"Unfortunately not." Juha shook his head. "Not this. Not primarily. It's a cloaked exoframe. It's *powered armor*."

"My God." The ramifications hit Greene like a physical blow. This would change espionage forever, just like they'd feared, but even worse than that, it was a game-changing military advantage as well.

"Shit," Ojukwu said.

"What has it got?" Greene asked.

"I've only seen it once uncloaked, and only for a few seconds. They've really leaned into the bulkiness of the projection unit. My guess it's based on the scout armor the military uses, although it's got pretty substantial mounting rails. You could put some big-ass guns on there."

"Jesus," Greene said. "Can you see it? When it's cloaked?"

"Yes. If it's close enough. And if it's moving."

"How close is that?" Ojukwu demanded.

Juha shrugged. "Anything past about twenty meters is iffy. You know, if you want to keep standing around here and talking, you might get a chance to see it—or not, as the case may be—for yourself."

Greene noticed a sign on the door on the far end of the junction, and a rush of new thoughts entered his head. "*Holding*. Is that where they were keeping you?"

"Yes, would you like a tour?" Juha asked. "Since apparently we're not leaving."

Greene moved to the windowless door and pulled on the handle. Locked. "Are there other people in there? Other prisoners? Test subjects?"

"For God's sake," Ojukwu said. "What are you going to do if there are? Try to rescue them?"

Greene fought down a swell of despair. He was used to the fact that other people didn't see the world the way he did, but God, if it wasn't frustrating at times. "If there are other people locked up, we can't just leave them here."

"That's not the mission. That was never the mission," she said, her tone mocking. "Christ in heaven, even if there are people in there, and even if you get them out before the Algary reinforcements show up and kill us all, how are you going to evac them? And then after we leave, you think Algary isn't just going to go out and grab some more?"

"You know that kind of logic doesn't work on him," Juha said. He was obviously amused, which irritated Greene further. "Much as I hate agreeing with her, I do concur that this would be a damned inconvenient time for you to be a hero. Fortunately for us, no, there's no one else in there. There were a couple ragged-looking people when they first brought me here, but that was the last time I saw them. I'm the cream of the crop; what do they need ordinary peasants for with me around?"

Greene stared at Juha. "You're sure?"

"You want to take the time to check? I promise: if there were people in there, I would be piggybacking on your quixotic do-goodery in a heartbeat. Lord knows I need all the good karma I can get."

Greene hesitated. He wasn't sure he believed Juha. He freely recognized that such a detour would be a strategically terrible decision, but for him, it was the principle of the thing. Which Juha knew.

Would Juha lie if he thought it would get them out of here? Yes, he absolutely would. But *was* he lying? Greene had no idea. A part of him felt he might as well flip a coin.

Ojukwu stamped a booted foot on the metal staircase. "What is the matter with you? Come apart at the seams on your own time!"

What *was* the matter with him? It was a good question.

Greene took a deep breath, then stepped away from the door. "All right. Let's keep moving."

The staircase ended one floor up in a junction identical to the one below except that it had two doors instead of four—one of which had been obliterated by a plasma grenade. Blood splashed the floor in numerous places, but there was no sign of any Algary forces, alive or dead.

"You guys have been pretty busy," Juha said. "Good for you."

Greene shook his head. "I was expecting reinforcements, not this. Where is everyone?"

Rifle raised, Ojukwu went to the blasted door and peered out. "I know I hit a few of them, obviously. I don't know how badly, though."

"They didn't go downstairs, or we would have run into them," Greene said. "And I don't think they would have tried to go out the way we came in. They must have gone out through there." He nodded at the door opposite the destroyed wall.

"Did you make them think you've taken the facility?" Juha asked. "If so, it makes sense that they'd prioritize getting their tech out of here. Wait, *have* you taken the facility?"

"No, it's just us," Greene said.

"Well now I'm even more impressed."

"I don't trust it at all," Ojukwu said. "They didn't know we were coming, and this site clearly wasn't set up for defense, but Algary isn't nearly that incompetent."

"No indeed," said a deep, rich voice, foreign yet familiar.

Carandini!

Greene went tense all over. "He's here!"

With the sound of a blow, Ojukwu went airborne, her rifle flying from her hands. She landed on her back near the jagged hole in the floor, and her momentum carried her over the edge and below. She hadn't even had a chance to cry out.

"Oh, shit," Juha said. "I'm sorry. I didn't see him. I didn't know, I couldn't—"

"Can you see him *now?*" Greene backed toward the nearest wall. He had absolutely no idea where Carandini was.

"Yes, now that he's moving," Juha said. "He must have been standing still in here the whole time. You know, we're lucky he doesn't have the guns mounted on that thing, or else we'd—"

"Where is he?" Greene almost shrieked.

"Duck!" Juha said, leaping away from him.

Greene threw himself hard to the floor as an unseen mass whooshed over his head. He rolled sideways, toward Juha, hoping he had guessed right.

He must have, because Juha was already pulling him to his feet and half-dragging him around the room.

"You know, we could leave her here," Juha said in his ear. "We'd be safe, she'd be off my ass, and you could pin this whole thing on her company. It'd be really convenient."

"It would," Greene said. "And I'm not doing it."

"I know you aren't. I just thought I'd— *Down!*"

Greene let Juha yank him down and backward, then up again, feeling unpleasantly like a puppet.

Carandini's booming laugh filled the room. "I am going to take my time with you," he said. "And I am going to enjoy it. If this really is all of you, it's quite a remarkable achievement. Seems a shame to destroy you, but it's imperative at this point, I'm afraid."

They didn't necessarily have to defeat this thing, Greene realized—they just had to get back to the car. However, that meant retrieving Ojukwu from downstairs, whatever state she was in, and then navigating the zoo. But Carandini would have even more of an advantage in the open because of the speed of the powered armor.

"We need a plan," Greene said. "Can we stop him here?"

"I could try to grab onto him from the back, but then what are you going to do?" Juha asked.

Greene drew his pistol and handed it to Juha. "See what you can do with that."

Juha took it. "Get behind me."

Greene obeyed, pulling out his heat ray as he did so.

Carandini laughed again. "Pistols. By all means, go ahead."

Juha fired three shots toward the center of the room, and Greene heard them ricochet off an invisible object before striking the metal walls.

No wonder Carandini had targeted Ojukwu and her high-powered rifle first.

Aiming where Juha had, still seeing nothing, Greene pulled the trigger on the heat ray and felt no small degree of satisfaction when Carandini bellowed in pain.

"Oh, shit," Juha said, starting to back up and bumping into Greene. "Move, you have to—"

Still roaring, Carandini flung Juha sideways, sending him headfirst into the wall.

In the next instant, a blow spun Greene around, pain exploding up his arm, the heat ray falling from his mangled fingers.

Gasping, oblivious to everything but the agony in his hand, Greene sank to his knees, his vision blurring.

"Again you surprise me," Carandini said. "But I must confess, I've had about my fill of surprises for today. Now: if either of you tries to get up without my command, I will break both your legs."

Cradling his shattered hand against his chest, attempting to keep it still, Greene planted one foot and turned himself back toward where Carandini must be.

Juha sat against a wall, fresh blood pouring from his nose. He made no attempt to rise. "We aren't allowed to score *any* points?" he said. "That's not very sporting of you."

Carandini laughed again. "My good fellow, if I were a sporting man, would I have spent untold fortunes developing this suit?"

"Don't forget stealing the bits you couldn't work out yourself."

"Quite. Although technically, I hired *you* and *you* stole the one. But you've got the spirit of it."

"Awesome. So now what?"

"Now you go back in your cell. Your friends will go there too, although their stay will be quite a bit shorter than yours. Just long enough for me to discern who they are."

"I've never seen these people before in my life," Juha said.

"Pardon my incredulity." The smug amusement in Carandini's voice was maddening. "Shall I take a guess myself?"

"I've got nowhere pressing to be," Juha said. His eye had swollen, but the spark hadn't gone out of it.

"Very well. How about Xiong Holonautics? I understand you're fairly well connected with them. With Mister Green Greene in particular. And he is well known to be a man of action. Why, this could be him sitting there now, with us at this very moment. We shall soon see."

Greene flinched, immediately hoping it would be interpreted as a reaction to his considerable pain. How many of his fingers were broken? Possibly all of them. Never before had he been as acutely aware of just how many bones the human hand contained.

"Whether you are Xiong or someone else," Carandini continued, "please know that the reprisals will be considerable. You will not leave here alive, but you will appreciate knowing that you have earned misery and suffering not only for yourself, but also for your organization, your associates, your friends, and perhaps even your family. Hm? What's that? Nothing to say?"

Juha wiped his nose on his sleeve but only succeeded in smearing blood across his cheek. "Well, go ahead," he said to Greene. "I'm excited to see how you think us out of this one."

Despair buffeted Greene in waves. No, there would be no thinking their way out this time. Never mind that his hand was broken, that Ojukwu was gone, that maybe Juha couldn't even walk—Carandini had been toying with them the entire time.

He'd shocked them before, with enough charge to incapacitate them. He hadn't needed it now. With that weapon on top of the invisibility and the incredible strength bestowed on him by the powered armor, Carandini possessed an embarrassment of riches. They'd never had a chance.

There was no escaping the stealth suit, either down here or up on the surface. Greene accepted that as fact. And what next? He'd be unmasked and identified, and then God knew what they would do to him before they finally killed him. And they would do the same to Ojukwu as well. Juha, too, was damned—there would be no more attempts to rescue him.

At least Burg and Sonnenschein were safe. That was significant. Even catastrophic failure had a silver lining, Greene thought.

What did he have left? Greene mentally took an inventory. His pistol was gone. His heat ray was gone. His grenades were spent. The only thing that remained was Garcinia's prototype device, but that was designed to reveal the stealth suit, not to damage or disable it.

If only he'd had a chance to use it earlier! Still, it would be better to use it up now, if he could, than to let it fall intact into Algary's hands.

The device was clipped to the harness under his jacket. He had no idea at any given moment where Carandini was or how much of his attention was on Greene, and he wasn't sure whether it would be better to go for it fast or slowly.

Another dose of Power-Through would be really nice right about now, he reflected, but there was nothing to be done about it.

The thought ignited an unexpected rage inside him.

He was going to die here, likely tortured to death, certainly disavowed by his company, and he was thinking about painkillers?

Nisha would never find out the truth about what had happened to him. He would never get to hold his daughter. But he was focused on self-medication?

Had he gotten himself addicted to Power-Through? He'd thought he was better than that. Quite possibly, he'd been wrong.

One more thing to add to his long list of failures. Failed rescuer. Absent husband. Soon-to-be absent father. Not up to the challenges the world threw at him, unable or unwilling to alter the course of his life even when he recognized the need for change.

For I do not understand my own actions. For I do not do what I want, but I do the very thing I hate. Et cetera.

But it was too late to do anything about any of those things. What yet could be done? Nothing. Nothing but to go down fighting. To die well.

Anger—at his circumstances, at his choices, at being trapped in his own skin—ignited a flame inside him. Greene planted both feet and scooted himself back to the wall. When he felt the cold metal against his back, he pushed with his legs until he was half standing, half leaning.

"Juha, where is he?" he said.

Juha wore an uncharacteristic look of concern. "He's right in front of you."

"That's correct," Carandini said, his voice startlingly close. "I'm going to rip that mask off your face, for starters, and then I'm going to break your legs, because I'm a man of my word."

Fast, then. Greene jammed his good hand into his jacket and yanked out Garcinia's grenade. "Stop talking and come do it, then."

"What is that?" Greene detected a note of panic in Carandini's voice. "What are you do—"

Greene closed his eyes and pressed the trigger.

It made only a soft click, but the flash of light the device produced was painful even through his closed eyelids. The acrid odor of burned plastic and wiring filled Greene's nostrils, and an instant later, the device had become so hot that he had to drop it.

The light faded quickly. Greene opened his eyes. Before him stood Victor Carandini.

He wore thick armor of heavy pads, black with a pattern of gray triangles—presumably a design that facilitated the cloaking technology. A metal exoframe, powered by a mechanism mounted on his back, enveloped Carandini's torso and the outsides of his legs and arms, leading up to rails that ran high over both shoulders like roll bars. Carandini was fit, but a man his age would likely be incapable of moving the bulky apparatus without the power supply. Bundles of red wires and blue pneumatic hoses streamed down the suit like countless tentacles, giving it a rough, unfinished look. Carandini himself was clearly dazed, not looking at anything in particular, holding his arms up in a defensive posture.

After all Carandini's actions, after all his talk, after all his threats, finally seeing the man—his angry blinded eyes, his metal-framed fists, his yellow teeth—was too much for Greene to bear. The fire inside him became an inferno, consuming his reason and his senses.

Roaring his fury, Greene hurled himself at Carandini. When the top of his head impacted Carandini's nose, he barely felt it. As Carandini cried out and stumbled backward, Greene seized the suit's shoulder frame with his good hand and was pulled along.

"Enough!" Carandini bellowed. "You will—"

Greene headbutted him again. He had no other weapon, and Carandini had no other weak point.

The older man fell back again, and again Greene closed, unwilling to give any distance. A third strike, this one mis-angled, broke Greene's Spec-Trons and made him feel giddy.

Then Juha appeared behind Carandini, pulling at the machinery on his back and yanking at the cables.

"Oh *yes*," Juha said cheerfully. "You can get *all* the way fucked."

Flailing blindly, Carandini clubbed Greene on the back of the neck, and he lost his grip. Carandini shoved Greene away with a blow that took the wind out of him, and it was all he could do to keep from falling.

Greene braced himself against the wall and tried to catch his breath. His furious energy was spent. As his reason returned, he became aware of the pounding ache in his head and the blood—whether or his or Carandini's, he didn't know—in his eyes, in his nose, saturating his gaiter.

Through blurred red vision, he saw Carandini swiping at Juha, who still clung to his back. But only with one arm—the left hung dead. Juha must have disabled it.

Carandini lurched backward, no doubt intending to crush Juha against the nearest wall. But his left leg had been disabled as well, and he stumbled and fell.

Greene didn't have the air or the presence of mind to cry out. He had no idea how much the massive armor weighed, but it could likely do considerable damage if it pinned Juha to the floor.

But Juha let go—or lost his grip—and tried to maneuver out of the way. Carandini's bulk knocked him down nonetheless. Carandini landed on top of him, pinning his legs.

Juha immediately twisted around, grabbed a handful of Carandini's hair, and yanked. "Damn it, man, personal space."

Greene wiped his eyes and braced himself to charge again. He probably couldn't get Carandini off of Juha in his current condition, but maybe he could do enough to enable Juha to free himself. And just maybe, he could disable a bit more of the suit.

Carandini touched a control panel on his torso that Greene hadn't noticed before. Electricity crackled, and Juha cried out in pain and let go.

Carandini planted his hand on the floor, got one leg under him, and vanished.

Greene froze. Whatever disruption Garcinia's device had caused had worn off.

An instant later, Juha scrambled free and got to his feet. "Watch out. He's limping, but he's up again."

Greene nodded. He fixed his gaze on Juha's eyes, looking for cues.

Juha turned his face toward the center of the room. "Your move, you raggedy old bastard. Come at us again and we'll rip every last wire out of you. I may not be able to see you properly, but I remember where they are, I promise."

A horrendous scraping sound emanated from the center of the room—Carandini dragging his disabled leg across the floor, Greene realized. He tensed and glanced at Juha, who looked toward the door opposite the one Greene had originally entered through.

"This is not over." Carandini sounded shaky and short of breath. "This is only the beginning. You will suffer for this affront. All of you will suffer. I will identify you, and I will find you, and I will make you wish profoundly that you had never come here."

Juha held up a middle finger. "I already wish that."

The door opened. The scraping sound came again from that direction, and the door closed. An instant later, Greene heard locking mechanisms activate.

"He's gone," Juha said.

Greene let out a breath and nodded.

Juha came over to him and put his bloody hands on Greene's shoulders. "Holy shit," he said, beaming. "Jesus Christ. I'm not sure what I was expecting out of you there, but that was definitely not it. I've never been prouder."

Greene turned at the sound of another set of footsteps, tensing again.

Ojukwu stood at the top of the stairs, holding her rifle awkwardly in her left hand. Blood soaked through the gaiter on her face. Her right arm hung at an awkward angle—Greene's uneducated guess was that her forearm was broken.

Greene unzipped his jacket and wiped the blood from his face with one side. "Are you all right?"

"It was not a good landing." Ojukwu's voice was oddly thick. She leaned the rifle against her body, then reached under her gaiter and winced. "But I think I collected all the teeth I lost. You *won* against that thing?"

"Naturally," Juha said.

Her eyes narrowed. "I can't believe it."

Juha jerked his thumb toward the door Carandini had gone through. "We can go after him if you want, and you can ask him yourself. Or—and this is only a suggestion; I don't mean to be pushy at all—we could just get the fuck out of here."

"Seconded," Greene said.

They headed for the dark hallway that led out, but the huge gap Greene's that plasma grenade had made in the floor stopped them immediately.

Juha peered into the break room below. "That's got to be two and a half meters. I could jump it easy if I wasn't down about a liter of blood, but it's all part of life's rich pageantry, I suppose. Which one of you broke that table down there?"

Greene's ankle was throbbing now. He didn't like his chances, either. "If one of us can make it across, they can help the others."

Ojukwu handed her rifle to Greene, who took it in his good left hand. "I have two working legs," she said. "Give me some room."

Greene moved out of the way, and she took a three-step running start and cleared the gap easily.

"Toss me the rifle," she said.

Juha shook his head. "Don't you do it. She could just leave us here. Or shoot us and then leave us here."

Ojukwu sighed. "I'm not going to do either of those things. But if you can't jump across without it, how are you going to jump across with it?"

As far as Greene was concerned, she'd earned that much trust and more. "Okay, here it comes."

But as he prepared to throw the rifle, he realized he couldn't figure out how—it was bulky and unbalanced, and he'd never thrown anything substantial with his left hand.

He made a face under his gaiter that she couldn't see. "I'm sorry, I'm right-handed. I don't—"

"God, we are never going to get out of here, are we? Let me do it." Juha held out his hands for the rifle, and Greene gave it to him.

"Thank you," Ojukwu said.

"All right, here we go." Juha held the rifle in both hands, bent down, and lobbed it underhand. The throw was well short, and the rifle fell into the gap and clattered on the floor of the room below them. "Oops."

"You did that on purpose." Ojukwu pointed a finger at Greene and said, "I'm going to bill you for that."

Greene opened his mouth to rebuke Juha—obviously he'd done it intentionally—but the absurdity of the situation suddenly struck him. "*You're* paying for it," he said to Juha.

"Jesus God, this man is making jokes." Juha looked across the gap at Ojukwu. "I trust you understand the severity of the situation. This is very concerning. He needs medical attention immediately."

"We *all* need medical attention immediately." Ojukwu held out a hand. "Who's coming next, then?"

"I am," Juha said. "But I've rethought the situation. I'm not going to be beholden to you one iota more than I absolutely have to, so stand aside."

Ojukwu shrugged and gave him space.

Juha checked the bottoms of his shoes, then wiped a spot of blood from the floor with his hand. "All right."

He got a running start and jumped. For an instant, Greene was afraid Juha wasn't going to make it, but he landed at the far edge of the gap, windmilling his arms for balance. Ojukwu reflexively reached out a hand to grab him, but Juha waved her off.

"I'm fine, thank you," he said. "I said I didn't need the help."

"I wasn't going to help you," she said. "I was going to push you down the hole so you could go get my gun."

Juha turned to Greene. "Now *she's* making jokes. Maybe. How do you want to do this?"

Greene was certain that he didn't have the strength or ankle stability to run fast enough to make the jump. The walls on either side of the gap were crumbling from the plasma blast, so trying to vault off of one of them was out.

"I'm just going to have to do my best, and I think you're going to have to grab me," he said.

They both nodded.

"And please don't grab my right hand."

"Just come on already," Juha said. "You can take down an invisible suit of powered armor like an absolute badass but you can't jump over a hole?"

Greene took a deep breath and tried not to overthink it. Only two and a half meters. The last obstacle—he hoped—to being done with this place once and for all.

Running wasn't an option. He rocked back on his right leg, then leapt off his left—and then felt an immediate pang of terror as he realized that he wasn't going to make it.

The toe of his shoe hit the jagged edge of the metal floor, and for an instant, he seemed to hang in space. Then he began to tip backward.

Ojukwu grabbed his left wrist with her good hand, but his momentum didn't change. Greene wondered fleetingly whether he would carry her into the pit with him.

Juha, his eyes wide and hard with resolve, lunged forward, grabbed a handful of Greene's jacket, and yanked, twisting his hips to harness the full power of his legs and back.

Greene found himself suddenly pitching forward headlong, but in the right direction, at least. Instinctively, he raised his arms to stop himself from smashing his face on the floor, realizing too late what a terrible mistake he'd made.

His crushed right hand gave way instantly to his mass, although he managed with his left to keep his face from smashing against the floor. The pain was excruciating—it seemed to short out his central nervous system.

He curled up, panting, unable to process what he was feeling—for how long, he didn't know. He had to close his eyes—sight was more sensation than he could handle.

Then, all at once, it rushed in on him, unbearable.

Greene screamed, raw and primal. His pain poured out of him until his air was gone, until his throat caught, until white bursts appeared against his closed eyelids.

He lay on the cold metal floor, sweaty and shivering, and when he finally opened his eyes, he saw Juha, a bloody wreck himself, kneeling over him.

"Feel better?" Juha said, his face warm. "Let's go. You're all right. No real harm done, eh?"

Greene labored to process these words. "No ... harm done?" he repeated.

Juha hooked Greene under his arms and pulled him to his feet. "I mean, your hand was already broken, right?"

Greene put a hand on the wall to steady himself. The desire to hit Juha flitted through his mind. Instead, he said, "Thank you."

Juha nodded. "Home stretch, yes?"

Greene began to make his way down the hall, keeping his hand on the wall. "God, I hope so."

When they reached the foyer, Ojukwu looked up at the sealed freezer door at the top of the ramp. "Damn it, I forgot about this. Now what?"

Juha reached into a pocket and held up an access card. "Allow me."

"Where did you—"

"I took it off that guy who was trying to vivisect me. My mother didn't raise any foolish children. Well, except for my sister, but anyway, let's just go."

Juha headed up the ramp, and they followed. He tapped the card against the reader, and Greene felt a surge of relief as the door opened immediately.

"Well," Juha said, "except for all of us almost dying, I'd say that went remarkably smoothly."

They emerged into the wreckage of the Algary concession stand, now barely more than a foundation. Greene took deep breaths of fresh air, glad to be outside, delighted to be alive.

Juha began to laugh, first softly, then so uproariously that he had to lean forward and put his hands on his knees.

"What's the matter with you?" Ojukwu asked.

"Just look at this place," Juha said, tears in his eyes. "Oh, man, you guys fucked them up good. It makes me so happy."

"Browne! Raptor!" Burg's voice crackled in Greene's ear. "Do you copy?"

"I copy," Greene said. "We're out, and we've got Jester."

"Am I Jester?" Juha said. "That's nicer than I was expecting, honestly. You guys run a real pro operation. Class acts all around."

Greene waved him away. "We're on the way back to you, and we're ready to go." He suddenly remembered Sonnenschein, and a pang of guilt lanced through him. "How is she?"

"I got her patched up in time," Burg said. "It's nothing a prolonged stay in Medical won't fix."

"Thank God," Greene said. "All right, see you soon."

"Copy that."

Greene turned to Juha and Ojukwu and indicated the path. "This way."

"By all means," Juha said. "Lead on."

"Just a minute," Ojukwu said. She hadn't moved.

Greene stopped. "What's wrong? What's the matter?"

She had taken off her Spec-Trons, and her eyes were cold in the moonlight. "Has this operation concluded to your satisfaction?"

"Yes, obviously," Greene said, confused about why she was asking this, especially now. "Thank you for your help. You were invaluable."

"You're welcome." She removed her earpiece and handed it to him. "And your company makes no claim on this place?"

Greene took the device from her, switched it off, and put it in his pocket. "As far as my company is concerned, we were never here."

Ojukwu nodded, then pulled out a phone, dialed, and held it to her ear. "We are clear to proceed," she said a moment later. "Send them in on my position."

Greene felt a jolt of terror run through him. "What are you doing?"

She pocketed the phone. "Even if we've missed the chance to get our hands on the stealth armor itself, we could be sitting on a treasure trove here, and it's wide open for the taking. If you aren't going to take advantage of it, then we are."

"Damn," Juha said, still looking amused. "Classic Ojukwu. I was wondering why she agreed to help you."

Greene shook his head. "This is a terrible idea. It's too risky."

"You have no right to lecture anybody about risk," Ojukwu said. "Not after today. Besides, we've already done the hard work."

"And what about tomorrow, or the day after? What if you start a war with Algary? Crestridge couldn't possibly hope to win. What if you incriminate yourselves?"

"Or what if they incriminate Xiong instead?" Juha tapped a finger to his temple. "I'm wise to these megacorporation games."

Greene stared at Ojukwu, suspicion churning in his gut. "He's right. You could do it easily. Plant whatever evidence you want."

"Yes, we could," Ojukwu said. "But we won't."

Greene scowled. "How do I know? What assurances do I have?"

She shrugged. "None. You'll just have to take my word for it. But if it makes you feel better, you can consider your acquiescence in this matter as repayment of a small part of the debt you owe me. Oh, and I'll even check the holding area for you when we get back down there."

Greene ground his teeth. He hated every bit of this. But what could he do?

Ojukwu held up a hand. "Listen, Greene. You're right: we can't win a war against Algary. Not by ourselves. But Crestridge and Xiong—together, we could win. That door is open, and I'm not going to be the one to close it."

At the sound of rotors overhead, all three of them looked up into the sky. An unmarked and unlit autocopter descended to the open space near the picnic area.

"If you'll excuse me," Ojukwu said, "I'm very busy just now. Plus I'm sure you're all eager to go get medical attention." She pointed a finger at Juha. "I'll be around for you later."

Juha raised an eyebrow. "Just like that?"

"Just like that. Greene will hold you to it."

Juha looked at Greene. "Really?"

"Yes," Greene said, scowling.

Ojukwu was already walking away, toward the autocopter, from which eight armed figures had emerged.

Greene realized that his one hand capable of making a fist was clenched, and he made himself relax it. No, he conceded to himself, there was nothing to be done. Not now. Whatever else happened here tonight was out of his control.

Greene turned away in disgust, his exhaustion taking hold. "Come on," he said to Juha. "Let's go."

TWENTY-ONE

The instant the doors opened, Greene stepped out of the elevator onto Xiong Tower's one hundred and seventy-fifth floor. Juha followed more slowly, taking in the glistening onyx walls, the golden Art Deco inlay, and the opulent chandeliers hanging high above them.

"Oh, it's a cruise ship up here, too," Juha said. "Very elegant."

"Listen," Greene said. "Before we go in there. What we did—coming to get you—that was not a Xiong-sponsored action."

"I figured that, seeing as our old boss was there, and momentarily on our side, even. That's fine with me; it just means I don't owe The Bear anything."

Anger surged through Greene. Even after half a night's sleep and a fresh course of medication, his exhaustion and pain trampled his self-control. He had no more patience for Juha being Juha.

"*Owe?*" Greene said. "Get this straight: I didn't do what I did to make you owe anyone anything. At this point, I shouldn't even have to tell you why I did it. But if you want to bring up what you *owe*, then you can't possibly—"

"I owe *you*," Juha said quietly. "That's a better debt. One I'm happy to carry."

That might be as close as Greene would ever get to expressed gratitude from Juha, not that he was particularly expecting it.

Greene raised a finger under Juha's nose. "Coming to get you, I put myself at risk. In doing that, I put this company at risk. I'm not telling you that for any reason other than that once we go into that office, you can either be helpful or you can shut up. Got it?"

"Sure thing," Juha said. "No problem."

Greene's phone buzzed, and *Incoming call: Satu Karjalainen* appeared on his Spec-Trons' display.

He pulled out his phone and held it to his ear. "Hello."

"Green!" Satu's voice was a mixture of worry and frustration. "I'm sorry to bother you. I haven't been able to get a hold of my brother in two days. It usually goes from annoying to concerning after about the first night, but with everything that's happened—"

Greene wasn't sure how much she knew about what had happened, but he guessed it wasn't remotely close to *everything*. So he said, "I think I can help you with that, actually," and held out the phone to Juha.

Juha frowned at the phone, shrugged, then accepted it. "Hey, Satu. I was going to call you. Eventually. No, I don't know how many missed calls it was. I don't even know where my phone is."

Greene couldn't make out what Juha's sister was saying, but he could hear the agitation in her raised voice clearly.

Juha rolled his eyes. "Yes, well, it's a long story, but I spent all of this past night in Xiong Medical. I'm alive and in one piece; you're welcome for that. I suppose you're wondering what happened to— Oh, right, the gym."

Juha looked at Greene, who gave him a wrap-it-up finger twirl.

"So, yes, there was a fire at FatAss. The investigation is ongoing. Dealing with that situation is my top priority, I promise you. Anyway, let me finish up here and then I'll be in touch. All right. Bye."

"Everything all right?" Greene said as Juha returned the phone.

"Yeah, fine, fine, I mean apart from absolutely everything being a complete disaster." Juha nodded at the hard brace covering Greene's right hand. "How about you? You going to be all right?"

Greene shook his head. "Thirteen broken bones. The doctor says it'll be quicker and easier just to take it off at the wrist and bioprint me a new one from scratch."

"Probably. Is that the same one you lost last month?"

"No, that was the left. But I had the original reattached." Even with that experience, Greene still felt leery about having his hand replaced. The shorter recovery time was extremely appealing, though—and he had to put in the time down in Medical anyway to get his eardrums redone.

"Unlucky," Juha said. "Man, where would you have been fifty years ago?"

"Dead. Five times over. The same as you."

Juha raised a hand to the bruise under his eye and nodded. "Thank God that technology can paint over nearly all of our foolishness and bad decisions. What a time to be alive."

Greene glanced at the time on his Spec-Trons, then resumed his walk down the hall. "Come on."

When they reached Marlena's reception area, Sundstrom looked up from his desk and nodded. "You can go on in."

"Thanks." Greene grabbed the handle of one of the immense leaded glass sunburst doors, then paused and looked at Juha. "Can you please behave yourself?"

Juha grinned. "What is even the purpose of saying that to me?"

Greene opened his mouth to demand, to exhort, to beg, but closed it again. Juha was right; there was no use. He smoothed the front of his security uniform, pulled the door open, and entered.

Marlena sat at her desk, engrossed with something on her computer screen. As they approached, she held up one finger without looking at them.

Greene stood straight, his hands behind his back, waiting. He glanced over at Juha, who was taking in the opulence of the office—the rich red décor, the designer furniture, the giant golden Xiong logo on the wall—or maybe he was just staring at Marlena.

After a minute or two, she pushed her chair back from the desk and gave them each eye contact. "Gentlemen, welcome. Please, have a seat."

Greene chose his usual of the four leather chairs available. Juha chose the one nearest the desk.

"I'm glad to see you both here, and in such good condition, all things considered." A smile tugged at the edge of Marlena's mouth. "Now then, Chief, completely off the record, and speaking purely as a friend, I'd be interested in hearing what you did last night in your free time."

"Yes, ma'am." Greene related the events of the previous night, attempting to be concise but including everything he thought might be relevant. Juha, thankfully, cooperated, chiming in only to corroborate points of importance and to mention the occasional detail that Greene missed.

When Greene had finished, he said, "Bottom line, we didn't blow our cover. Whatever they know, or think that they know, there's no evidence. Beyond whatever blood we left there, anyway."

"And you got everyone out, let's not forget that," Marlena said. "By all accounts, you did a fine job all around."

"Thank you," Greene said.

Marlena toyed with a lock of her hair. "You know, it might even turn out to be a good thing for us that Crestridge went in after you. A big team like you described might not be as clean as you were. They might draw Algary's attention their way."

"Maybe." Greene had been busy running through all the worst-case scenarios in his mind. "Or given everything that's happened, they might assume it was us and step up their aggression."

"Or," Juha said, "maybe Ojukwu didn't tell you the truth, and Crestridge will plant some evidence that it was you guys, frame you up nice, and then sit back and watch The Bear and The Dragon go at each other."

Greene shook his head. "I don't think Ojukwu would do that."

"Mm, assumptions," Juha said.

"I know her. And *you* know her. She's an honorable person."

Juha chuckled. "And you insist on going through life expecting the best out of everybody. It's amazing, really. Nobody's so one-dimensional. Not even you, and you're a magical unicorn of virtue."

Marlena held up a hand. "Maybe Greene's right. Maybe she wouldn't do that. But Juha is correct: you're assuming. And more to the point, she's not the only nor the final decision-maker at her company. We can't rule it out."

"Fine," Greene said. "But putting that point aside, I don't think Crestridge is in a position to take such a big risk. Especially given that we've built the foundations for a working relationship after Algary hit us both. My guess is they went for a quick intel and tech grab and that they tried to keep it as clean as possible."

"That's a fair analysis," Marlena said. "I'm inclined to concur."

"Thank you," Greene said.

Marlena crossed her arms and turned to Juha. "Now then. Mister Karjalainen. Not to put too fine a point on it, but you've caused a lot of difficulties for a good many folks over the last week or so."

"Yes, I'm sorry about that," Juha said. "It's kind of just who I am as a person."

As neither of the other two were looking at him, Greene rolled his eyes.

Marlena looked similarly unimpressed. "In fact," she said, "I'd say you're becoming quite a problem. Not only for those around you, but also for yourself. What do you think the odds are that Algary won't try to grab you again, if not cut to the chase and just kill you on sight?"

"I guess it's possible," Juha said, as unfazed as he said everything.

"What *are* you going to do now?" Greene asked.

"That question assumes that Perseverance Ojukwu isn't going to kill me or lock me up in the Crestridge dungeon like Algary just did. What exactly did you promise her, anyway?"

"You're going to walk her through exactly how you breached their security and stole their device. And then you're going to give them a bit of technical consulting with your maximum effort and complete honesty."

Juha raised an eyebrow. "Is that all? That's not so bad. You got off cheap. Nice work."

"Hm," Greene said. He still owed her his own debt, whatever that might involve. "Anyway, you'll have plenty of time to get on with your life, whatever you're planning on doing."

Juha took a deep breath and let it out slowly. "I don't *know* what I'm going to do, honestly. My gym is gone. I could rebuild it, but that doesn't solve the problem of having an angry megacorporation up my ass."

"And what about your financial debt?" Greene asked.

"The insurance money from FatAss getting burned down by *Algary*"—Juha gave Greene a pointed look—"should cover most of it. Probably the smart thing to do is leave town and start over somewhere else. Unfortunately, it's probably too late for me to go to Los Estados and start an illegal zombie safari operation of my own. Oh well."

"Juha—"

Juha looked at Greene, a rare earnestness in his eyes. "Thank you. For coming to get me."

Everything Greene could think to say in response was a banality. After a moment, he nodded and simply said, "You're welcome."

Marlena cleared her throat, and they both turned their attention back to her.

"You know, Juha," she said, "it occurs to me that we might solve a number of problems all at once if we brought you on staff here at Xiong Holonautics. *After* you've paid your debt to Crestridge, that is. Chief, what do you think about adding Juha to the Security team?"

"I'm sorry, I don't think that's a good idea," Greene said immediately.

"Absolutely not," Juha said at the same time.

Surprised, Greene looked pointedly at Juha, who returned his accusatory gaze with one of his own, then shrugged.

Marlena made no effort to hide her shock. "Explain yourself, Chief. Right now."

Greene sighed. "Juha is my friend, and I've defended him as much as anybody. But he's erratic and unpredictable and probably not entirely trustworthy. There's no doubt that he has a lot of valuable skills and that in certain situations, he'd be extremely handy to have around, but he could also turn out to be unreliable if not outright disruptive. No offense."

"Absolutely none taken," Juha replied.

Marlena looked at Juha. "And what about you?"

Juha gave her an apologetic smile. "Look, Green is a wonderful human being, obviously, and I'm sure this is a swell company, but I don't know if getting tied down as his underling is what I'm looking for in my life right now."

Greene opened his mouth to retort, then closed it. The boss had a twinkle in her eye.

"Fine," she said. "You both have valid points. All right then: what if I hire you to work directly under me instead?"

Greene felt his eye twitch, and it was all he could do to keep silent. His further opinions were not desired at this time.

"Work for you?" Juha raised an eyebrow. "You personally? Doing what?"

"Troubleshooting," Marlena said. "That's what we've traditionally called it. Or 'special projects,' if you prefer. And in between jobs, you could head up our corporate fitness program. Our facilities are top-rate, but we could use someone with the drive to change the culture around here."

Juha stroked his chin. "Hm. That *is* tempting. But like we've discussed, I'm not sure if it's safe for me to stay in Portsmith right now."

"I'll give you a suite here in Xiong Tower. You'll be safer here than anywhere else in the city."

"True, unless Algary gets tired of this elaborate dance you've got going on with them and just airstrikes the building. And otherwise, what? I've got to wear a holographic collar if I want to go out? God, I can imagine the migraines already."

"That's the best I can offer," Marlena said. "Take your time. Think it over."

"All right, fine, I accept," Juha said. "But you have to hire my sister, too. And give her a room of her own. I refuse to live with her."

Marlena shrugged. "That shouldn't be a problem. What skills does she have?"

Juha seemed to ponder this deeply. Finally, he said, "She looks good sitting behind a reception desk is the main thing."

"We'll figure it out," Marlena said. "We have a deal then? You'll take the job?"

Juha nodded. "As you wish."

Marlena turned back to Greene. "I trust that this is all right with you?"

Greene hesitated. None of it was up to him, and any objections he might have at this point would create more problems than they solved.

Professionally speaking, it was probably smart to have Juha on board. Juha was a considerable asset, and Marlena would put him to good use, never mind that however long her leash might end up being, at least he wouldn't be off working for the other megacorporations. And this way, Greene would be able to keep something of an eye on him.

Plus, in spite of everything, Greene was forced to admit to himself that he liked having Juha around.

"Sure," Greene said. "Sounds good."

"Thank you for that ringing endorsement," Juha said. "*Chief*."

"Please don't ever call me that."

Marlena's phone beeped. She glanced at the display, then picked it up. "Go ahead, Burg." She scribbled notes on a pad as she listened. "Good work. No, I want you to see this project through to completion yourself. The Chief is going to be taking some leave."

By the time she hung up, Greene could barely contain himself. "What is she working on?" he asked, trying his best to keep his tone neutral.

"We're adapting Garcinia's prototype grenade technology to the scanners at the building entrances. Once we've gotten that working properly, we'll focus on adding some lines of defense around our more secure areas. We don't know exactly how Algary's tech works, so I expect we've got a lot of testing ahead of us."

Greene frowned. "I should be involved in this process. For several reasons. Firstly—"

Marlena held up a hand, and he stopped talking.

"This is not a discussion," she said. "I am simply informing you."

Greene opened his mouth to argue, but she was looking at him sharply, and he remembered what she'd said the other day about delegating, about trusting his team, about managing his insecurities. Plus he felt as though he could sleep for two days straight through.

"All right," he said.

She nodded. "Very good. Now then—"

Greene's phone vibrated in his pocket, and a text message appeared on his Spec-Trons' display.

"Oh, God," he said, before he could help himself.

Marlena looked at him sharply. "What is it, Chief? What's wrong?"

A wave of excited anxiety unlike anything he'd ever experienced crackled through him, filling him with an energy he didn't think his battered body was capable of generating. "The baby's coming. My wife's gone into labor."

Juha leaned over and clapped him on the shoulder. "Congratulations! Don't forget, it's not too late to name her after me."

"Chief," Marlena said, staring intently at him.

"Yes?"

"What are you doing still sitting there? Go! Go be with your family."

Greene blinked. "Yes, ma'am." He jumped to his feet and headed for the door—for his future.

Acknowledgments

I am grateful to Emily Asad, a voice of unrelenting encouragement. Honorable mention to Emily Carry, first-time pregnancy consultant. Special thanks to Bella M. for the same-day janitorial services.

About the Author

Joshua Danker-Dake lives in Tulsa with his longsuffering wife, their three irrepressible children, and a tank full of cannibal guppies. Things he gets rather excited about include bombastic European power metal, *He-Man and the Masters of the Universe*, St. Louis Cardinals baseball, and conversations about science-based health and fitness.

Visit him online at www.dankerdake.com.

ALSO AVAILABLE

Made in the USA
Columbia, SC
10 October 2022